ONE DOWN

DIANA WILKINSON

Boldwood

First published in Great Britain in 2023 by Boldwood Books Ltd.

Copyright © Diana Wilkinson, 2023

Cover Design by Head Design Ltd.

Cover Photography: Shutterstock

A CIP catalogue record for this book is available from the British Library.

Paperback ISBN 978-1-83751-010-8

Large Print ISBN 978-1-83751-006-1

Hardback ISBN 978-1-83751-005-4

Ebook ISBN 978-1-83751-003-0

Kindle ISBN 978-1-83751-004-7

Audio CD ISBN 978-1-83751-011-5

MP3 CD ISBN 978-1-83751-008-5

Digital audio download ISBN 978-1-83751-002-3

Boldwood Books Ltd
23 Bowerdean Street
London SW6 3TN
www.boldwoodbooks.com

To Neil, my crossword buddy in crime

PROLOGUE

It's been a long time coming, but May third is finally here.

I lean against the fence. Count down from ten. I whisper in a soothing rhythm. Ten, nine, eight, seven... It'll take me ten seconds to reach the front. That's how long it takes.

I look down. The pitted driveway, its yawning chasms of neglect, tells me off. Slovenly reproof of my disinterest. A rampaging weed, thick, lush with sharply pointed talons, taunts with a strangulated grip as it waves at me through a crack. I yank it out, fling it aside but not before a prickly coating sears my skin and leaves an angry rash across my hand. My eyes squeeze against the pleasant pain.

I pick my way across the rotting asphalt. Silver Birch, a once majestic home, towers above me. Its carcass has been greedily devoured, deboned by filthy maggots. Beneath the darkened porch, I catch my breath, then nudge the door ajar, flinching as it creaks a rusty welcome.

A vein pulses in my neck. I exhale heavily, the sound like the hiss of air from a deflating tyre, and step inside. A slather of sweat coats my neck, my forehead, and I wipe a palm across my brow before I start a slow ascent.

The stairs creak, they're familiar, the fourth and sixth risers groaning in irritation despite my attempts at stealth. My damp fingers slide along the wooden rail as I creep upwards. I pause halfway, as my insides rumble with increasing wrath. Volcanic fury builds as mad compulsions knock back the measured rationale.

A few more steps and I'm on the landing, the holding cell between Flats B and C. The airless space suffocates my thoughts, and my body tenses as I turn the key. The unoiled hinges groan.

Inside the flat, the solemn silence of the stairwell fades, replaced by scuffle noises, agitated movement, puffs of rasping breath. I follow the sounds with gentle tread, and through a crack in the bedroom door, take in the scene. All as I hoped.

It's hard not to smile.

* * *

Blood spatters appear as aftershocks, and dot my skin and clothes like measles. I fall backwards as her eyes spring open on hearing the crack.

I gulp, swallow down the nausea, and put a hand across my mouth. My tongue has a bitter tang, a metallic taste. But I keep my eyes locked on hers. I think she's trying to speak. I lean closer.

'What's that?' I ask.

'Hmm.' She giggles, in conspiratorial mirth, and replies, 'What's the noise?'

She doesn't scream, although I wonder why. The crack was like a crash of thunder. I'd expect a reflex yelp at least. But she slips away into unconsciousness, and thanks me with her glassy eyes. It's gratitude enough.

Claret-coloured plasma seeps like soft-boiled yolk across the bedding, an Ebola flow of death. It's quite startling.

I freeze when I hear a phone but puff out my lips, release the air, when I remember it's the timer on my mobile. Ten minutes is up. I need to move, get out before the cavalry arrives. I spin, check behind me. Boo. I jump. But there's no one there.

I check out the scene, the final curtain. It was a convincing script if I say so myself, and the players have more than lived up to expectations. But I've one more thing to do, before I tidy up, clean my hands, and wash my face. I glance down at my black top, smug at the forward planning, its darkness mingling with the bloodied scarlet hues.

I gently unfold her fragile fingers, rigid to the touch, and thread the implement inside them. It'll be enough. Shakespeare at his best.

I move away, and by the door unlace my trainers, peel off my socks, and slip them in a bag. My feet are cold, numb like climbers' feet. But the pallid whiteness is clean. Pure. No trace of guilt.

I skip lightly back down the stairs. In the hall I prick my ears, picking up a restless spirit. I hear ghosts laughing through the flimsy walls, their skeletal fingers beckoning. It takes a second to realise the gentle hum is mine.

Outside, I pull out my phone, check the time, look heavenwards. Thank God it's all over.

My bare feet weave left and right, back the way I came, playing dodge with the thorny weeds that laugh through the fissures. They'll not catch me out again.

Up against the fence, I take out my socks and shoes and prepare to drive away.

Once out on Brewer's Hill, I don't look back.

SUNDAY, MAY THE THIRD

1

AMANDA

A metal bundle of twigs for a tree (6,5)

I'm fast, flipping across the cryptic crossword puzzle grid, my terror ratcheting up with each conundrum. The clues could be random, a sneaky theme weaved through the teasers like fine thread in tapestry, delicate, subtly telling a mystifying tale. Perhaps it's some smart-arse cruciverbalist, a crossword-puzzle setter, new on board with worth to prove. Someone I've never met. But I know that's not true.

Sweat globules bobble round my neck, pale beads of panic. They tell me otherwise. Who am I trying to kid? I'm the target of an online stalker, a word-troll maniac, who's been methodically toying with my sanity for six months now, give or take.

My bare feet slap against the hardwood floor as I get up and circle the lounge. By the window, my gaze dips from the London skyline with its smoky early-morning outline to the dense communal undergrowth below. A rampaging weed-infested wilderness is steadily advancing, a determined army, towards the fortifications of Flat A, soon to cover the walls like a serial killer's lair, the rendered surfaces invisible to the naked eye.

My arms circle my upper body, a futile hug of comfort, until a shiver pulls me round and I slump back into the chair, biro poised and chattering against my teeth.

Paranoia grips with every new clue. The Christmas Day Giant Crossword Puzzle is full of seasonally themed clues and answers: *mince pies, crackers, plum pudding, Noel, stuffing* and *cranberry jelly...* words evoking festive magic with simplistic formula, but for one day only.

Perhaps today the subject is death.

* * *

Each morning as I sip my coffee, from the lofty heights of Flat C, Silver Birch, I wait for my neighbour to wake up. Get ready for work. On autopilot, I listen for movement beneath the floorboards, of Flat B coming to life. But today there is no welcoming death rattle from the pipes. The daily violence that shakes the building like the precursor to a seismic earthquake, and heralds my neighbour's shower time, is eerily missing.

Agaves is my neighbour. His real name is Edward Heath, Teddy to his friends, but mine and Nathan's nickname for the guy in Flat B will forever stick. Nathan, my estranged husband, came up with a whole host of belittling nicknames for our handsome neighbour, who is now my lover, but my choice of sobriquet finally won the day.

Today the silence screams, a loud reminder of my absent lover who has gone away for the weekend. I miss the juddering crescendo of metal which then crashes to a halt as the power shower springs into action and spikes the frustrated fantasies which grip my thoughts daily. I imagine Agaves' tanned and rippling biceps as I listen to the cascading deluge. But today the comforting sounds of life are absent, replaced by the morgue-like atmosphere and a biting fear.

I peek at the crossword puzzle through slit eyes and carry on, my morning sourdough breath gaining strength as my gut gurgles and churns. On my scribble pad, I scrawl, checking, reading through my thoughts as I study the clues, the tiny equations of perfection.

'Keep a pad close, don't deface the newspaper. That's sacrilege.' Nathan's voice would join me in our speed of calculation. Solving the daily puzzle became a gladiatorial battle between us, fought to the bitter end. But now I face the clues alone.

So far today, each clue is linked to death and menace. And to me.

The bare walls echo my laugh, a nervy noise of disbelief as the sound, tinged with mania, bounces back at me.

'Alcohol does that, Manda. It feeds paranoia.' Nathan would admonish me with holy certainty that my psychosis was down to drink.

The clues have Nathan's stamp all over them. Dark humour laced with payback. I stare at the words, swivelling the pad on the glass top table, and swallow the answers. They're all correct, no ambiguity possible. But I can't be positive he is today's setter.

The anonymous puzzle setters at the *London Echo* newspaper are famous in a Banksy way, enigmatic, invisible yet brilliant in their cryptic clue construction. If the setter today for the newspaper is *Adnam* – my nickname, Manda, backwards, a phoney pseudonym – I know him only too well. My husband. But I'm not certain it is him. A ghost seems to be communicating through the words and perhaps it's someone else. It could be anyone. Maybe someone I've never even met.

I go back to the first clue. The other clues so far might just be random, imagined menace. That's how the police would see it if the worst happens. No one would believe me. Delusions of an addled mind.

But *A metal bundle of twigs for a tree (6,5)* is specific. My eyes flick towards the window. A light breeze is tickling the drooping branches and heart-shaped leaves of the tree outside which stands sentry in our front garden. A rich green canopy is slowly growing back after the winter frosts. It covers the light silvery bark which shimmers in the sunlight.

The clue is easy to solve.

A metal, six letters, is *silver*. *Birch* is another name for a *bundle of twigs*. The whole relates to a tree. The answer is *silver birch*. It comes easily, because I remember me and Nathan toying with a possible clue for the name of our building when we moved in. He told me that birching had been used as punishment in schools and prisons up until the mid-nineteenth century.

'Bundles of twigs were secured and used to punish schoolboys and prisoners on their bare buttocks.' I can hear Nathan's knowledgeable pronouncement in my head. Outside of work and setting puzzles for a living, his hobby is constructing cryptic clues for names. People's names. Place names. Names of foods, countries, animals. And names of trees and plants. The day we moved in, Silver Birch was already tagged with possibilities.

The next few clues take me longer to solve, until I sense the theme. My brain speeds up, soon racing headlong like a runaway train.

Two fools one country for murder (13)

The word *murder* jumps out before I get the answer. Another word for *fool* is *ass*. *Two fools* could be *ass* followed by another *ass*. *One* is often denoted by the single letter *i* and another word for *country* could be *nation*. *Murder* is the whole thing and *assassination* is the answer.

Nathan enjoyed teaching me, imparting knowledge like a schoolmaster hungry for adulation. That's who he was.

'One bit of the clue relates to the whole thing. Like in a quick crossword puzzle. The next section, often following a comma, gives you clues as to how to make certain you have the right answer.' Nathan was patient, keen to prise me from the bottle that sang with heady promises and nearly cost my life. But the images of death are never far away.

I carry on, my mind twisting this way and that as my eyes fixate on the grid. *Silver Birch* is where I live. Can *assassination* be just another random answer? Zigzag sparks zap around the edges of my vision, and warn of a building migraine.

I'm certain that the clues are linked, and sending me a threat.

2

AMANDA

If I lived in an airy open plan apartment with sleek lines and marble tiles, and wrap-around balconies framed by shining glass, the silence surely wouldn't be as terrifying. But trapped inside Silver Birch, with its solid masonry shell, I feel the waft of vengeful ghosts passing through the walls.

Silver Birch, the name given to the property that houses three separate flats, reminds me of Cerberus, the hound of Hades, whose three monstrous heads guard the gates of the Underworld to prevent the dead from leaving.

The trio of snarling properties within Silver Birch share one heart, with its tangle of clogged-up arteries that filter amenities through the robust but cracking torso. Our garden is the serpent tail that swishes from the creature's thunder thighs. A hissing mesh of weeds, thorns, and wild abandon that chokes the healthy growth.

I imagine our majestic property in its infancy before it was christened with the name of the burgeoning tree that dominates the front. Built over one hundred years ago, for the landed gentry if rumour is to be believed, the structure has grand but asymmetric form. A central staircase once linked three sprawling levels. It reared up on the left-hand side of the main entrance, winding its way up several floors, before developers, sometime in the seventies, had it truncated on the landing shared today by Flats B and C. Inside Flat C, the narrow stairs creak on upwards towards a skylight. Sun beams through by day, stars twinkle by night and when the heavens open, rain seeps through the joints. This is our flat. The flat that belongs to my husband, Nathan, and me.

Flat B was carved out into an eclectic mix of shapes and sunk into the underbelly of Flat C, which became its loftier neighbour. The conversion into three flats was higgledy-piggledy to say the least. Cracks, crevices and crooked edges abound, and in one corner of our bathroom is a creaking floorboard, so loosely fitted that I can slip it aside and peek through a tiny gap into the kitchen of Flat B which lies directly underneath.

From our elevated skyline, we look out over the heady sights of London, but our neighbour's view from the flat below is of the newbuilds across the road.

The entrance to Flat A is on ground-floor level and incorporates a basement and musty cellar. With its own front door and more than generous floor space, it has '*potential*'. That was Nathan's word for the dungeon whose view is stifled by the dankness of suffocating foliage and overhanging branches.

Nathan scoffed and said the chaotic layout of the flat conversions reminded him of childhood Lego, blocks locked together without form or aesthetic. Although I fell in love with our flat the moment I stepped over the threshold, it was the shared exterior of Silver Birch, with its imposing facade and towering dimensions that sealed the deal.

In the centre of the small communal front garden towers the *Betula pendula*, the scientific name which Nathan loved to spout when describing the grand tree, the grandeur of the elegant drooping branches, heart-shaped leaves, and diamond fissures at odds with the roots' destructive properties which buckle unevenly underfoot like ancient burial mounds, creeping ever closer to the foundations.

The first day I came to look around, to compare reality with the online airbrushed photos, it was the luscious summer foliage on the striking centerpiece, with its silken adornments of midsummer magic, that swept away any doubts. There was no hint of the barren crisp white bark, like tissue paper, which shivers in winter, void of leaves and life or of its gnarled and nobbled arthritic branches. Today, after a long, hard winter, the Silver Birch is only slowly coming back to life.

When Nathan began his quest to save my soul, he forgot.

Forgot that one heart, one soul, can't be divided into three. The flimsy partitioning of paper-thin walls, and shared communicating echoes, saved me from certain death.

3

AMANDA

I've been up since dawn and my body is exhausted, my limbs still entwined with leaden slumber. But my mind whizzes with alertness, gripped by the macabre. It's hard to shake the nightmares, which reach hellish depths in the dead of night.

Each morning, I somehow shake myself awake and flick the lamp, flooding the room with light. Mindful vigilance knocks the ghouls aside, although I know they're patient, waiting in the wings.

I try to calm my breathing, stem the panic.

I move to carry on with the puzzle. The morbid theme is thickening and I'm almost scared to look.

I crave the daily rap against my door. *Yoo-hoo. Have a great day.*

Each morning, Agaves' deep throaty fog schmoozes through the wood before he marches down the staircase, size twelve brogues smacking on the risers. The ridiculousness of early-waking paranoia gets momentarily squashed by his steady tread, but today, a slam, a sudden crack of wood against a door frame, bangs against the silence and shocks me rigid.

Tory, the lady who owns Flat A on the ground floor, has just left the building.

With Agaves in Brighton visiting his mother, I'm now totally alone. Trapped inside Silver Birch.

* * *

Old Bob finds amusement at home but not here presumably? (14)
The answer takes me two minutes, no more. *Slaughterhouse.* The working out was easy. Nathan taught me well.

'Single letters can, in "cryptic-puzzle speak", relate to certain things. You'll get to learn them. "S" can be used to mean old shilling... as in Old Bob.'

Nathan went through letters, one by one, trying to hold my waning concentration. As I study the clue, his words come back to me. *Old Bob (s) finds amusement (laughter) at home (house) but not here presumably?*

The next two clues make things even worse. They need little reasoning, and I've seen them both before.

Accelerator or choke (8). I fill in *throttle.*
Undertaking final tax demand (5,6). *Death duties.*

* * *

It's now 11.10. I know coffee isn't the best idea, but I crave another caffeine fix. I've been refilling my mug all morning. It's a comfort thing, my lively daytime companion. Nathan worried that caffeine overdose was likely, an alternative addiction in place of alcohol, but I laughed, assuring him my liver was in better hands.

I take my empty mug through to the kitchen. The tiny room feels safe, a stuffy space with a broken fan that Nathan never fixed. It's stacked with wholesome foods, herbal teas and full-strength coffee which keep me company when loneliness bares its teeth. I slump back against the sink and will the hissing coffee machine, with its bubbly effervescence, to quell my fears.

But as I skulk back to the lounge, gripping the hot drink with shaking hands, the dread returns.

4

AMANDA

There's one final section of the grid to solve, bottom right-hand quartile. I tap my pen above the clues, push my mug aside and let my loopy scrawl do the thinking.

Soon there are only five clues left. But the first one needs no thought.

A male attorney for the girl (6)

I recognise the clue as the one Nathan came up with when we first met, in Shoreditch. The Boat Yard pub.

'I'm your male attorney,' he announced after I told him my name. His wolfish grin and wicked eyes glinted wild reflection as he handed me the wine.

'Whatever,' I roared at the weirdo who would become my husband.

My name, Amanda, he explained, after telling me he was a cruciverbalist, a crossword setter, could be broken down.

'*A man* is the same as *a male*,' he said, writing on a beer mat in nursery letters, large and clear, with a thick black pen. '*Attorney* in the US is a *DA*, an abbreviation for a District Attorney.'

'I know that,' I scoffed, amazed that I was telling the truth. Too many US crime dramas.

'Put it all together. What do you get?'

'Duh.' I wasn't quite there yet and too tipsy to really take it in.

But he leant across and brushed my cheek with generous lips and whispered the one word. *Amanda*. It was afterwards that he promised he would forever be my *male attorney for the girl*.

Four clues to go.

Ice-cream dessert, we hear, for the Sabbath (6)

Sabbath relates to the whole answer. It's easy. *Sunday* is the answer. *We hear* is a sound-alike pointer. The answer sounds like an ice-cream dessert. Sundae.

Three to go.

It's 11.30. I'm desperate to finish and get out of the flat. Breathe again, but I'm not prepared for what's coming. If I'd known, I'd have left much sooner.

Japanese play at the scheduled hour – twelve! (8)

It takes me ten minutes to work this one out. *Noontime* was easy to guess at as relating to twelve (as in o'clock) but the rest needs Google help to be sure this is the right answer. My damp fingers slither over the keyboard. Noh theatre, also spelled No, is a traditional Japanese theatrical form, one of the oldest in the world. If *No* is linked to *On time* (at the scheduled hour), the answer is *noontime*.

Two clues left.

When I solve the penultimate clue, my chest constricts, my vision blurs.

Tim Hardy makes a date (3,5)

Makes (an anagram pointer) tells me what to do and the only anagram I can get with the letters in *Tim Hardy* is *May third*. A weird flood of relief washes over me, and I let out a shaky laugh. Today is 2 May. Not *May third* as in the clue.

I pick up my mobile, check the date. But I'm wrong.

No! No! No! Today is the third!

The final clue, the answer to which runs along the very bottom right-hand line of the grid, is seven letters long. It's at the end, which is apt.

Commendation for being late! (7)

It takes a further three minutes to solve. *Late* (as in dead). A *commendation for* the dead is an *epitaph*, a short text inscribed on a tombstone. The answer is *epitaph*.

The list of answers is a story told in shorthand. It's a story for me. A story to give me nightmares. I know it's meant for me because who else could it be for?

Amanda. Silver Birch. Noontime. May third. Sunday. Assassination. Slaughterhouse. Throttle. Death duties. Epitaph.

My pen slips to the floor and my heart speeds up, trying to catch my brain, the coffee firing my pulse and thoughts round as if negotiating a serpentine chicane.

Oh my god! Oh my god! I double-check the time, the date. It's 3 May. And it's a Sunday.

Sweat blinds my vision as I hurry to the door. I jiggle the safety chain, secure it in place, reach up and bend down to re-bolt the bars top and bottom and press an eye to the glass viewer. The landing is empty. It's now 11.50. Ten minutes till midday.

I've no idea what to do, who to call or where to go. Who'd believe me anyway? I don't want Agaves running scared. It's too early days in our relationship, and he'd think I was crazy.

Suddenly I freeze. There's a knock at the door. I don't move, too scared to breathe or make a noise.

'Amanda. Are you in there? It's only me.'

A second rap beats harder, more persistent.

Relief catapults me to the door. I peek through the spyhole, yank back the chain, undo the bolts and rip it open.

'Oh my god. Am I glad to see you. Come in. Come in.'

Once we're back inside, I slam the door shut behind us.

THREE YEARS PREVIOUSLY

5

NATHAN

Nathan, a man of words and a crossword setter by trade, succumbed to numbered lists, which he used to organise his life. He woke with purpose, his tasks numerically ordered before the day began, a meaningful modus operandi to help him face the hours ahead.

Until Amanda came into his life, and her chaos ripped his plans – and world – apart.

Each morning an urgent to-do list greeted him, hand-drawn emojis scribbled on the sheet, silent sign-language companions. During breaks from puzzle setting, he'd perfect emoji drawings, and toy with emoticon construction using signs and punctuation marks.

On his bullet-pointed schedule, a smiling emoji face was linked with pleasant tasks. A jog. A pint with Joseph, his best friend, and hopefully, one day, his best man. A takeaway supper. Angry red emojis, with downturned mouths, explosive cheeks, got knitted with unpleasant jobs. Blocked drains. Car repairs. Encroaching damp patches that craved attention. He saved the smiling, big teeth grins for the rare events he'd relish with mild anticipation. A blind date. A theatre trip. But the first time he used a love-heart emoji was after that fateful day in 2018. Three years ago, almost to the hour.

After they were married, Amanda's derision challenged these well-worn habits.

'You must be joking.' She would snarl when he waved his weekend list. 'Can't we just go with the flow? Bin the bloody schedule.'

'If we go with your flow, nothing will ever get done.'

'Why not draw up a wish list instead, and plan something exciting?'

Her face would pop up from below the duvet, flushed from slumber and too much wine, and in the early days of marriage Nathan would give in. Back then, he would have done anything to keep Amanda happy.

He first encountered the chaos one late spring morning, when a sunbeam grinned through his bedroom window, heralding the arrival of an early summer heat wave, and encouraged a rare moment of procrastination. And a minor touch of madness.

Nathan drew a sunny face with six pointy spikes at the bottom of his list, and with cautious abandon, he made a snap decision. With unaccustomed impulsiveness, he left the flat, forgoing his tasks, and hopped on the Tube to central London. He had no idea what lay ahead and how his life was about to change.

An hour later he was standing to one side of a queue that snaked around the entrance to the London Eye, indecisive about whether to buy a ticket and climb on board.

He was on the verge of passing, encouraged by the blasts of shell-fire laughter that came from the selfie-snapping tourists and the sweaty surging crowds, planning instead a lazy lunch, when he spotted the woman who was to become his wife, the redhead reeling in his direction. If not love at first sight, it was indeed a heady fascination. Her flaming lion's mane swirled across bare shoulders, a light jumper hanging loosely over one arm. Sharp pointy heels craved attention, as they crackled across the pavement. She veered from side to side and when her ankle buckled on a wonky slab, her burly suited companion grabbed her arm and hoisted her upright. The guy, dressed in a slim-fit suit, its cheap sheen glinting like a sheet of polished glass, laughed in a forced explosion of exaggerated merriment. She brushed him aside, swishing hair off her forehead with scarlet glossed fingertips and tripped unsteadily ahead.

Nathan couldn't look away. He downed the Diet Coke he had been holding, crushed the empty can and chucked it in a bin.

As the couple merged with the queue, he wandered over and slipped in behind.

The thing he remembers most clearly about Amanda was her voice, the highs and lows of emotion, the giggling, the whispering. It wasn't posh, and there was a dearth of accent, colloquialism. From her colouring, he assumed she might be Celtic. Scots perhaps, or maybe Irish. But from a few inches away, all he heard was the flirtatious lilt, the energy, the throaty timbre of suggestion.

Once the doors closed on the air-conditioned pod, it began a slow cantilevered ascent above the Thames. Nathan counted fifteen people in the egg-shaped capsule. He nestled himself in between a group of Japanese sightseers. He took his sunglasses off the top of his head, and together with a baseball cap, blocked out the glare from the sun which dazzled through the glass.

Zero point six miles per hour. That's the speed the capsule moved. He gripped the leaflet between his hands, reading, rereading the words. *From its 443 feet above the ground, the London Eye is the fourth-largest Ferris wheel in the world. More than 3.5 million people use the Eye every year.* But on that late spring afternoon, Nathan was intrigued by one thing only. The lady with the flaming red hair.

Five minutes in, something startling happened. The fiery beauty slithered like a rag doll towards the floor, her back against the metal surround. Her breathing came in laboured gasps.

'Amanda. Are you okay?' Her companion hunkered down, his cheeks reddening as he spoke in muffled tones. The woman clasped her head between shaky hands. Nathan watched as her hair fell like silken curtains across her face.

He slid the rucksack off his back, unzipped the top, and lifted out a paper bag, which he upended, pouring the sticky sweet contents directly back into the holdall. Then he moved towards the couple.

'Here. This might help. Just put it over your mouth and breathe normally.' Nathan spoke directly to the woman, but her companion took the bag, fiddled with the paper before passing it on.

'Thanks,' the guy said with a mere tic of acknowledgement.

'You'll be fine. Inhale slowly, count out as you exhale.' Nathan persevered and nudged closer until his body was centimetres from the woman's. 'Are you claustrophobic?' he asked, his voice soft, gentle, as he dared to lay fingers on her bare arm.

She nodded, keeping her eyes closed as she rocked from side to side. When the bag was secured over her lips, Nathan moved back across the pod.

After some minutes, she staggered to her feet, gentle sobs hiccupping from her glossed lips. Under the brim of his cap, Nathan watched the man shove thick hands into his trouser pockets and step back from the lady, taking in the view outside instead.

It was then that Nathan made assumptions. That's what he did. He watched, weighed things up and made assumptions. The man was married, and he'd soon be making excuses about needing to get back to work. A busy afternoon. He'd call her. And then he'd skulk back to the security of his mundane life.

Nathan could decode the smallest action, his observations picking up the merest nuance of deceit.

When the doors reopened, the tiny band of trippers dispersed. Nathan hovered, and as the unlikely duo strolled away, he realised that not only was the woman claustrophobic, but she was also very drunk.

He held up his phone, feigning the taking of a solo selfie, and caught the pair on camera. His stomach lurched, the short reel of video capturing the collision of pouting lips as the couple's bodies pressed together. In blatant view of milling crowds.

6

NATHAN

After they left the London Eye, Nathan moseyed along behind the duo, until a taxi suddenly drew alongside them and threw him off-kilter. Fearing he'd lose them completely, he dithered between ceding defeat, or waving down another cab. Such was his fascination for the redhead, he chose the second option and moved kerbside to hail a ride.

And as fate would have it, Amanda hopped into the taxi while Justin Blakemore, whose name Nathan would learn some ten minutes later, slapped a palm against the shiny black door and waved the driver off. Even before the taxi merged with the thick rumbling traffic, Justin was striding off with a renewed spring in his step. Before Nathan could hail another cab, follow Amanda, her cab had disappeared from view.

Instead he followed Justin, from a space of some twenty yards. He had to dip behind a tourist kiosk when Justin paused outside a tapas bar. Inside the eatery, a wooden counter ran along two sides of the peripheral dining area, the layout allowing Nathan to continue with a swiftly formulated plan. The tightly packed row of seating faced outwards and offered a stunning panorama across the Thames. The high-backed wooden stools, which discouraged loitering, offered five-star watching-the-world-go-by views of passers-by.

Nathan hovered a minute before ambling in behind Justin, who, as luck would have it, sat down next to a second vacant stool. Nathan approached and tapped the empty seat.

'Hi. Is this free? Do you mind if I push in?' Nathan asked.

'Sure.' A flicker of recognition and Justin stood up. From his six foot plus frame, he gazed down at Nathan. 'Hey, you're the guy from the Eye.'

Justin shook Nathan's hand and with the other pulled out the adjacent stool.

'Thanks. What's the food like? Any good?' Nathan plonked his rucksack on the floor and sat down.

'I hope so. The menu looks okay, but I haven't been here before. It's not my usual stomping ground.'

'Me neither. Do you work locally?' Nathan set his cap on the counter and slipped his sunglasses into a plastic case which he'd extracted from an inside pocket.

'No. I work in Shoreditch. A financial advisor. What about yourself?' Justin asked.

Justin flipped the A4 menu card back and forth in his large hands.

'Me? I work from home. I'm a crossword puzzle setter.' He didn't use the word 'cruciverbalist' because he didn't want to encourage the likely conversation that would follow, and waste precious time discussing what he did for a living. He was keen to do the listening.

'Really? Sounds interesting.' But Justin's disinterest was palpable, as he flicked his fingers towards a hovering waitress. 'What's your poison? Beer? Wine? Fancy sharing a bottle of something?'

'Sounds like a plan. Red wine would be good. Merlot? Malbec? You choose.'

Justin ordered food for them both, and as wine loosened the stranger's tongue, Nathan learnt some interesting facts. Nathan prided himself on being a good listener, having had a father who never let him talk and a mother who never stopped. At a young age he learnt that silence was the best way to glean information, and he'd mastered the art of nodding, smiling, and laughing on cue.

'Has your girlfriend gone home? Nasty things panic attacks.' Nathan sipped his drink, eyes locked on Justin's.

'Oh, Amanda. I didn't realise she was claustrophobic. She's just a friend if you know what I mean.' Justin grinned, a lopsided affair displaying an uneven incisor.

'I see. A friend with benefits.' Nathan's lips upturned, but the smile didn't reach his eyes.

'You could say that. If I must be honest, I'm a happily married man.'

Nathan's hand jerked, and for an awful moment he thought he might chuck his wine in the prick's face.

* * *

An hour later, the bill split two ways, and having swapped business cards, Nathan and Justin headed off in opposite directions.

As he neared the Tube, Nathan stopped and keyed in the name of the pub Justin had mentioned. The Boat Yard in Shoreditch. Having drunk the lion's share of Malbec, Justin let slip, in the strictest of confidence, that every Friday night for the past two years he had met up with Amanda there, the pub a stone's throw from his office.

'She's good fun. Likes her drink. And more besides.' Justin

shouldn't have winked because it helped Nathan make up his mind.

He set to work, planning how to make sure Justin didn't turn up next Friday at seven o'clock.

For he intended to take his place.

7

NATHAN

On Friday night the following week, Nathan arrived at the Boat Yard pub. From inside the heavy oak-doored entrance, he watched Amanda swivel unsteadily on a bar stool before he inched forward and introduced himself properly.

His future wife showed no recollection of having met him before, which was as he had surmised would be the case. When she had lain slumped on the capsule floor, she hadn't looked up, her one concern being to breathe more easily. If she did recognise him, his plan was to feign surprise at the amazing coincidence, but Amanda never linked him to the man with the paper bag, and Nathan never told her.

And if Justin Blakemore had confided in Amanda about the tapas lunch with the random stranger, she never joined up the dots. Only Nathan knew the subterfuge that had gone into this fortuitous event.

Nathan used his work phone, the one attached to his crossword setting work, to put his plan in motion. At the *London Echo* daily newspaper, Nathan worked under the pseudonym of Hercules, a name he had chosen himself. All cruciverbalists, crossword setters, worked anonymously but Nathan's choice of moniker meant his mental genius, in the eyes of the puzzle enthusiasts, would be coupled with the physical prowess of the mythical Greek god. Though no one was supposed to know who he was, he enjoyed the imagery of superhuman strength, bravery and masculinity that added fascination to his intellectual brilliance.

It was on Thursday, a week after his day in London, and the day before he turned up unexpectedly at the Boat Yard pub, that Nathan, using his private Hercules phone, keyed in the mobile number of Justin Blakemore, and attached the short video of his steamy clinch with Amanda. Nathan edited and cropped the clip, fading out the background, so that Justin wouldn't link the footage with the sunny spring morning when they had all visited the London Eye. Nathan opted for a night-time background with stars twinkling overhead, and only pressed 'send' when he was happy with the result.

He added a short succinct message.

Wouldn't your wife love to see this video? Keep away from Amanda, or else.

Five minutes later a reply bounced back.

Who the fuck is this?

It was then that Nathan switched off his phone.

THREE MONTHS BEFORE MAY THE THIRD

8

AMANDA

Chaperone shredded corset (6)

Chuffed, like a puffed-up pigeon, a crumb in its beak, strutting its stuff. That was me, the first time I tackled a clue single-handedly, and won.

My squiggly flamboyant answer looked like *effort*, but I knew what I meant as I creased the paper in a victory clench. I've never mastered longhand, preferring the flit of my fingers over a keyboard. Fast and furious, that's me, and my fingers match my brain. My crazy chicken neck bobs back and forth as I solve anagrams at lightning speed. *Escort...* a chaperone, and anagram of *corset*. Easy-peasy. The word *shredded* gave the clue that an anagram was involved.

'Fast is positive, but can we drop the furious.' Nathan's voice, with its sage pronouncements, using words like Michelangelo wielded brushes, isn't far away.

My husband's neatly clipped head, like a topiary TV set, is what I see every time I fill in the blanks of a crossword grid. Inside his skull I imagine criss-cross wiring that links up nerve endings, as lexicographical data gets analysed and stored on a hard drive.

He studies words the way an entomologist studies insects, dissecting phrases into the smallest possible components and always on the lookout for a rare species of word formation.

But his calm, logical personality, sunny and precise, breaks down when assaulted by a crumpled newspaper.

Square it off. Neaten the corners. For Chrissakes eat your toast first and wipe your sticky fingers. World War Three would break out if a circlet of honey ringed the clues, and each time I would imagine flashing red lights inside his cranium, warning of a logjam.

Escort was the first clue I ever solved. Well, the first time I tackled the enigma code of the cryptic puzzle on my own. My disinterest in all things verbal was who I was. I was the numbers person in our marriage; maths perfection my way-to craft. I was a maths teacher, a career well suited to my numerical skills, along with a heady love of being around kids. But last Christmas at the sixth form party, I got in trouble. Disrespected boundaries with staff colleagues, being overly familiar and raucous. After one drink too many, my rock and roll routine got a warning from the head teacher.

Nathan, the well-respected 'words man', was an obvious match. Our similarly wired brains collided in a galaxy of words and numbers. The symmetry of equations was soon likened to the neatness of the palindrome, *Madam I'm Adam.*

'Go on. What's that? *Madam I'm Adam,*' I had asked.

'It's a palindrome.'

'What the heck's a palindrome?' My finger hovered over the remote control, impatient to get the evening started, the latest Netflix crime drama almost as magnetic as the alcohol. But not quite.

'A word or phrase which reads the same forwards and backwards. Look at the letters. Read it in reverse and then read it normally. Fun, isn't it?' Nathan's eyes glistened.

'Cool.'

Back then, I didn't really understand Nathan, or even try to understand, my disinterest in my husband's work palpable, though I listened out of respect. So no one was more surprised than me when I finally got hooked on crosswords.

In the early days of our relationship, my eyes preferred the TV screen as I channel-hopped and poured out the wine, large medicinal goblets filled to the brim. 'Cheers,' I'd purr, my lips lapping up the crisp dry nectar. The alcohol made life seem much more interesting, coating our dull existence in glossy hues. But it soon became the poison that helped tear us apart, although I won't take all the blame.

By the time Nathan left, I had the drinking under control. Or so I thought.

9

AMANDA

Today is a big day. I have a date, a challenge to myself. This evening, I am going to have a single celebratory glass of wine to congratulate myself on my progress, and for having come so far.

This morning, I settle on the sofa early, to do the crossword puzzle. I'm half-expecting some hidden clues from Nathan, as he's started communicating and toying with me through the grids. I'm sure it's him. It's quite a novel approach, but to be honest, I'd rather he'd pick up the phone. Talk to me, after so long.

I slowly settle, puff out pent-up air, and begin to read through the clues. My mind whizzes back and forth until I relax into a steady rhythm.

Key state of America? (7)

Country Stuart shortly revolutionised in song (7)

Spanish town where girl receives amazing tan (8)

Key state of America? – seven letters. It's on my wish list. The question mark hints at word play. Key is the hint. It's easy to solve. *Florida.*

The Florida Keys, the string of tropical islands stretching about 120 miles off the southern tip of the US state of Florida. Nathan and I had planned a trip for the Christmas after he left. Palm trees, beaches, sun and sand for me. Fishing, snorkelling, scuba diving for him.

Country Stuart shortly revolutionised in song – seven letters. A country. My pen chatters between my teeth. Aha. Another place on our wish list. Skiing in the Alps, cable cars and après-ski. Cocktails for me, the slopes for Nathan.

Stuart shortly revolutionised... Aust (*shortly*) indicates not all of the word *Stuart* going backwards (*revolutionised*); *in song* – *ria* (*'air'* the word for song in cryptic speak). The answer is *Austria*.

The clues are like Nathan's hovering ghost. Slight irritation makes me shiver. I check the time. Ten minutes before I need to shower.

I crank open the window, inhale the morning dampness and let raindrops patter on to my upturned palm. I raise my eyes heavenwards towards the blackened sky, finding comfort in the darkness for a few moments before I sit down again.

Spanish town where girl receives amazing tan (8). I fill in *Alicante* straight away. *Spanish town* is the whole answer. The girl referred to in the clue is *Alice*, the letters encasing an anagram of *tan*. The word *amazing* hints at an anagram. *Ant* is received in the middle of the girl's name. *Alicante*.

I don't need to solve the clue. The place-themed puzzle is made up of Nathan's and my travel wish list. He's toying with me from goodness knows where. Part of me is pleased he won't let go, another incensed that I can't get hold of him and that he's blocked me from making contact.

'You've been officially ghosted,' my girlfriend Cheryl tells me, relieved that my husband has disappeared. She never felt easy in Nathan's company, and now she's gone, she phones occasionally to see how I'm getting on. She was my good-time friend, bars and nightclubs our go-to places. But I keep my distance, scared of her unhealthy influence. Nathan was right in that regard, I need to keep company with sober people.

As I finish off the puzzle, I wonder if Nathan is taunting me with memories for a reason. Maybe he's ready to meet up, softening after all the time apart. But it's all a bit too vague. A bit too random, and to be honest a bit too freaky.

Also, a bit too late.

10

AMANDA

The clock ticks with relentless precision, the gentle rhythmical march towards six o'clock becoming a crescendo of insistence as I stare at the bottle. It's teasing me to be its friend, to forget the enemy within.

Joseph, my sponsor, the guy with the Jesus locks and thonged sandals who is tasked with guiding me through my AA recovery programme, proffers daily sober suggestions which I scribble on a fresh sheet of paper, ripped from an A4 pad. He texts me every morning with little survival tips. I've been doing it for the last four months since Nathan moved out, taking with him my life support. I used to sit with Nathan, plan the day and learn to take no risks. But now my help comes from a distance, though from a guy only ten minutes round the corner.

Joseph is a religious zealot where diet is concerned. He spouts the theory 'the body is a temple' with monotonous holiness and regularity. By omission, I lie about the chilled chocolate bars, nodding in rapt assent at his suggestion to eat five pieces of fruit and veg a day, as per his gift of the magnetic healthy-eating chart stuck to the fridge. Each morning, the oatmeal muesli with its dried papaya and bowel-shifting dates, stares at me like a wrestling titan, battering my feeble willpower into submission.

Today is 'day one' in the second stage of my recovery plan. I must admit this 'second stage approach' was my idea. I've been feeling confident in my progress – so much so, that Joseph has reluctantly agreed that it's worth a try, but he's far from happy. He battles my stubborn confidence that I can beat the alcohol at its own game and my belief that I'm a winner, a conqueror of all tasks. *Enjoying a glass or two, what's the harm in that?* Still battles the tagline of addiction.

'Whatever.' He shrugged, resigned to allowing me a one-time attempt. Today's the day.

The clock ticks through the minutes:

5.51

5.53

5.56

5.59

And hey presto. It's all OK. I can pour a glass – just one, mind, to help me climb the mountain that others call the evening.

6.05 p.m., and a self-congratulatory smugness pats me on the back for having sat it out an extra five minutes. I whoop at my success, presenting the glass trophy with its 125 ml of glistening liquid. I hold it to the light, distraught that the thimbleful is the recommended dosage, drowning in its meagreness.

I take a sip and curse the pleasure. It's been ten months and three days since I first suggested to Nathan that my goal was to become a social drinker, a glass or two in company and occasionally with food. Nathan's holier-than-thou face had puckered with scepticism. He came close to giving up trying to help me achieve my goal. But after that fateful day in June, when our lives changed forever, he proved his worth. In sickness and in health, he didn't waver. When I succumbed to joining AA, he knew the journey would be filled with obstacles, but heads down, determined, we set forth as one. My addiction bound us closer than our previously mismatched union. And with Joseph as my sponsor, coincidentally, also Nathan's long-time best friend, things were looking up.

Outside it's black, but the casement window that stretches from one wall of the living room to the other, a luxury length of polished glass, reflects the romantic glistening lights of London. The twinkling stars, flashing fairy lights, could be from another galaxy, rather than night lights from concrete office blocks only a mile or two away. From our master bedroom on the opposite side of the building, a second mirrored length of glass displays more scenic glory. In the distance Alexandra Palace nestles on a pedestal with its domed outline and opalescent glow. And beyond, who knows? Romance waves its teasing fingers through my prison bars.

When Nathan and I were ready to buy our first home, I spent hours and hours googling until I finally found 'THE' flat. The one that set my pulse racing, like an elusive lover who suddenly appears and fills a mundane life with meaning.

At first, I viewed the flat alone, and afterwards persuaded Nathan to come and have a look. While I was euphoric in the building's rotting shell and grand potential, Nathan wandered round, as if strolling through a graveyard, his orchestral silence resounding off the bare scuffed walls. The noisy clacking of his leather brogues was the earplug that muffled his concerns, drowning out any screaming doubts.

'Well? Go on. It's fabulous. You've got to love it,' I screamed in delight.

Resigned, he knew he didn't have a choice; I'd already made an offer. The wooden floor – 'real oak. Isn't it amazing?' – was bare, angry splinters like sharks' teeth teasing with their bite.

We hadn't been long married, early days and all that, and lust was still the powerful heady force that assured Nathan's acquiescence to my wishes. His malleability, like a bendy doll, had helped me fall in love. I wasn't 'in love', but I really loved him. His capitulation in all things contentious helped me sleep at night. Well, that was how it all began. Early days indeed.

When Nathan finally gave up the marriage fight, left with his furrowed battle-weary face, he had called my unilateral approach to decision-making manipulative and controlling. Sad, because when he left, the alcoholic battle was on course, victory nigh.

But none of these were the reasons why he left.

11

AMANDA

The next morning, the first thing I do is automatic: make sure there's no sweaty torso slumped alongside me. Memories flicker like a faulty lightbulb, but I'm alone, no random guy reminding me of foggy regrets.

I drag myself out of bed at 7 a.m., sleep not worth the effort, and slither towards the front door. I fumble with the key, my fingers shaking as if from cold. On the landing, I hover for a second, then grip the banister before tiptoeing down the stairs. In the hallway, I shiver as my bare feet pad across the frozen black and white tiles which bubble like an Aero bar, playing havoc with my balance. Whenever I'm dizzy from drink or lack of sleep, they seem to scatter in all directions, in an optical illusion of chaos. Like unfathomable Op Art, the boundaries are ill defined and stifle a steady focus.

A smack through the letter box makes me jump. I wait until the footsteps outside retreat before I bend and pick up the newspaper which has been tossed on to the mat. I glance upstairs. Agaves is unlikely to be up, but still I tug down my T-shirt, tuck my hair behind my ears, and scuttle back to the flat. I lock myself in and flop hard against the door till my racing pulse steadies. I don't want Agaves to see me hungover, and in such a state. Although we've only reached the stage of small talk when we meet outside or on the landing, or occasionally when he needs to borrow milk or tea bags, increasing flirtation feeds me hope of something more.

I slink towards the lounge, the failure of last night a staunch companion. I haven't drunk for months, and was so convinced I was ready to enjoy a single glass. But Nathan was right. Alcoholics can't drink a single glass, yet I've been so determined to prove him wrong.

A calm early morning sunrise creeps up outside the window, smiling, beaming hope through the glass. The sadness, dull despair of failure, is trapped inside the walls. Its misery will shadow me for days.

I slump on to the sofa, tucking my legs under me, and flick to the back page of the newspaper, to find the crossword puzzle. I carefully fold the paper in half, then in half again, place it on the coffee table in front of me and use my fingers to iron a sharp crease along each fold. Only then, do my eyes start to focus and scoot across the grid.

'Work methodically,' Nathan would say. 'Start at the top left quartile, then the top right, finishing with bottom left and then bottom right.'

But Nathan is good enough to do that. I like to spot the clues that will be easiest to solve. Short clues. Or clues denoting sayings, phrases, containing more than one word. I fill them in at random across the grid, but Nathan works with method, left to right and downwards in a steady rhythm.

Today, my heavy brain skitters back and forth until it lands on 9 Across.

Drinking too much finishing up with a broken bone? (7,9)

When the answer doesn't pop up immediately, I motor on.

A male attorney for the girl (6)

Twenty down. It's easy. Too familiar. Seeing the clue in black and white, Nathan's personal creation, I guess my husband is today's setter. Monday always used to be his day. The setters at the *London Echo* originally used monikers, made up aliases, which were printed against the cryptic grid. It was an old-fashioned tradition that let readers connect with different setters. There was never any doubt when Nathan was the culprit. But recently the paper ditched the name tags, for greater flexibility and to make use of freelancers.

Nathan has begun to keep in touch through the clues, as if by telepathy. He won't pick up the phone, and ghosting me has been his chosen stance against my sins. He won't meet up, talk through a handset, or by Facetiming. There'll be no discussing the future like grown-ups. I forfeited that right. He now uses the crossword puzzle to communicate using words as menace, a way to punish without fear of repercussion. He's gagged my mouth while he carries on the dialogue. Typical of Nathan, always after the last word, but the drinking jibes are really starting to wind me up. More so, after last night's failure.

This morning my concentration is that of a gnat, the pointless pest without a memory. I drop my pen and push the puzzle aside, letting my gaze wander round the living room and out through the window where the sun is gaining strength as it creeps skywards. The illusion of heat beams with chill sarcasm as I pop to the bedroom, pick up a fleece and tug it over my head.

Damp is creeping up the walls.

'Down the walls,' Nathan would correct. 'Damp comes in from outside, from up above, not through the middle of the wall.'

Who cares? Either way the train tracks are getting longer, darker, closer. Beep, beep, not far to the station. Wet, dripping, leaking, sloshing. Everything feels damp, drenched. My soggy brain is like a marsh, thick and muddy as if someone has hiked across in heavy boots with hard ridged soles.

I'm a happy drinker.

Of course, I don't need to drink.

Don't be ridiculous. One drink doesn't make you an alcoholic.

I would spout the words with tedious regularity.

I know the mantra, off pat. Who am I kidding?

Joseph, of the lanky locks and angry skin, the psoriasis making country shapes across his face, picked up my call at three this morning. It's the last thing I can remember. My wild animal howls surrendered to wracking sobs and bouts of choking phlegm before my sponsor could be heard above the orchestra of despair.

To Joseph I'm a random addict, someone he's taken under his wing, like stray dogs are rescued by the kind and caring. But he's also been there. He knows the pitfalls, where to look for booby traps. You see, Joseph is also an addict.

Joseph must have used his key, the one Nathan gave him when he and I began the battle to get me sober, because I don't recall letting Joseph in last night. But my discarded clothes were folded neatly, and my curtains drawn. I must have been out cold, as I don't remember him leaving either. When I woke around six, the flat was eerily quiet.

I suspect the empty bottle, which still sits accusingly on the windowsill told Joseph what he already knew, after I'd phoned and blabbered down the line.

12

AMANDA

As the whistling kettle comes to the boil, jolly morning birdsong, I drag my leaden limbs through to the kitchenette. The 'ette' appendage is something else that reminds me of Nathan.

'*Ette* means miniscule, a fancy verbal appendage to fool the buyer,' he had said, exiting the 'ette' room, as he liked to call it, with a robotic backwards slide.

I'd swivelled, 360, arms thrown wide to prove it was no 'ette'.

'Wide enough to swing a cat.' I'd laughed. 'The kitchen's twee, class, bijou, beautifully proportioned. Like your wife,' I said, beaming like a siren and managing to coax a smile with my flirtatious patter.

Nathan gave me a face of resignation like that of a ventriloquist. Jaw rigidly clamped, his barely upturned generous lips emitting a low buzzing hum as if a bee was trapped inside. A crinkle at the corner of his eyes reminded me he's human, but only just.

My hands curl round the mug, fingers threaded through the handle, hoping that the morning ritual will soothe the pain. Not the headache, the dry throat, scratchy eyes, and acid bile, but something deeper.

Yes, I'm an alcoholic. One drink isn't possible. I used to lie at the meetings, pretend I believed the spiel, but no one was fooled. Especially not the other expert liars around the circle. But this morning there's no room for doubt. Ten months dry, one night drunk. The percentages don't seem fair, but then what is?

Life was homely with Nathan; he was warm, loving, and for the first time in as long as I could remember, I felt safe, part of my own little family. All the past bad boys and sordid incidences were brushed under the carpet, the dirt and disgust with them. Nathan didn't know the half of it, but it didn't seem to matter, and he didn't pry. What Nathan and I had felt real, untarnished, in a magnolia-coated kind of way. Nothing fancy. But clean and neat, with empty walls of life waiting to be filled with excitement. With holiday memories. Safari trips to Kenya. Cycling breaks around Lake Como. Far-flung destinations would be paired with homely memories. A few years down the line, we might add to our coupledom. Things were steady, but spontaneous excitement, danger, had, all too soon, flown the nest.

It was only at dinner parties, when the *old married couple* jibes were tossed around, that my wicked side rebelled, and drink re-loosened my tongue and my inhibitions. Wine would fight the ennui that very soon came knocking.

Doing the cryptic puzzle after supper became a nightly ritual. Nathan would make a copy, letting me keep the wrinkled rag, and then place his grid down neatly, waiting for the green flag. Our competition was like Formula 1: La Mons, Monaco, Silverstone. Go, and we were off, adrenaline pumping through our veins as we steered our minds around the word track, my wine briefly forgotten, set aside.

A few months in, no longer a beginner to the puzzles, I became more eager to win. One night, when Nathan called a loo break, my nodded assent that I would hold fire sent him scurrying to the bathroom.

'Wait till I get back,' he yelled, but that was the red rag. I concentrated even harder.

That first time he caught me cribbing from his copy, a dark, black mood blanketed him. That's how important winning fairly was for him, so vital that he crawled silently to bed later that night, unaccepting of my apology. I was no longer a beginner. If we played to win, there'd be no cheating.

I didn't follow him to bed. Instead, I stayed in the lounge, drank two whiskeys and finished the grid.

I celebrated with a third glass and fell asleep, the victor without the spoils.

13

AMANDA

After the accident, I took time off work and concentrated on recovery.

The school where I teach maths set up online tutoring classes so that I could keep my hand in. Mrs Parmenter, the head teacher, dangled the constant threat that if I didn't make a reappearance in the classroom, even on a part-time basis, they would have to consider a full-time replacement.

It was Nathan who helped me build a website, angry on my behalf at the school's inflexible approach to my trauma, and at their unemotional ultimatum. As he didn't work on Mondays, he insisted that I also keep the day free, so that we could enjoy 'together' time. 'Quality time' was spouted like a repetitive litany, which for him meant not letting me out of his sight. When agoraphobia kicked in and I couldn't leave the house, the whole twenty-four hours of every day morphed into 'together' time. When Nathan did go to work, he'd phone me every hour, text me smiley faces and ask me what I'd like for supper. While he grew in stature, grew more confident, I became childlike, my dependency tinged with frustration and increasing fear.

Today's clues aren't difficult, but perhaps it's because I've become more adept at solving, but as I look at the puzzle, the teasers are irritatingly familiar. I recognise previous clues, ones I've worked out before. They have Nathan's stamp all over them.

It's a well-known fact that the start-of-the week clues are simpler, with the difficulty level building through the week. That's what the *London Echo* management demands. But Nathan likes to throw in rogue toughies like obscure exam questions that sort the 'A' students from the rest. He likes to showcase his genius at every opportunity and doesn't like to be linked to the simple grid. He never told me on which other days he set, but he made it known he set the tougher grids as well. Without the Adnam moniker appearing, it's not easy to pick out which days he's involved.

Since Nathan left, I've been regularly googling puzzle setters, digging round the *London Echo* regulars, curious to learn about my captors, the masterminds who hold me spellbound throughout the week. But the paper's cruciverbalists remain anonymous, even though the monikers no longer appear. When Nathan first introduced me to his colleagues, they masqueraded using their pseudonyms. A weird boys' club that no one else would want to join, but a club which gave its members kudos. At least among each other. I wonder how they feel being totally anonymous. No way to link their genius to even a fake ID. Nathan was certainly against the paper's scrapping of tradition.

As I reread the clues, the coffee tickling my brain to action, I know Nathan is toying with me, publicly naming and shaming. OK. No one else is interested, apart from Nathan whom I sense is soaking up satisfaction at his creative take on revenge.

My paranoia has certainly been fed by last night's bottle of full-strength, 14.5 per cent proof Chianti, but using that particular devil as an excuse for my exaggerated assumptions seems a bit extreme. Yet intuition, the sane partner of paranoia, has joined the party.

I chew the end of my pen, tapping it between my teeth which are set on edge and wonder how Nathan knows I would be drinking last night. He would have set the puzzle at least a week ago. Perhaps he's guessing, or perhaps he's just messing with me, teasing with the assumption that I'm bound to fail, falling off the wagon sooner or later.

Then, of course, there's Joseph. Nathan and he likely keep in contact and my sponsor probably shared my illusion about the myth of social drinking. A glass or two can't hurt. Surely not? Joseph has known for quite some time that last night was earmarked as *day one of my stage two* plan. A personal mountain I was so certain I could climb. Nathan, if Joseph had confided in him, would have guessed I'd fail and took a chance to gloat, from a safe distance.

As I fill in the answers, the more certain I am that Nathan is indeed today's setter.

Drinking too much finishing up with a broken bone? (7,9) Getting plastered

A male attorney for the girl (6) Amanda

14

AMANDA

A heavy fist at the door, thumping through my concentration, makes me jump and sends the pen careering from my fingers. Although I've been very quiet, sitting down most of the morning, I still my features, gnaw the inside of my cheek and rein in the blinking.

'Amanda. Can you answer the door please? Now. It's an emergency.' A loud deep voice booms as if from a loudspeaker and I glance at my trembling hands as the shakes increase. I almost, but not quite, forgot the tremors that quickly take root in the compost of booze.

It's Agaves from Flat B who is knocking.

* * *

He'd hated war breaking out in the Tory Party (6,5)

Nathan came up with the cryptic crossword clue for our neighbour, a clue aimed at belittling the handsome chisel-jawed bachelor from across the landing. *He'd hated war* when rearranged, anagrammed, makes up the name of a famous politician. *Edward Heath.*

Edward Heath is Agaves' real name, but he prefers to be called Teddy, happy to distance himself from the Tory prime minister who sailed around the world in his yacht. When Nathan shared this knowledgeable piece of information and about how Edward Heath was screaming to be anagrammed, Agaves laughed.

'I hate politics and I'd certainly not sail around the world. I can't even swim!'

I remember when he said this, his wide engaging smile. He was shaking Nathan's hand and at the same time swishing back a dark wavy fringe that flopped in front of his chocolate-coloured eyes. But mostly I remember my husband's mirth.

'Really? You can't swim?'

As a norm, Nathan doesn't laugh loudly. He laughs politely, holding his emotions in check. But later that night over supper when we were alone, his shoulders shook from the hilarity in replaying the conversation.

'Do you think he has a rubber ring? Maybe he wears armbands.'

While Nathan carried on with his disparaging put-downs, Teddy, overnight, became my fantasy. I began to watch him through the window, and was soon planning coincidental meetings on the landing, in the hall or in the garden. I'd listen to his movement down below but kept my eyes averted when Nathan was around.

'Is that the prat that hated war?' Nathan would ask facetiously whenever Teddy knocked. He never used our neighbour's name, preferring labels of anonymity.

Nathan was constantly amused by his superior intellect. 'Nothing to declare except my genius.' That was my husband, accepting second place only to Oscar Wilde, whose famous quote has joined my husband's list of self-obsessed beliefs. Words are Nathan's thing, but the verbal gusto, I soon learnt, was the outer shell of deep-seated insecurities.

When we started dating, Nathan's modest blush, quietly spoken voice and gentle gestures sucked me in and I soon recognised a soulmate with matching vulnerabilities. He told me he'd been the weedy kid at school, craving acceptance from the bullies. I understood, having cried myself to sleep, with chants of 'carrot-top' screaming through my brain.

Ten marathons down and counting, Nathan constantly toils to prove his worth. Although his random boasts aim to inspire awe in self-centred colleagues, they also strive to build his self-defences.

Really? Wow. I could never do that. Run a marathon? Ten marathons? Jeez, you must be so fit. Nathan sops up their adulation like a dry sponge does soapy water.

But I became obsessed with *the man that hated war*.

Teddy is *muscled, square jawed, thick, hunky, savage, gorgeous, macho, eye-watering...* I drew up the word list one drunken evening after Nathan's dislike of our neighbour exploded. He insisted that Teddy was flirting with me. He'd seen us in the driveway. Nathan blamed Teddy, of course, but our neighbour was the perfect gentleman. I was the one who'd egged him on, and I couldn't help myself; old habits die hard.

I wrote down the adjectives on two separate sheets of paper, topped up our wine, and in an endeavour to lighten Nathan's darkening mood, challenged him to turn the words into anagrams. Nathan snatched a pen, moved away from me, and settled further along the sofa.

'Whatever,' he said. But his eyes narrowed when I set the timer.

His usual determination to prove his brilliance was slow to wake, the petty rivalry with our neighbour festering like an open sore. But my whoops of early victory soon spurred him on. For a few minutes he forgot the jealousy, his concentration set on thrashing me at his game of expertise.

I didn't really try. I wanted him to win, plus the wine blurred any coherent thought.

The next morning, I felt guilty, wrong for having wound him up. I cried and blamed the drink for having set the challenge. The words had meant nothing, plucked from thin air. I tried to turn the blame, saying that Nathan had spurred me on by his constant, ridiculous belittling of the man.

'Of course, I don't fancy him. It's you I love.' I pleaded, as I pulled my husband close. After we made love, I felt safe again. And I thought Nathan did too.

'I love you too. Mine forever,' he said, as he emitted silent, heaving, child-like sobs.

But when I drink, the alcohol pops the cork on the bottled fizz of passion. It always has. Drink reminds me that it's there, a physical longing that simmers close to the surface. But Nathan nudged the lustful thoughts away by holding me tight, calming me down and telling me that he loved me. That I belonged to him. Together forever.

But my inner passion sizzled on, desperate for an outlet.

I remember some of the anagrams that Nathan and I came up with that night.

'*Argues* is an anagram for *square*... The Argues is a river in the Seine-Maritime department of northern France.' Nathan jabbed a victory nib at the words.

'Did you google that? You've cheated.' I waggled an admonishing finger in his face. 'Never heard of the Argues. How did you know that was the name of a river?'

'Just did. And no, I didn't google. We agreed.'

'OK. One to you.'

I then came up with an anagram for *thick*.

'*Kitch* is an anagram for *thick*... Kitch is art that's garish and in poor taste.' I enunciated the words for effect.

Nathan burst out laughing, saying an 's' was missing and it was spelt 'kitsch'. The only kitch he'd heard of was the café in the High Street with the same name.

But I beat him with my anagram of *savage*. Fair and square.

'*Agaves*, the plural of agave,' I said.

'What the heck is agave?'

'Agave is the name of a plant. I've got some agave syrup in the cupboard. Want to see?'

'No. You're all right. I believe you.'

But my little victory niggled Nathan, especially when I started ribbing him, reminding him. I would wiggle the syrup in his face over breakfast. It went on for days.

One morning when Teddy banged on our door to borrow some tea bags, Nathan said he'd go and let Agaves in.

'Who?'

'The savage from next door.'

In my mind, Teddy will forever be Agaves. The sweet guy who feeds me with savage longing.

15

AMANDA

As the rap on the door grows louder, I've no option but to answer. Agaves will know I'm at home.

'Coming. Hang on.' I scoot into the bedroom, rifle through the clothes mountain, the chaotic pile that's grown since Nathan's departure, and throw on a red top and ripped jeans.

Another bang at the door increases the panic. I forgo a hairbrush, running my fingers through my hair to loosen out the strands, squirt scent behind my ears and stumble into the hall. Through the spyhole, a concave face with a distorted guppy-fish mouth stares back.

'Christ. Hurry up. Water is leaking into my kitchen.' Agaves is now yelling.

The chain rattles as my damp fingers slide it off and inch back the door. Agaves lifts his T-shirt to wipe sweat from his face, displaying a corrugated stomach, and a meaty hand rakes through his matted hair.

'I need to know where the water's coming from,' he says, his six foot two frame trying to squeeze past, to push me aside.

Shit, shit, shit. My bathroom is directly over Agaves' kitchen. I suddenly remember inching aside the loosened floorboard last night, when the drink kicked in, to eye the peepshow in the kitchen down below. While I try to resist the sneaky compulsion, it's a hard habit to break. In the early morning, the sight of his naked body holds me rapt as I watch him jiggle a frying pan of sizzling bacon. When his flip-flops slop across the tiles, I can't contain the giggles.

'Give me a second.' I swivel too quickly, stub my toe against the door frame, but manage a nimble sidestep and reach the bathroom before Agaves catches on. The locking bolt cuts him off.

'Sorry. It's such a mess,' I shout.

'Bloody hell. Forget the mess. Can you just let me in?'

I kneel, re-slotting the floorboard into place before I open up.

Agaves, or Teddy to all his friends (two that I'm aware of), bought Flat B in 2016, three years before Nathan and I moved in, when my husband threw me, fireman-style across his shoulder, raced up the stairs and deposited me upright alongside our new fridge-freezer.

Teddy reminds me of the past I left behind, dark, dangerous, bursting with illusions of a happy-ever-after, of possibilities where lust and love entwine, the forever twins of fairy tales.

While it was my dreams that were filled with all things Teddy, for Nathan, it was his nightmares that our alpha neighbour dominated. In the mornings I'd watch Nathan glide with stealth, his bony feet slick across the floor, to take sentry by the window, waiting for the front door to slam. Occasionally, he'd raise an arm and wave, using a mean-finger gesture if our neighbour didn't glance up.

'He's such a moron. Who gels and styles their hair at eight in the morning?'

'No one to think about, other than himself.'

'Selfish git.'

Back then, I used silence to mellow Nathan's morning mood, the grumpy seventh dwarf. I humoured him with coffee, gentle nods and sighs, ignoring the jealousy and insecurity simmering beneath the surface.

Since Nathan left, I've tried to work things out, get some answers to the puzzle: *what is love?*

I still can't solve it. Years spent trying to tie down guys who needed a challenge, an alpha female to stoke their fires of passion, but these were also men who craved approval, a woman's gentle touch. A wife.

I couldn't make it work, get the balance right. I'd even left the ring, given up the fight. That's when Nathan came along, the prince with un-gelled hair and understated ways who saved me from myself, his love blanketing me with its warmth.

But I still fantasised.

And I am no nearer to solving life's greatest cryptic clue. *What is love?*

* * *

Agaves plonks his heavy rattling toolbox by the bath panel and wrenches the plywood off using both hands.

'I'm really sorry.' I don't know what else to say.

'It's not your fault.' He twists his head round and smiles. 'I need to find out what the problem is.'

'Coffee?' I glance at the mirror by the sink, twizzle my hair behind my ears.

'Please. Two sugars,' he says, his red face now intent on action. Yellow-handled tools – spanners, wrenches, pliers and weird-shaped implements – get randomly spread around the bidet.

Before he started any work, Nathan would line things up, neatly, methodically. In the garden shed, hoes, rakes, spades would be ordered, like numbers in an Excel spreadsheet, side by side, column by column, before his brain could get to work. My husband (ex-husband?) plans simple moves with extreme precision, like an army general in the thick of preparations.

'Coffee coming up. Are you sure the leak's coming from the bath?' I ask.

Agaves doesn't answer, the whirr of an electric screwdriver screeching as if in pain. His jogging pants have slipped and a tiny thatch of black hair teases me as it appears above his bottom crack.

When I reappear, mugs in hand, he's kneeling on the bathmat, as if in prayer, prising off some loosened screws. His fingers, with their neatly squared-off nails, gently coax them out. With a victorious whoop, he tugs a section of rotten casing apart.

'See. The waste pipe seal is cracked. The bath water has been leaking through the floorboards rather than draining away.'

'Shit. I'm really sorry,' I repeat.

'It's not your fault. It's easily fixed. I'll come back later but don't use the bath till then.' His eyes glint, relief freeing up the wolfish grin.

What big teeth you've got. My stomach flips, months of fantasy revealed by rosy cheeks.

'Great. Thanks,' I say. 'Let me know what I owe you.'

'Oh, don't worry. Just glad to solve the problem.'

He rounds up the implements, the clank of metal harsh, and snaps the box lid shut. He stands up, a muscled tower of threat, gulps his coffee and hands me back an empty mug. An electric current shoots through me as our fingers brush.

'If you fancy, I'll cook supper. A thank you,' I say.

'Why not? Sounds good.'

And with that Agaves is gone.

16

AMANDA

This morning after Agaves came around, I was tempted to give the AA group a miss. But Nathan's warnings haunt me.

'It's not a party you can drop out of if you don't feel like it. You have to go.' Nathan would use his schoolteacher tone, and he'd walk me to the meeting hall, make sure I went inside. It took a while to twig that he was working more regularly from home, unwilling to leave me alone in the flat.

Following on from last night's drinking session, my dry mouth, thick head and the waves of nausea remind me why I need to come. Shopping for my pending supper date and tidying the flat will have to wait. I thought I was on the mend, the right path to being an occasional drinker, but as I hover outside the leaden swing doors of the meeting hall, the reality hits that I've a long way to go.

I push against the metal plate to squeeze the door ajar. It creaks, like a hoarse master of ceremonies, heralding my entrance. I tiptoe across the wooden floor, but all heads pivot towards my squeaky shoes.

The lunchtime circle of our local AA group is neat, no ragged edges where addicts lean towards the door with excuses set for speedy exits. Our group is filled with hard acceptance, by old-timers who no longer battle in denial. The reverence is like that shared by a Bible study group, everyone linked in a round halo of sanctity.

'Hi, all,' I whisper. 'Sorry I'm late.'

Joseph pats a pale freckled hand on top of the red plastic chair beside him, and I slip in alongside my sponsor.

* * *

Before that fateful day in June, I was still convinced I wasn't an alcoholic, able to fully function after a couple of drinks, the life and soul of every party.

I was in denial, even when I'd wake up some mornings mortified by what I'd done. Or might not have done. I often wasn't sure. Guys took advantage, and although I hoped for something more, they helped themselves and rarely called me back. Perhaps I should have joined the #MeToo movement, but saw no point, as I always blamed myself.

The *not remembering* was the worst part. I'd wake in empty beds, foggy headed, mouth parched, yet powdery as if coated in sawdust. With trembling hands, I'd retrieve discarded clothes strewn across the floor and after a hurried coffee I'd be bundled out the door by a colleague, or, worse still, by some random stranger.

The shame would cling for days, but I'd soon hoist myself back in the saddle. Boasting that I had hollow legs, I would start all over again, downing vodka shots in one.

We close our eyes, a group hug of silent prayer. The hall echoes with the silence but as eyelids peel slowly open, the noise returns.

Dry coughs, fumbling hands and restless legs make warm-up sounds like an amateur percussion section.

'Are you okay?' Joseph's voice breaks through the memories, as he leans close. His breath is thick, soupy, past its sell-by-date.

'Fine.' I nod.

'I'm glad you've come,' he says. 'I wasn't sure you'd make it after last night.'

I'm too embarrassed to look Joseph in the eye, and simply nod.

My smile paints determination, as it slaps a coat across the peeling façade. But today it's easier to partake because of the thought of Agaves, our dinner date not far off. As the addicts talk, recount their week, my mind races on to supper. What to buy. What to wear. How to behave. It'll be tough without wine, but I'm determined and a few hours down the line, the heavy-headed hangover should have broken. A butterfly of hope flutters in my stomach.

Joseph gives an understanding smile when I decline to share.

When the meeting is over, and the members of the circle, one by one, start heading for the exit I pick up a carrier bag from under my chair and hand it to Joseph.

'Your favourites. To say thanks for last night. It'll not happen again.'

I listen to my voice shake like a nervous child's. I trust my words. I feel safe today, the enemy having been forced to retreat for now, but I know it'll come creeping forward when I'm not looking, crawl out from the undergrowth with a twitching finger on the trigger. But, as an addict, Joseph also knows the dangers.

He pats my shoulder, glances inside the plastic bag.

'I'm always here. Anytime, remember that. And thanks for the chocolates although they'll not help my waistline.' He runs a finger under the waistband of his baggy jogging bottoms. 'But I'll put the diet to one side. Just for you. I'll be a *cool cheat*.'

'Sorry?' My voice travels over Joseph's head as he turns towards the last member of the retreating group, a young woman, mid-twenties, who pulls him to one side.

I trill my fingers, keen to leave the claustrophobic hall and it's only as I step out into the watery sunshine, that Joseph's parting words make sense.

Cool cheat. An anagram of chocolate.

17

AMANDA

A month after the accident, sometime in early July, I attended my first meeting. Nathan's insistence wore me down, and my misery and self-loathing finally ceded to the inevitable. Nathan strode in front as we walked up Brewer's Hill to the community hall on the corner. He glanced round every few seconds to check I hadn't run away. Petulance dragged my feet, a sullen child unwilling to admit wrongdoing, but the recall of those few fateful minutes when the car spun out of control, changing so many lives for ever, is never far away. It fills my days and nights with nightmares which I fear will never go away.

Nathan led me through to the cavernous hall where the meetings are held, and I remember the mingling stench of mould and disinfectant. A dampness hung in the air as small widely spaced fan heaters whirred with futile endeavour. Joseph shook Nathan's hand with a tight supportive grip, and landed a conspiratorial slap on his best friend's back, while Nathan gave a gentle nod of resignation. He hung around, sitting some rows back, and let his eyes weigh up the members. Although a mild rebellion threatened within, I acquiesced and took my seat, succumbing to a future that seemed to lie in these two men's hands.

After several sessions, I began to wonder if Nathan only came to check out the members, vet them. At first, he said he came to keep me company, make sure I didn't sneak away, but when I said I'd like to go alone, he carried on. Even when I convinced him that I wouldn't miss a session, with Joseph as a solid witness, he wouldn't listen, insisting that he liked to be there. We were on the recovery road together.

I soon realised Nathan didn't really trust me. Not for my commitment to the programme, but being in the company of other men. I'm still not sure who he trusted less. His wife or the men. But when he began to joke and anagram the addicts' names, I knew he was boxing away an imagined threat. Nearly three-quarters of attendees were women, the random men pale and insipid, their machismo having succumbed to defeat, but still he insisted.

Joseph, Nathan's best man at our wedding, his best friend for as long as he could remember, soon got included in the levity of wordplay. A gentleman's agreement of schoolboy trust locked the two men together, but I remember my surprise when Nathan let slip a mocking edge directed at Joseph.

Joseph, impossible to anagram easily, became J-Hopes.

'Like J-cloths. Wet and soggy, good for wiping up.' Nathan thought he was hilarious. When he told me Joseph's birth name was Ian, that he'd been reborn by deed poll as Joseph, father for the greater good, Nathan laughed even more. But he didn't leave it there. That night in bed, after he'd had his fun, he continued to ramble on about Joseph and wouldn't let up.

'Ian,' he said. 'I'll have to look that one up.'

'Look what up?' I asked, already dozing off.

'See if there's an anagram for Ian. I doubt it, but who knows.' Nathan sat up, switched on the bedside lamp, picked up the iPad and began to google. A minute or two in and he coughed, bringing up phlegm as a fit of mirth catapulted through the darkness.

'Here we are. Ani.'

'What's an Ani for goodness' sake?'

'It's the name of a black tropical American cuckoo. That's Ian. Cuckoo all right!'

18

AMANDA

On the way back from the meeting, I cling closely to the property boundaries that abut the pavement. The gentle incline of Brewer's Hill has morphed into a dangerous winding slope and the imagined steepness reminds me daily of my irrational fear.

What started out as an illogical fear took a couple of months to morph into a full-blown phobia. It began as a nagging anxiety, but one day in September my heart began to race, and as Nathan and I walked down Brewer's Hill, I couldn't breathe. We had to turn round and head back up towards Silver Birch where I finally collapsed on to the icy tiles in the foyer.

Nathan hugged me to him as I convulsed and gave in to a full-blown panic attack. He talked me down with soft words of encouragement. As my pulse calmed, Nathan turned my face towards his.

'I think you're suffering from bathmophobia.' He spoke in a measured monotone like a consultant giving a terminal diagnosis.

'What the heck is that?' I hauled my knees up, tucking them tightly to my chest as Nathan hunkered alongside me.

'It's an irrational fear of slopes, stairs. It'll have been triggered by what happened. The accident.'

'At least it's not a fear of baths.' I tried to joke, make light of another manifestation of my PTSD. Nathan took my arm, coaxed me up with animated congratulatory gestures, for what achievement I wasn't sure, but with praise worthy of a gold medal winner.

'Well done. It'll get easier. I promise you.'

Later, I wondered if he'd needed to look up the word. Bathmophobia, my new condition. I doubted, even with my husband's titanic vocabulary, that the word would have come easily to him. But he was so invested in my well-being that I didn't put anything past him. The more labels of weaknesses he could attach, the more I'd lean on him. That this was his intention became more evident as the weeks passed.

That day, when we finally reached the safety of the flat, Nathan made me sweet tea. He enjoyed the role of carer, minder, saviour of my soul. It was like a hobby, one he embraced with vigour, and while I battled panic and anxiety, Nathan maintained a calmness with overwhelming, yet suffocating, patience.

* * *

When I arrive back at Silver Birch after the meeting, and shopping for tonight's date, I exhale the bottled-up air as I round the sagging gatepost into our driveway. I bend down, plucking out a few weeds that have drilled through the cracked crazy-paved pathway leading to the porch.

When I banged into Agaves outside the property a while back, we agreed to pencil in a date to clear the garden, front and back, joining forces in a two-pronged attack against the woman in Flat A. Tonight, I'll remind him.

Silver Birch Ltd is the name of the management company that was set up years ago to look after the upkeep and maintenance of our shared property. The owners of the three properties have equal say in decision making, with expenses and effort also supposedly split equally. But so far, the woman in Flat A hasn't shown willing to be involved in either discussion or graft. I've never even spoken to her.

When Agaves and I chatted, he made me laugh when he referred to our mysterious neighbour as 'the Woman in the Window'. He asked if I'd seen the film.

'I haven't, but I've read the book,' I said.

'She never seems to come outside.'

'I've only seen her a couple of times since she moved in but, I agree, the garden outside her window is a mess.'

Flat A, where the Woman in the Window lives, takes up the right-hand side of Silver Birch. The original entrance for the whole building is her front door, with its flaky green paint a slovenly declaration. Ivy straggles up her outer walls, a creeping display of ownership but she seems unconcerned by the destructive powers of the *Hedera helix* as it eats through the bricks and mortar. The taming, cutting back and nurturing of the flora is our joint responsibility, but currently Agaves and I are the only two active members of the three-man management company. We promised that we'd discuss it further.

I survey the property's framework from the front. It is one of two distinct asymmetrical halves. The left-hand section, which wraps around Flats B and C, has an ornate tessellated flat roof and balcony, a Romeo and Juliet feature. Nathan once jested that he was Romeo and would scale the walls to save his trapped and house-bound spouse.

A sudden breeze makes me shiver as I slip my key into the newly glossed green door which leads into mine and Agaves' shared foyer. Agaves rubbed it down and repainted it a few weeks ago.

When I viewed the property on my own, Mr Pritchard, the

estate agent with the spiky hair, goatee beard and shiny shoes, jangled a large set of keys as he led me across the black and white cracked tiles in the shared hallway, past a pair of gunmetal mailboxes pinned to a whitewashed wall and onwards up the steep central staircase.

When we reached the space outside the door of Flat C, a cool steady stream of air made me tug up my collar. Goosebumps popped up along my arms.

'Oh. The ceiling fan is controlled from inside. Someone must have forgotten to turn it off,' Pritchard said, glancing upwards as his bony fingers struggled with the lock. The whirring ventilation system clicked through revolutions, buzzing like an insect in its death throes. I should have taken note of the relentless stuttering ticking with its ominous fanfare. But back then my mind was closed off to any negatives as I had already fallen in love with what was to become our new home.

As I now stand outside the door, it all comes back. Perhaps the broken fan was an omen, a warning that things weren't quite so perfect as I imagined on that sunny day. Even before the agent and I stepped inside, I was already mulling over finances. How much we'd need to borrow. How much we'd offer. Deep down, I knew I'd be prepared to fork out the full asking price no matter what.

Stepping inside now, the quietness of Nathan's and my first home has the claustrophobic feel of an empty prison cell. The hopes and dreams that followed us have long evaporated and even the ghosts of days gone by have left the building.

19

AMANDA

Agaves is one of those guys whose appearance requires minimal maintenance. Even his early morning unkempt thatch and baggy boxers crave attention when he puts the bins out. He's so effortlessly attractive that if he was a woman I'd hate him.

He arrives, 8 p.m. sharp, in the same jogging bottoms he was wearing this morning but with a fresh blinding white T-shirt which sticks to his chest like cling film, hugging his biceps and outlining his six-pack.

'Hi. Bob the Builder is back. Hm. Something smells good.' He sniffs the air like a gundog.

'Lamb casserole. It's still stewing.' I blush, hoping he'll not remember my vegetarian aspirations. I know that Agaves is a meat man, the local curry house his favourite restaurant. With his full-blooded and wholesome appearance, he reminds me of a rare cut of beef.

Tonight, I've put to one side the recipes of lentil bake, peanut slaw with soba noodles and vegetable paella which Nathan collected and neatly arranged in a lever-arch file. Even my rebellious stomach is gurgling with excitement as the gamey aroma escapes from the covered pan.

I'm feeling slightly ridiculous in my skirt which skims my kneecaps and twizzles when I turn. My freshly washed hair bounces, and the sight of Agaves' flip-flops mocks my sparkly sandals.

While he knuckles down to work, fixing the waste pipe with seals and fiddly attachments, I hide in the kitchen. The emergency bottle of cooking wine is under the sink and tempts me like the serpent holding forth an apple.

Try another type of drink. Something long and fizzy. Nathan's voice rasps in my head.

He bought up to thirty varieties of non-alcoholic drinks: fruit liqueurs, grape concoctions, rum-flavoured iced coffees, gin and tonic taste-alikes, fizzy, non-fizzy, sweet, and sour. They're stashed like tenpin skittles in a lower cupboard. There's a different option for every day of the month, a quirky calculation by my husband to help me scale the Everest of addiction.

But it's not the taste of wine I miss, it's the heady buzz of confidence and excitement, the feeling that anything is possible. Nathan didn't really get it. He preferred me sober, safer, calmer, less reckless. I pooh-poohed his suggestions, unconvinced that I had a problem until there was no other choice.

Agaves' head pops round the kitchen door followed by the rest of him, wearing a grin like a gold prospector who's struck lucky.

'All done.' He waves a spanner in the air, the tool that claimed the victory.

'Brilliant, thanks. I'm really grateful.'

'No worries. A pleasure to be of service.'

I give the stew a last stir, then hold out a tasting teaspoon and smile as Agaves laps up the flavour.

'Delicious,' he says. 'Here. Let me.' He nudges me aside, and with proffered oven mitts, lifts the sizzling pan. 'Lead the way.'

We settle by the window, at the table I've extended for the occasion. Small dumpy tumblers speak sobriety and have replaced the wine glasses, the delicate long-stemmed crystal goblets, which are boxed and stored.

'Sorry, there's no wine.'

No need to explain. Agaves knows the story. Well, most of it. The part I'm prepared to share, in that I go to AA and it's a daily battle.

'No worries. I've brought some non-alcoholic beer,' he says, flipping the top of a smoky brown bottle and sharing out the contents. 'Ooops.' He frowns when foam cascades over the sides. He uses a paper serviette to sop it up.

'Don't worry. I'm usually the one to miss my mouth.' I laugh, remembering Nathan's humour when I spilled my food. I didn't mind when we were alone, but in company he used his forefinger once too often, as an indication for me to remove the speckles round my mouth.

'Here's to my plumbing genius,' Agaves says, beaming as he leans his towering frame across the table to clank the stumpy glasses. It feels good to celebrate. 'Next time, I'll wow you with my mocktails.'

'Mocktails?'

'Mock cocktails. Non-alcoholic.'

It's the words 'next time' that warm my heart.

'Cheers,' we say in unison.

20

AMANDA

'Have you seen Victoria recently? Or should I say the *Station Queen*,' Agaves asks, his chuckle like a baby's gurgle. A long tongue appears and travels round his generous lips to sop up bubbling foam.

Agaves had used a growing enthusiasm for crosswords to come up with the cryptic clue for the Woman in the Window on the day she moved into Silver Birch.

'*Station Queen*,' he said in a loudspeaker announcement when the removal men blocked the street. Agaves and I were standing side by side and watching through the window on the upstairs landing when our neighbour arrived.

'Pardon?' I remember thinking I'd lost the thread, misheard, when he said the words *Station Queen*.

'Our new neighbour in Flat A is called Victoria. That's the name of both a station and a queen.'

Agaves' eyes shone, and the urge to fling my arms round him took me by surprise. His childlike thrill at the simple clue construction, warmed my heart. So far removed from Nathan's calm pronouncements when he cracked a tough conundrum.

'Brilliant,' I whooped.

'Yes, I thought so too,' Agaves said, faint pink splodges fanning out across his cheeks.

It seems so long ago, but it's only been a few months.

'No, I haven't seen her for several days. She's a bit of a hermit. Any idea what she does for a living yet?' I ask, as I get up to tidy our dishes away. Agaves' plate is spotless, having used bread crusts to sop up all the juice.

Once I've put the coffee on, I play it safe and sit back down at the table, conversing from a distance. Agaves' long legs stretch along the floor, his flip-flops neatly set aside and every so often he wiggles his perfectly formed toes.

'No idea. I haven't seen her for a while either. What say when we do the garden tidy-up at the weekend, we light the barbecue and invite her along? Maybe lend her a set of shears.' His sarcastic suggestion makes us grin.

'Sounds like a plan.'

When the coffee's ready and I bring it through from the kitchen, Agaves is sitting upright, ankles neatly crossed with his shoulders hunched in concentration. The newspaper is bunched between his hands.

'Hair of the dog,' he says without looking up.

'Pardon?'

'*Hair of the dog.* Answer to clue 28 across. *Fine thing from Skye, say, as homoeopathic remedy?' (4,2,3,3)*

I set the mugs down and, throwing caution aside, push in beside him until our shoulders are nudging.

'How the heck did you get that?' I stare at the puzzle, wondering how Agaves has worked out the clue. Even I'm not certain what *homoeopathic* means.

'Ha.ha. I'm a genius, aren't I? Seriously, it's just a wild stab by filling in the spaces. You gave me a head start with letters from the down clues you've already solved.' As if reading my thoughts, he asks, 'What does *homeopathic* mean?'

'No idea.' We giggle conspiratorially.

I take my mobile and tap the screen, then read aloud. 'OK, it means "an alternative approach to medicine based on the belief that natural substances, prepared in a special way and used most often in very small amounts, restore health".'

'Well, smart-arse, would you like to explain how the clue relates to my clever filling in of the squares?' he asks.

I reclaim the paper, study the words, and imagine Nathan racing through the code, trying to solve it first. It takes a couple of minutes for me to work it out.

'*Fine thing* relates to *hair. From Skye, say,* is misleading. It's not the island of Skye, but Skye is also a type of dog. A bit of wordplay going on there. When it uses the word *say* that gives a clue that Skye possibly could be this. *As a homeopathic remedy?* relates to the whole answer. *Hair of the dog* is an alternative remedy to fix a hangover. The question mark tells us it's a possibility, and in this case *hair of the dog* certainly could be!'

I slump back, throw my hands behind my head and whoop. 'Piece of cake.'

* * *

With the puzzle finished and coffees drunk, Agaves uncoils his long legs, gets up and hovers over me like a nervous schoolboy.

'Thanks. It's been great. Although I might have eaten too much.' He pulls up his T-shirt and pats his stomach which is flat, solid and copper-tanned. I have to look away.

'Thanks for coming. And for the plumbing.'

He wanders towards the front door, and I follow close behind.

'A pleasure.' He pauses for a moment. 'See you at the weekend.'

'Sorry?'

'The garden clear up. Barbecue? Hope you haven't forgotten already. I'll put a note through Victoria's door.'

He then leans in and kisses me on the cheek, and I'm scared to close my eyes. His lips linger until I pull away.

'I'll be there.'

'Great. See you then.'

With that he gathers up his toolbox and departs.

21

AMANDA

A clammy silence fills the flat once Agaves has gone. I feel deflated, like a dingy lost at sea. I kick off my sandals and turn on the central light, which flickers on and off like a lighthouse beacon, never reaching full strength. Through the walls of my flat, outside on the landing, I hear a key grate in the lock before I hear Agaves' front door slam with an almighty goodnight thump.

In the half-light, I sit down and take one last look at the cross-word grid and mull over the clues. As well as the two answers that made me do a double-take this morning, *Getting plastered* and *Amanda, hair of the dog* now hits a nerve. It flashes accusation.

Nathan used to tell me that my mind worked overtime, all the time. I was always looking for problems. Seeing slights that didn't exist and feeling guilty when I'd done nothing wrong. In a quiet voice he told me this was a trait of alcoholics, barely concealed paranoia swimming like a predatory shark too close to the surface.

'If you don't believe me. Google it.'

'Google what?'

'Alcoholic paranoia.'

I did, but with wan enthusiasm. At first, I ignored Nathan's claims, guessing it was just his way to make me quit the drink. But back then, before the accident, I wasn't ready, or willing to admit I had a problem. Besides I enjoyed the buzz. It was only later, when depression clung like rancid mould, that I realised he was most probably right all along.

The clue, *Fine thing from Skye, say, as homoeopathic remedy?* *(4,2,3,3)* is slotted into the bottom right-hand quarter of the grid, the place where Nathan liked to finish, methodical in his workings, whereas I still flit all over the place, using easy answers to lend me letters for the nasty teasers. Nathan says I'm skittish, disordered, but when my speed of thought got me there before him, he'd grind his teeth, rubbing his molars together, side to side. His lips would droop in a mild expression of disinterest.

The alcoholic theme rattles me, pierces my flimsy psyche. Although my early morning hangover has slipped away, it's left a muddy landslide in its wake where the doubts, real or imagined, are festering. I wonder how long Nathan is going to carry on with the childish payback clues. It's as if he's stalking me, playing weird mind games. It's not easy to ignore. It's as if he knows what I'm doing, even from a distance. The occasional random drinking clue which I picked up in the puzzles shortly after Nathan left, is gradually being replaced by a stream of more targeted darts.

I go and yank the curtains closed, peeking out through a slit. The garden down below is in darkness, and the perimeter of Silver Birch is shrouded in a black veil. I tug at the slit where the curtains don't quite meet, and rip a section off the runner.

It's midnight by the time I get ready for bed. But first, I check the front door bolts, rattle the chain across, and peer through the spyhole. I fear an eye up close, but there's no one out there. The landing is empty, lit only by a small night light.

In the bathroom, after I've brushed my teeth, I bend down and have one last look through the loosened floorboard. But there's no sign of life in the kitchen of Flat B. Agaves must have gone to bed.

Finally, I slide under the duvet, pulling it over my head and ears, but can't quite block out the faint creaking sounds that chatter throughout the night. Nor the loneliness that talks to me, reminds me I'm on my own.

22

AMANDA

It's been several days since I cooked Agaves supper. I'm not sure why I've been avoiding him because my pulse races whenever I spy him through the window, and my night-time fantasies are escalating, the loosened floorboard beckoning like the bottle in *Alice in Wonderland* even though I know I shouldn't look.

I wait anxiously for the daily knock, fearful of an altered pattern but so far Agaves hasn't changed behaviour, still rapping at my door on his way to work and whistling as he hurries down the stairs with a lightness of tread.

My sober state reminds me how I used to be. A few drinks in, a handsome man, and I'd jump headlong into the fiery pit of lust. But now I'm scared. Scared to face rejection. Scared of my wild and beating heart. Scared of what's to come.

But today, I won't be able to avoid him as it's garden clear-up day. At least the weather's good, the sky a Côte d'Azur sapphire blue, not a cloud in sight. Through the master-bedroom window, I see him outside already, far below, pacing up and down the back garden, stopping every now and then to finger plants and bushes.

He looks up, and before I've time to duck, he waves and motions me to join him.

I rifle through a musty bin bag of Nathan's scrunched-up old clothes which he set aside for gardening. Nathan would often talk pruning, cutting hedges, lopping trees, weeding beds, fence repairs and erecting garden sheds. But Nathan was good at talk, action lagging well behind.

'It's too wet. Can't mow the lawn in this weather.'

'I've got to go to work.'

'The garden will have to wait till next weekend.'

'Ask that lazy savage from next door to get the finger out.'

Other than long-distance running and marathon challenges, Nathan got little pleasure from physical graft, much more at home with mental workouts. His fastidiousness where cleanliness was concerned didn't help. Blackened fingers, muddied clothes and earthy smells churned his stomach.

I haul out an old red T-shirt with 'Harvard Hopeful' emblazoned across the chest, matching holes eating through the H's. I sniff a pair of navy jogging bottoms and pull them on, then tie a jumper round my waist.

I lock up, scoot downstairs and yank open the lobby cupboard where a single hanging bulb displays the chaos. Flat B and C share the space, but as with the garden, Nathan shirked responsibility. His reluctance to tidy up was fuelled by the sight of Agave's weights and muddied hiking boots. I rummage in a wicker basket and dig out a small hoe and spade, a pair of gardening gloves and a kneeling pad before I head outside.

The air is crisp, the bright blue canvas overhead an illusion of heat. I quickly pull the sweater over my head, tugging my straggling hair through the gap. I then turn left towards the small wooden gate that leads into the garden.

As I pass the fogged-up window of Flat A, I scrunch down, but with a sidewards glance I see Victoria drinking, both hands gripping a black receptacle. As I haven't met her properly, I'm embarrassed to wave through her window. I scurry past and only slow when I reach the damp steps that lead down to the sunken lawn below.

Agaves is in the middle of the garden, hauling at the mower cord to kick-start the spluttering machine.

'Shit, shit, shit.' He grimaces as his angry trainer kicks the side and then pirouettes a full 360, the pain evidently biting.

'Hi. Having trouble?'

'You could say that.'

'Here. Let me have a go. Did you twizzle the choke? I'd turn it off completely. Nathan showed me how.' I set my tools on top of a rickety table.

'Be my guest,' Agaves says, stepping aside.

With one almighty tug, the machine coughs to life.

'Not just a pretty face then.' He smirks, our fingers brushing as he takes back control.

23

AMANDA

Victoria appears an hour later, dressed like a sixties hippie in a floaty flowery skirt billowing round her ankles. Maroon-painted toenails poke out through the ends of flimsy leather sandals and a virginal white blouse is at odds with dark-nibbed nipples poking through the braless top. The crisp March air has painted rosy circles, like make-up on a clown, on to her pale cheeks and a thick woolly jumper is loosely knotted round her shoulders.

She's taller than I realised, as it's the first time I've seen our neighbour up close since she moved in several weeks ago. We've never really spoken, the only communication between us being polite nods from a distance.

When Agaves and I watched her moving in, back in January, I didn't go down. He eventually went to lend a hand, and from the upstairs window, I watched him bustle round, lifting and carrying manly weighted boxes while our new neighbour floated in and out of view. A few times I had to dip behind the curtain in case she caught me spying.

I remember thinking how skinny, fragile she looked, like a

maiden in distress. The sort to entice a knight. On that day, I waited till she'd gone inside, and the removal men had driven off, before I sneaked out to attend an AA meeting. I wasn't ready to be sociable.

As Victoria approaches, Agaves cuts the mower to kill the noise, and slops a palm across his brow before extracting a scrunched-up handkerchief from his pocket to mop away the sweat. The smell of freshly cut grass mingles with his wholesome appearance. I get up from the kneeling pad, wincing as my knees click, and slip off the gloves.

'Hi, Victoria. Good to see you,' Agaves says, extending a hand.

'Call me Tory. All my friends do,' she says. 'Sorry, I'm not much good at gardening but I've brought refreshments.' She pats a broad bag slung across her shoulder which is bursting at the seams.

'That'll do nicely.' Agaves' eyes light up. 'You must have met Amanda. Flat C?'

She looks at me for a second, her eyes moving from my head to my feet, and back again. 'Hi. We've passed each other a few times, but never been properly introduced.' She smiles, her small perfect teeth reminding me of my childhood dachshund.

'Hi. It's good to finally meet. We're ready for a break and I think Teddy's just about to light the barbecue.'

'Yes. It's all set, just needs a match,' Agaves says as he wanders over to the rusting grill, pulls out a tiny swatch of matches from his pocket and fires up the bag of instant coals.

'I've got some salads here and when the barbecue's ready, I'll go and pick up the marinated meat skewers.' Tory starts to unpack her bag, like Mary Poppins unloading goodies for the children, setting the contents atop the round rickety metal table. Agaves unstacks the chairs and sets them out. He's buzzing, a bee round a honeypot of queens. A twinge of jealousy gets me flustered.

'I'll pop back up to the flat and get some glasses. I've made up a jug of home-made iced lemonade,' I say, my voice croaky, nervous.

'Here, I'll help you,' Agaves says and follows me back up the steps and round to the front of the house.

'Blue Station Queen,' he calls as he follows me up the stairs.

'Sorry? What's that?'

'Tory. Right-wing or blue. That's the Tories' colour, right? Station Queen... Victoria. I'm getting better, aren't I?' He laughs, the sound thick and throaty, as he catches up with me on the narrow landing between our two front doors. He faces me as I fumble to find the key and makes triangles with his arms by stuffing his hands in his pockets.

'Okay, clever clogs. Well done. But maybe best we keep the nickname to ourselves. Also, your clue's not quite right. If the answer is *Victoria*, the clue would be *Station Queen*. *Blue* relates to the word *Tory*, so that would be a separate clue.'

'Don't forget I'm still a beginner, but whatever you say. You're the boss.' He makes a stern salute.

It's hard to tone down the smile as a warm flutter tickles my insides.

* * *

When we return, Tory has covered the table with a red-checked vinyl tablecloth and arranged three place settings with cutlery, sunny serviettes and hard plastic plates. She's furiously wiping the mildewed chairs with kitchen roll.

I pull up several yards away and lean against the back wall of the house. Agaves has gone ahead with the pitcher.

There are two bottles in the centre of the table. No mistaking even from a distance. Red wine. White wine. And the Blue Station Queen is slowly, carefully, prising a champagne cork from another bottle. Agaves jumps aside as the cork shoots past him like a bullet and spume spurts up in the air.

'Phew. That was close,' he says.

She hands Agaves a glass and holds another in the air, motioning for me to come and join them.

24

AMANDA

Addict rues mistake (4)

As I slowly approach the table, like a tortoise with a heavy shell, I concentrate. Conjure up an early cryptic clue that Nathan made me solve. *Addict rues mistake (4)*.

'Come on. That's an easy one. Even you can work it out.' Nathan willed the tears away, by trying to trick my brain. But it didn't always work. With droopy jowls and sullen pout, I doodled on a pad. *Addict* is the definition. *Mistake* suggests wordplay, an anagram. *Rues* is the anagram. An anagram of *user*.

'*User* is the bloody answer. You've made your point,' I screamed, slamming the door behind.

I watch Tory lower the glass when Agaves gently places a hand on top of her outstretched arm. He's telling her, confiding in my failings. I give him time before I move forward.

'I'll go and fiddle with the barbecue. It's smoking like a chimney.' Agaves collects some dried kindling from a box under a lean-to and wanders down the garden. With a stick, he churns the coals until flames escape through the blackened grill.

'Sorry, I didn't realise.' Tory's voice is sombre as she purses her lips in a sympathetic gesture.

'Why would you? Drinking problems aren't easy to spot and not the best conversation opener.' My levity aims to make it easier, but who am I kidding? Admission makes me feel a failure. It reminds me I'm a user. Like her, I was once a social drinker. Quick witted with a flirtatious nature, I'd rock the room until I fell asleep or fell over.

'Here. Let me.' She lifts the pitcher, sunny slices of lemon floating among the icebergs, and pours me a glass. I'm like a child with allergies.

'Thanks.' The acid bite stings my throat and tears prick my eyes.

Tory quietly sips champagne, small ladylike mouthfuls, and soon refills her glass before excusing herself and disappearing through the back entrance to her flat.

'Can't I just have one glass? Go on. I can do it. You can keep an eye on me.' My cajoling tone fooled Nathan a few times, my sincerity fickle and delusional.

Tory's plastic fizzing flute is now calling out to me. Through her downstairs kitchen window, I see her looking out. She's motionless, her hands holding up a large platter.

A few yards away, as I wander over, Agaves is flapping a piece of cardboard, sending thick smoke over his shoulder which makes him cough.

'It'll be another fifteen minutes at least. I think the damp's got in. Are you OK?' He concentrates on the flickering spark which rears up and dies down like a fiery dragon.

'I'm fine. Thanks for telling Tory.'

'No worries. I'll stick with non-alcoholic beer if that helps.' He lifts a bottle, takes a swig. 'Not big on lunchtime drinking anyway.'

I want to hug him. I'm not sure whether it's loyalty to Nathan that holds me back, or fear of how Agaves makes me feel. Then there's an unease that Tory is nearby.

'Tory seems OK,' he says. 'She felt bad when I told her you didn't drink.'

'Thanks.'

* * *

Tory likes her drink, that's for sure. The champagne bottle was half empty when I left her and Agaves in the garden, feigning a burgeoning migraine rather than admit the real reason I was leaving, that I'm not yet ready to be around alcohol. I lied to save face.

'Sorry to spoil the party. At least the garden looks a bit neater,' I said.

'Yes, it does. Thanks for the help,' Agaves says. 'Maybe take a couple of paracetamol and a hot cup of tea.' He stood up as I made to slope away.

'Good to meet you at last. We'll get together again soon.' Tory didn't get up, but I felt her eyes follow me up the steps as I disappeared out of sight.

I'm now sitting beneath the bedroom window, peeking out over the sill. Tory has poured out two glasses of red wine, and with the merest upward glance in my direction, passes one to Agaves. She then leans across and chinks his glass before she throws back her head and joins him in a drink.

'Cheers,' I guess they're saying.

I slowly get up and in an instant Tory and Agaves' heads turn as one and they wave up at me like synchronised swimmers. As I lift my arm in response, I watch as Tory inches Agaves' reluctant hand off the top of his glass and fills him up.

My stomach churns, the sickness of rejection coming back. Waves of despair wash over me as I draw the curtains and collapse on to the bed.

25

AMANDA

It's been four days since the fateful barbecue, but routine has pulled me through.

I've concentrated on simple things, like rising early, scalding showers and healthy eating. Wholefoods, multicoloured fruits and vegetables, lentil soups and home-made smoothies have fed mind and body.

My online tutoring business is picking up, my resolve pulling in new clients. Uni students struggling with degree coursework are now my bread and butter, paying way more than the classroom slog. For now, working from home is easier, and a strict schedule keeps me on the AA recovery track.

After two hours of intensive Zooming, I close my laptop and head to the kitchen where I switch on the coffee grinder. The beans grate and smash, ricocheting off the Perspex like atoms in the Hadron Collider. Where drinks, as well as food, are concerned, I'm practising substitution, and coffee is hard to beat, offering a buzz without the liver damage. Freshly ground beans from all parts of the globe vie for my approval and I smell their bouquets the way I once did wine. Vietnamese Robusta is hard to beat.

Nathan said I should work on the addiction angle itself, not on replacing one craving for another. That said, in the grand scheme of things, the sweats, palpitations and insomnia from coffee over-dose are bearable. Yet, Nathan had a point, so I continue to try to work with him. He's still in my head, if no longer in my life. I remind myself to drink slowly, whatever I'm drinking, and when doing the puzzle, a single sip is a reward for each clue solved. Now, as I wander through to the lounge with my mug, I sniff the comforting smell of coffee.

The quietness in the flat spooks me, even in the daytime, and it's worse when I know Agaves has left the building. Over the last couple of days, his early-morning rap and sing-song greeting, have lacked spontaneity and chirpiness. There's a hesitancy, which could be down to guilt that he hasn't been to see me since the barbecue, although he still calls out, 'Have a good day. See you later.'

I grip the sofa until he's gone, but then can't help myself from scooting to the window. Visions of him and Tory are clouding my judgement. I watch them walk, side by side, towards the tube station. There's a new familiarity about them as their shoulders sway more closely, and when she's around, Agaves' stride seems more purposeful. Although I know I shouldn't look, the masochism gnaws away.

I spread the paper, using my palms to flatten it out across the table and skim the headlines. I then neatly cut out the once-a-week Crossgram puzzle for Mr Beckles, our elderly neighbour one door down, and set it aside. Although easier to solve than the cryptic puzzle, the Crossgram with its simple quick clues *down*, has *across* clues made up of anagrams which can be tricky. Beckles likes us to tackle it together over a bowl of home-made soup, although his mind is getting sharper, and he's started nudging me aside until he's had a go himself.

With religious concentration I then refold the paper, firstly in half, then into quarters, and sharpen the edges of the broadsheet. Thursday's cryptic setter can be a tricky git, and on first glance I suspect Poseidon, one of Nathan's setter colleagues, who used to set on a Thursday. I've no idea of the guy's real name, as I was only ever introduced to him as Poseidon, god of the sea. I had to bottle up a snigger when he bowed and introduced himself.

Nathan shared with me certain tricks his individual colleagues would use to ratchet up a grid's complexity. The clues today have Poseidon's stamp. But as my eyes hop from corner to corner, up and down, and back again, I sit up straighter. My feet and legs begin to jiggle as my chest constricts.

The drinking theme is back. As well as something more macabre.

26

AMANDA

The converse of 'in vino veritas' (5,5)

The pen knocks back and forth against my teeth as I dissect the individual words.

The converse means the opposite. *In vino veritas* means 'in wine, there is truth'. For Nathan this is true. After a glass, his words bubble like a mountain spring, inhibitions loosened, and his honesty shines through. But I'd embellish after several mouthfuls. Confident, arrogant, I would aim to trick the listener. False flirtation led me down murky alleys.

The clue hits a nerve. The opposite of telling the truth would be lying. I curl my legs under my thighs, scrunch my shoulders and then I twig. My 'Aha! Moment' as Nathan called it. The opposite of a drunken truth would be a *sober truth*. I can hear Joseph's pious voice in my mind as he skims the AA circle with his pale grey eyes, telling us we'll never know the truth until we're sober. It's addict recovery speak.

The first sip of coffee tastes bitter, a sour reward for solving the clue, but the next answer doesn't come so easily.

Island doctor and I live only to drink (6)

The word *drink* irks, mars the moment. Nathan would have beaten me to this one, it's not coming easily. He knew what to look for, the instant markers. Five minutes in, I break my rule, and have another sip of coffee, my tongue already furred with a metallic taste.

The whole means *to drink*, I'm almost certain. The whole might be an *island* or perhaps the clue is tricking me with the word *doctor*, to think about an anagram... perhaps I need to doctor *I live*.

Then I work it out. The first letter of the answer is *i* from *island*. The *doctor* is represented by *MB*, (Bachelor of Medicine). *I live* can be turned into *I be* and yes... the whole clue means to drink. *Imbibe*.

I neatly fill the squares and then carry on working clockwise round the grid.

An alcoholic can gain nothing (4)

I've already filled in two of the letters, the second and the fourth; _i_o needs only two letters.

I stare into the bottom of the mug. All that's left is a thin layer of black molasses lining the base. The caffeine hangover has begun, the three-shot strength kick-starting the shakes.

The meaning is easy. The answer for the whole thing is another word for an alcoholic. The *gain* is *win* with *nothing* (a *o*) added on to the end. *Wino*.

My stomach is gurgling like waste water and I'm not even halfway through. Nathan would call a time-out when twenty minutes was up, preparing the stopwatch for reset in five minutes.

I get up, stretch out my neck and shoulders and wander through to the bathroom. I swipe a brush through my tangled hair, swill mouthwash round my gums and watch the brown spit dribble down the plughole. I hunker down and make sure the loosened floorboard is secured, slapping it firmly in place and make a promise to myself that I'll get it nailed down. Soon.

I return to the puzzle, agitated, and anxious to finish and get on with the day, but nothing has prepared me for the last few clues. They're not drink related. They're far worse.

Watch out for a worker encompassing conflict (6)

To be corpulent, boy, is disastrous (5)

Made a threat involving loss of living (5)

I get it the first one straightaway. I've seen the clue before. It means a warning. The whole means *watch out for. A worker* is *bee encompassing conflict. Conflict* is *war.* The word *bee* goes round the outside of *war* and the answer is *beware.*

The next answer is *fatal. Corpulent* means *fat,* and the boy is *al.* The whole means *disastrous.*

The drinking theme has really wound me up. It's no longer a joke, a pathetic means of payback. Nathan's gone too far. I'm already shaking with the real or imagined threat. But these three clues are different. They're warnings. They conjure up my worst nightmares. I may be paranoid, but the threats feel real, and combined with the earlier clues, it all becomes too much.

As soon as I've solved the last clue, bottom right, I launch myself back towards the bathroom. I'm just in time, before the coffee shoots up my throat and hits the sink in a projectile of creamy slime.

Made a threat involving loss of living (5)

The whole means *loss of living. Involving* is a marker that tells the solver that the answer is within *made a threat.*

I slink back to the lounge, and with a heavy nib I scrawl the answer in thick black letters until the grid is ruined. Then I rip the paper up. In half. In quarters, and finally into small confetti pieces which I launch across the room.

Death.

How can I forget?

27

AMANDA

The door to Mr Beckles' basement flat is ajar. He lives alone in the house next door. A rusting number plate dangles on its side, flimsily attached to a rotting gatepost, in stark contrast to the ostentatious brass sign on the front facade of Silver Birch.

My elderly neighbour is currently battling mobility issues, which I'm encouraging him to tackle. With Joseph spurring me on, tirelessly working on my recovery programme, I try to replicate this selflessness by looking out for Mr Beckles. He's a sweet old guy, but with no one left to care for him. His wife died recently, and his only son is settled in Australia.

As I peer down from the street above, a dank and musty rotting smell crawls up the stone steps to greet me. I sidestep the rubbish bags, which have been ripped and rifled by a night-time scavenger and pick my way over apple cores and chicken bones.

'Yoo-hoo. Mr Beckles?' I push the unlocked door, and step inside. 'Mr Beckles?'

Boffin, the cat, shoots past with a nasty hissing noise and skims my leg.

Boffin, the name Beckles gave the tomcat, prowls the neighbourhood and scavenges for food, but makes regular trips to Beckles where it knows there are likely to be leftovers. While my neighbour was in the hospital, I gave the cat milk until Beckles was well enough to come home. Boffin reminds me of myself, relying on wiles for its survival as a hissing tongue repels a careless hand.

'In here. Is that you, Amanda?' A wracking cough gets tagged on to the end of the question.

'Hi. Sorry I'm a bit later than usual, but I've got your soup.' I drum a hand against the saucepan, a percussive clang of welcome.

The lounge where Beckles sits is strewn with newspapers, plates and cans, and the curtains are still closed. A rusting Anglepoise lamp, bent and twisted like its owner, forms a halo of light as on a stage, and I notice it illuminates an unfinished puzzle.

'How are you?' I ask in a soft voice.

When he doesn't respond immediately, I set the saucepan to wobble on a pile of magazines and take out the Crossgram from my pocket. I unfold the cut-out, set it down and hand him his glasses and a pen.

'Why not make a start on the new puzzle while I pop through and warm your soup.'

He nods, his words getting drowned in a convulsion of thickening phlegm.

When I told Joseph about Mr Beckles, and how we had connected through my neighbour's feral cat, my sponsor encouraged me to help, saying a worthwhile cause can aid recovery.

'Looking out for others can help redirect negative thoughts,' Joseph told me, like a therapist spouting alternative behaviours.

When I realised Beckles was so isolated, it was easy to empathise. I now pop by three times a week, hoover, tidy up, and talk to him.

Nathan was encouraging, suggesting the quick daily puzzle might help sharpen Beckles' mind.

'Doing puzzles helps keep dementia at bay,' he announced. 'Much better than Sudoku.'

Nathan would print off the daily copies and stack them neatly for my visits. Now I've added the task to my own routine. I bring copies of both the quick crossword and the Crossgram puzzles every time I come, and the sight of the grids makes Beckles' eyes light up.

The kitchen is a salmonella minefield, but for once, I welcome the mess. Scrubbing, scraping, and rattling dishes sidetrack my deepening disquiet and jangling nerves. When I hold my hands out, they vibrate with a steady tremble and it's as if I'm looking at hands belonging to someone else. An overwhelming desire to have a drink – a shot of vodka, a stiff gin or a goblet of wine – teases my mind like an old companion knocking at the door.

Beckles' cupboards are black, inside, and out, thickly caked in grease. I tug the cord of the slatted blinds, but they lock a few inches up. Outside, the back garden jungle straggles over to the fence, which forms the boundary with Silver Birch, and as I turn my head ninety degrees, I notice that one of the wobbly posts has collapsed and is lying on the ground, leaving a gaping hole between our gardens. Agaves shook the fence recently, promising that he'd secure it when the weather picked up.

The pan suddenly starts to bubble and spit.

'Shit.' I swivel the gas knob to low, stir the contents, and give it a taste with a stained teaspoon. I then unfold the metal tray, cranking out the legs, gritting my teeth against the noise which grates like chalk on blackboard.

I carry the food through to the lounge and smile when I see Beckles curled over, his head against his chest as his pea-sized eyes glint through the thick glass lenses at the puzzle.

'How are you getting on?' I set the tray down and peer over his shoulder.

'Grand,' he says. 'Nearly halfway through with the anagrams.'

'That was quick. Here, let me see.'

Dust dances in the single beam of light and as an insect – midge, fly, or mosquito – settles on the red metal, Beckles spits it off. He sits quietly, waiting for approval, an 85-year-old man returned to boyhood.

His striped pyjamas are stained with yellow, likely from egg or custard, two of his favourite foods, and the top gapes, revealing thin wispy grey threads weaving across a concave chest. Although a carer pops in every day, he's adamant he can wash himself. He alternates between two pairs of pyjamas, and reluctantly lets me wash them in rotation. I've made him promise he'll dress in outdoor clothes soon, threatening otherwise to forgo the laundry.

Since his stroke, which followed on a couple of months after the death of his wife, Beckles hasn't left the flat. Each time I call round, I help him walk up and down the hallway, and he swears that soon he'll try to go outside.

'It's confidence,' he says. 'It's slowly coming back. My aim is to climb the steps up on to the street, but it'll be like scaling Everest.'

'You need to try,' I say, cajoling as if speaking to a child who's fallen off their bike. 'Try to get back out there.'

'Maybe when the weather warms up,' he repeats by rote, with a sullen determination not to be coerced.

As he slurps the soup, dipping doughy strips of bread into it, I skim the words he's entered in the Crossgram. I'm proud of Mr Beckles but also with myself. Not the prowess at having taught a skill, but at having taken up the task. It's given my neighbour a meaning, something to lighten up the daily darkness and a hobby to keep his brain alive.

'Well done, Mr Beckles. You're getting good at this.'

I'm not sure which of us it helps the most.

28

AMANDA

Suddenly, a dustbin lid bangs, flails on the ground outside, and I swirl round. Boffin is back.

All at once my head starts spinning, the heavy atmosphere inside the dank basement flat making it worse. I try to fasten a clean cloth around Beckles' throat, and as he puffs to cool the spoon, the exhaled air hits me in the face with a stench of rotten eggs.

'Hm. Tastes good,' he says, running his tongue round his lips. 'Thank you.'

My hearing has become mushy, a tinnitus of bell ringing. It's happened before when I'm stressed. While Beckles has been eating, I've looked at the Crossgram. The clues that he's filled in. I know my blood pressure is up, and I head for the window, tug apart the curtains. Through the cracked glass, I can just see up on to the street above. A motorcyclist screeches to a halt, his leathered legs swinging across the seat, and I watch him carry a parcel in the direction of Silver Birch. I'm scared to turn round, sit down again, and recheck the answers to the first two anagrams Beckles has solved.

In Tram – Martin
The Run – Hunter

When put together the two words make up the full name of the monster in my nightmares. The man who raped me. I can't forget the blurred outline of Hunter's chiselled jaw, teeth like sharks. Nor his hands. Thick, white, with black hairs that straggled up the backs like poison ivy.

The last thing I could recall, before I fell unconscious, was feeling drunk, swaying like a sot. When I came round my blouse, white, red trim, buttoned cuffs, flimsy, was torn apart. I remember the detail because I later chopped the blouse into a thousand tiny pieces. Martin Hunter was watching me when I awoke. He smirked as I rounded up my clothes, and laughed as I scuttled off into the night.

Nathan blamed me. It was my own fault, there was no one else to blame. I had chosen to meet Hunter, and that fact was enough. What happened next was of no import. The night of Martin Hunter was the night my husband left me.

The clank of Beckles spoon in victory, the metal clunking against the dish, brings me back to the present.

'Aren't you impressed?' he asks with a toothless grin. 'A clean white plate.'

'Well done,' I say. Before I lift his tray, I pause. 'If it's okay, I'll come back tomorrow and do the dishes, tidy up then. And fix the curtain. It's hanging off at one end.' I blush, realising I tugged the fabric too hard. But Beckles doesn't notice. His head has already lolled forward, hung like a cadaver's, but his sharp eyes and mind are refocused on the grid.

* * *

Outside, the sunlight sears my pupils, blinding in its fury. Before I climb the wet glistening concrete steps back up on to the street, I brush the rotting remains into a pile in the corner by Beckles' entrance and cover them with the stray dustbin lid. Clearing them away, like the dishes, will have to wait until tomorrow.

On my way up, I grip the iron railing for support. My legs are like jelly.

As I turn for home, I spot Tory walking into our driveway. A large handbag, damp green leather, dangles from a bony shoulder, and although she looks my way, she doesn't acknowledge me, instead taking out her phone.

I sit on our boundary wall, facing out onto Brewer's Hill, and look down at the screenshot on my phone that I took of the Crossgram before I gave it to Beckles. I'm confused as I stare at the clues. Crossgram puzzles aren't Nathan's thing. But the clues can't be coincidence. Maybe Nathan is helping out another setter. I'm certain the daily cryptic puzzle drinking clues are Nathan's bullets aimed at me. But the Martin Hunter anagrams are something else entirely. Instinct tells me they're not my husband's handiwork.

There's one other anagram that suddenly jumps out at me. As I stare at my phone, the words *Bad rat* make me freeze. I sit up, look up and down the road, and back to my phone. Beckles had answered this one as well. I remember the answer filled in, but only now pick up an alternative answer. Beckles had filled in the word *tabards*.

'I looked it up. It's a coarse sleeveless garment,' Beckles told me, stubbing his finger proudly against the word.

But I'm on another tack. My mind is seeing the same seven letters, but in a different order. Nathan spat the word, again and again. Up close. In my ear, drenching it with loathing. *Bad rats* had appeared as an anagram in a clue the day he moved out.

Before I solved the answer, which that day was *tabards,* Nathan hinted at another possible solution.

'I'll give you a clue. Think Martin Hunter.'

I then twigged. *Bastard.* As in my husband's loathing of Martin Hunter.

* * *

I put my phone away and walk up to the small gate by the side entrance to our property. The faded blue metal portal hangs off its hinges, creaking dangerously when pushed, and held in place as if by a thread.

'I'll mend that. Rub it down. Paint it. Secure the posts.' More of Nathan's promises. In sickness and in health. Till death us do part. But the gate has collapsed under the weight of insincerity. I squeeze through, twisting my body like a limbo dancer, so as not to bring it crashing down.

Tory, the Woman in the Window, is in her downstairs lounge looking out, wiping down the panes. In her hand she clenches a bottle of cleanser, squirts it on the glass. A fifties housewife in a sunny advert, she's dressed in a bright yellow apron; panels front and back.

Tory is dressed in a shiny sleeveless *tabard.*

29

AMANDA

Joseph asks me what triggers my panic attacks.

'What sets them off? I'm happy to listen,' he repeats. I'm not at ease discussing everything with Joseph. Knowing that he's undressed me, put me to bed when I'm unconscious, should help me open up. He's proven his worth. But he's too close to Nathan, and I'm not sure how much they share. Instead, I tell him that I'm fine and the moments quickly pass.

But they don't. After I returned from Beckles, I tried everything to calm my breathing. Paper bags. Camomile tea. Meditation. Nothing helped. To keep my mind off alcohol, I came to bed early, craving a safe cocoon. That was two hours ago, and I'm still tossing and turning.

My legs are like Mr Beckles', restless, uncontrolled. They thrash in and out from under the duvet. Cold air filters through the cracks of door frames, and the windows with their flaky seals. But I'm burning up, dripping, my brain on fire, rumbling to explode.

Even lying down, I crave a drink to calm me down. Slowly, I slither into slumber, but soon I'm desperate to get back to consciousness, reality. Back to the bricks and mortar of my cell, as the dark, macabre dreams suck me down. Tonight my nightmares take me back to the first time I met Martin Hunter.

* * *

It was early December, at the *London Echo* Christmas party. All the newspaper staff and half their spouses were crammed into a wine bar in Covent Garden. Grayson Peacock, the paper's editor in chief, had hired out the place, and as a live band belted out Christmas anthems, liquor from the free bar filled our veins.

I caught the Tube, thrilled to be getting out. Christmas cheer lit the carriage like a Nordic pine, the cold grey torso spun with gaudy tinsel. My playful reindeer antlers, red, brown, and white, were coiled inside my coat. A few drinks in and I'd plonk them on my head.

'I'll come home first and pick you up. We'll travel back into London and go to the party together,' Nathan had suggested.

'Don't be silly. I'll meet you there.'

'Are you sure?'

I was excited. It would be the first time I'd turned up at a social event on my own since we'd been married. Nathan liked me close, at all times, arms linked in coupledom. I found it stifling, unsettling, and now I understood what it meant to be a trapped canary. As the walls closed in, my wilful spirit got doused by Nathan's expectations. I told him I was too young to be middle-aged, boring and sensible, with no room for spontaneity.

'It's called maturity,' was his response.

It was our first Christmas as a married couple. We'd tied the knot six months before. Nathan liked to talk up marriage, and love, in platitudes. *Together forever. Work as one.* He'd swivel his wedding band and cite the word *belong*. When sober, I swallowed back retorts. But rebellion soon snorted through the drink, and while

Nathan played with building blocks, I puffed them down. He played happy families, while I played devil's advocate.

Then Martin Hunter happened. He was Nathan's boss at the *Echo*, the overseer of all the puzzle setters, and deputy editor at the paper. Nathan never liked him, calling him an arrogant supercilious prick.

Well, that first time nothing really happened. Rather I got punished for my behaviour, the overzealous Christmas merriment. Nathan called it flirting. Sluttish. Embarrassing. But I was only having fun, or so I thought.

I buzzed around the bar, like a fly on death row, skittering through the guests. Wild, euphoric, and very, very drunk. I threw off my spiky heels and shimmied on the dance floor, my hair flying wild with the reindeer antlers tangled in its mane. My slinky cocktail dress clung to my curves, rich in sweat, as I gyrated round the room.

Nathan doesn't dance. When I managed to drag him on to the floor, he shuffled like a robot from foot to foot. His fingers twizzled me round in an effort at taking part. But he didn't last, soon heading to a corner and joining a group of older colleagues.

But Martin Hunter was like me. A showman. A skilful mover with accomplished steps. That was how he seemed through the heady haze, and when we'd danced enough, I accepted his outstretched arm and accompanied him to the bar.

'So, you're Nathan's wife?' His lazy drawl flowed like syrupy treacle as he leant against the counter. 'A top-up?'

He gave me a fresh glass, wrapped his fingers round mine, and filled me up with cheap champagne. I knew Nathan was watching, but as the room spun like a speeding carousel, I didn't care. The devil me was back. Another person. Reckless. Wanton. And extremely drunk.

I didn't see Nathan leave, but as the party began to thin, and

Martin Hunter buttoned up, I asked him if he'd seen Nathan. I grabbed my coat, fear catapulting me back to reality. My eyes scoured the empty room.

'I think he's gone.' Hunter took my arm. 'But I'm more than happy to take you home.'

I remember frantically looking round for Nathan. I couldn't believe he'd left me on my own. When he'd asked me to rein in my behaviour, I'd told him to loosen up. I was only having fun. I never dreamt he'd leave.

In the early days of marriage, I didn't realise how much Nathan needed control, and it soon became clear that he didn't like to share me. When I got home, he snapped that he hadn't been prepared to watch me make a fool of him.

When I realised Nathan had left, I had to wrest myself free from Hunter's grip, before I staggered out the door, and into the middle of the road.

'You're OK. I can get a taxi,' I yelled. But flashbacks of Hunter's muscled arms, his deep insistent voice that he'd drive, and his grinding body as it pinned me up against a wall haunted me for weeks.

Sober, and in the cold light of day, I knew I'd gone too far. I had led Hunter on. He was handsome, the sort of bastard that had sucked me in once too often, but this was different. He was dangerous, determined to get what he wanted. On that occasion, I had a lucky escape.

Alcohol was the case for my defence. I assured Nathan nothing happened, but I was slurring when I got home and fell asleep on the sofa, which didn't help my trial. Nathan became both judge and jury. His argument for the prosecution was 'in vino veritas'. He said our hidden truths, desires, rampage after one too many drinks. Uncorked, free to drown, I was hung as the harlot my husband always feared. Case dismissed.

But I kept my head down, sobered up and played the long game. I waited. Waited patiently until Nathan believed me. *Actions, rather than words*, was top of my New Year's resolution list. Gradually, Nathan came round, and I swore it would never happen again. Slowly, I regained his trust.

I never told Nathan that Martin had tried it on, saying that he had also left the party before me. As the pair worked together, I didn't see the point. Also, I didn't think I'd see Martin Hunter again.

Even today, I blame myself, my stupidity, my drunkenness, for everything that's happened. When Nathan told me that Martin Hunter didn't drink, I knew the fault was mine. Apparently, his wife feeds him smoothies and protein shakes, his body like my own newly erected temple, fed and nurtured by designer food and healthy eating.

But Hunter knew I drank. That much is clear.

30

AMANDA

When I got up this morning, there was a scrap of paper on the hall mat which must have been slid under the front door while I was asleep.

Fancy popping round for dinner? 8 o'clock? Teddy x

The note twitches in my fingers as I turn it over. My name is scrawled in loopy letters on the front.

I'm not sure whether it's a date. A thank you for the night I cooked. A guilt thing after drinking with Tory at the barbecue. Or just my neighbour being friendly.

I've never been inside Agave's flat before as Nathan refused regular coffee invitations, and was adamant that he wouldn't enter his neighbour's flat, until eventually all communication, other than a passing nod between our two households, dried up.

* * *

It's now exactly 8 p.m. Pretence that I've been busy all day is Plan A. That I've been tied up with work, online lessons, Zoom calls and marking papers. There's no Plan B. The truth is that I've spent most of the day wandering round the flat, trying clothes on and off and counting down the minutes.

Before I met Nathan, date nights would be spiked with early shots to boost the fun, but more than that, to boost my confidence. Tonight, without the crutch, my nerves jangle and it gets so bad that I toy with the idea of staying in.

At one minute past the hour, a bottle of lemonade in one hand, two boxes of chocolates in the other, my elbow stabs the bell of Flat B. My throat is dry, scratchy with longing for a drink, as well as longing for something else. Agaves. He's become an obsession, lust and desire playing havoc with my insides, and my sanity.

The heat on the landing between our flats is suffocating. It's like a holding cell, the three thick walls boxing me in, locking in the panic. Unless I go back into Flat C, the staircase is my only escape. I glance over my shoulder and imagine a brick wall at the bottom which hems me further in. I conjure it in my nightmares when I can't escape from fear. From memories. The accident. Martin Hunter.

My breath grows raspy, uneven, and before I stab the bell again I put my back flat against the wall to steady myself.

Suddenly, Agaves appears, like the happy genie in *Aladdin* with his easy smile, bare feet and a drying-up cloth slung over one arm.

'Welcome. Come in.' He flings the door wide and ushers me through. 'After you,' he says. 'And excuse the mess.'

I mumble a greeting, glad of laden arms. I mull it over whether I should lean in and kiss him cheek to cheek. Long lost friend, hopeful lover, or familiar neighbour. I'm not sure what he is but since nine this morning I've been playing out scenarios.

Where will we have after-dinner coffee? Do I share the sofa?

Offer to do the dishes, tidy things away? There'll be no spur of the moment, merry-made decisions. No *go with the flow*. I already feel my juices blocked, caked with sediment, building up against a dam. But planning helps me cope, avoid the pitfalls.

'Hi.' The chocolate boxes slither from my grasp. 'Oops.' I feel my cheeks redden.

'Are those for me?' He dips to pick them up. 'My favourites.'

I trekked to Muswell Hill, ticked off a task by browsing round the handmade chocolate shop. Salted caramels, soft centres. Two boxes. One dark, one milk. Agaves told me these were his guilty pleasure.

* * *

Nathan was neat, meticulous to the point of insanity. He'd lift away my empty mug even before I'd finished, sweep up crumbs drizzled around my feet and plug in the hoover, letting the suction noise tell me off.

'Here. Let me help,' I'd tut, raising lazy legs as the machine rolled back and forth.

Agaves is the polar opposite. Jeez.

He leads the way to the lounge which is down a small tight flight of stairs. A second small flight of stairs lead off in the opposite direction. The lounge is like a junk emporium, the sort you browse on rainy days. Random shelves are filled with Warhammer models, congealed paint pots and caked brushes, but the space is filled with energy, warmth and a pleasant lived-in feeling.

'Sorry. Not had much time to clear up.' He lifts magazines, envelopes, mail, and an empty plate from a well-worn coffee table. He shuffles the papers into a neat pile and deposits them on the end of an already overflowing shelf.

'Don't worry. I'm fine here.' I sit on the end of a two-seater sofa, awkwardly lodged between worn tapestry cushions with suspect feather stuffing. As my eyes start to itch, I dare to poke a finger in the corners.

'Are you okay?'

Agaves looks concerned when I don't answer, until a sneeze bursts forth like a laden cloud.

'Sorry. I'm allergic to feathers. And pets.'

Nathan's sympathy for my puffed-up eyes and runny nose waned when he realised pets were off the table. In the early days of marriage, it was a sticking point that he couldn't keep a dog, but my tales of allergic reactions, blotchy skin and puffy eyes when around animals and feathers, eventually won him round. Or so I thought.

'Maybe one day. If we move out to the country,' I said, between lingering placatory kisses.

Joseph, who keeps in touch with Nathan, tells me I've already been replaced by a wiry mongrel.

Agaves disappears up the stairs with the dirty plate, and I hear him clamber down the other stairs, presumably towards the kitchen. I look round the room, comparing it to Nathan's bachelor pad when we first met, which was clinical, spotless, painted black and white. No decorative extras. But Agaves' walls are lined with posters, a random warrior spear, hardwood tribal masks, and randomly sized, dark-framed pictures.

My host reappears, two tumblers filled with ice and something pink, held between sturdy fingers, and a plate of olives.

'Pink gin,' he says. My mouth drops open. 'Only joking. Try it, it's the next best thing. No alcohol, I promise.' As I take a glass, our fingers brush.

The dining table is placed directly beneath where mine is one floor up but rather than looking out across the built-up London skyline, Agaves' window stares straight into the gnarled trunk of the silver birch. On either side of the tree, I glimpse the outline of the recently built cube-shaped flats across the road.

Reading my thoughts, Agaves says, 'Not as good a view from down here.'

The small path to the left of the silver birch is clogged with weeds, the slimy coating of the broken slabs just visible through the growth. The area around the trunk is bare, yellow, dusty and the barren tree has the timbre of a still-life painting, devoid of the summer waxen foliage, which hasn't yet begun to reappear.

From my flat, the evidence of neglect outside isn't as obvious, as my eyes tend to look up, across the skyline towards city lights, rather than at the tangled mess below.

A sudden merry ping sends Agaves shooting up the stairs again, and back down into the kitchen, which I know lies directly below my bathroom. The higgledy-piggledy layout of Agaves' flat is disorientating beside the more regular arrangement of Flat C.

Something smashes to the ground, crockery, a plate. A muffled 'fuck' seeps through the walls before he reappears carrying two laden plates held tight by a set of oven mitts.

'Voila! Fish and chips.' The strong scent of vinegar mingles with a ketchup smell, and mushy peas, like merry green gunge, brighten up the platters.

'Looks fantastic,' I say, suddenly feeling hungry.

'From the chippie up the road.' His admission makes me laugh, and as we sit down at the table, I finally breathe more easily.

31

AMANDA

Agaves is easy company. He eats with gusto, swishing the thick-cut chips through the ketchup and smothering each mouthful with a globule of peas. When he notices I'm struggling with the hearty portions, he spears his fork across the table and skewers my remaining chips.

'How did you get on with Tory?' I ask.

I've waited as long as I can before I ask the question, the one I've been bottling up for days. I need to know if anything is going on between Tory and Agaves. I straighten my knife and fork, and glance casually out the window. In the reflection I watch my host in his bright yellow T-shirt and glimpse a small gold chain circling his sturdy neck.

Agaves leans across and takes my plate, piling it on top of his before pushing them both to one side. He stretches his long legs out from under the table and plonks his feet on top of an adjacent chair. My eyes are drawn to his crossed ankles, his sculptured feet, slim and straight with their neatly clipped nails. His extremities are tanned like the rest of him. I've seen his perfect outline before, through the bathroom board – smooth and hairless except for the dark silken thatch that weaves across his chest.

'Tory,' he repeats. 'Yes. She seems nice.'

'What does she do for a living?'

'Interior design, I think she said, although I'm not sure if that's her job, or a hobby. She doesn't give too much away.'

'Maybe she can give you a few tips.' I look around the room. I can't help myself, but it lightens the awkwardness.

'Cheeky.'

His smile makes my stomach flip.

'What else did you learn? I wonder why she's single.' I reach across and pick up a leftover chip and nibble the end. It's something to do, help lighten my crisp inquisitiveness.

'Oh, she's divorced. Her husband left her, but I've no idea why.'

I want to ask what he thinks of her. As a woman. As competition. Instead, I ask, 'What about you. Ever been married?'

'No. I just haven't met the right woman. Yet.' He smirks, eyes twinkling as he flirts around the edges of the conversation.

* * *

When he goes off to make the coffee, I get up from the table and move back to the sofa.

On his return, Agaves sets down the mugs and then dips his hand below the coffee table from where he produces a crumbled newspaper. He waves it in the air.

'Yo! Look what I've got. Here, shove up. I need some help.'

He nudges in beside me and sets down the scrunched-up paper. A dark ringed stain straddles the edge of the crossword grid, but half the puzzle has already been completed.

'See what you've done?'

'What?'

'You've got me hooked. On crosswords.' His eyes shine.

I remember back to the first time I realised I was an addict. Not of alcohol though. I knew I was a crossword addict when one evening I spent three hours straight concentrating on words, without a thought of drink. But it's a healthy obsession, one that helps me relax, temporarily block out the world.

Now with our heads bowed, the puzzle loosely draped across Agaves' muscled thighs, it's not the words that quicken my pulse.

'Number four across. *Gibberish from Holland repeatedly? (6,5).* Any ideas?'

I don't let on I finished the whole grid in half an hour, at eight o'clock this morning. My tongue runs round my upper lip in feigned focus.

'Hmm.' Agaves hums in concentration, a furrowed ridge deepening on his brow. He taps the pen, his eyes glancing back to me.

'Okay, I'll give you the answer but you have to explain how I got there,' I say.

'Shoot.'

'*Double Dutch.*'

Agaves fills in the squares before he speaks.

'Aha. I get it!' He sounds like Nathan. 'How could I not have seen it?'

He swivels round, grabs me, and lands a wet kiss on my lips. When I laugh, he looks aghast.

'What's so funny?'

'Crosswords. They seem to be a new form of *flop year.*'

'What are you on about?' he asks.

'It's an anagram. Work it out!'

Wrinkles line his brow as he stares at the words. 'Come on, help me out.'

When I finally give in, offer up the answer, my cheeks redden.

'*Foreplay.* It's an anagram of *flop year.*'

32

AMANDA

Agaves asks me about Nathan. How we met. I'm not sure how much to tell him, but it feels good to talk, and he seems genuinely interested.

I don't tell him why I was at the Boatyard Pub on the night Nathan walked in. I'd been waiting for Justin Blakemore to turn up, feed me crumbs, and make empty promises which my drunken brain was only too happy to sop up.

Agaves moves along the sofa, retracting the warmth of his shoulders, but he's listening.

I tell him how I was sitting at the bar of the Boatyard, swivelling side to side on a bar stool, when Nathan appeared alongside. I remember his frayed denim jacket, and wiry sunglasses perched atop his flattened hair. I recount how I'd been waiting for someone, but they hadn't turned up. Nathan didn't pry, but slipped into easy conversation and kept my glass regularly topped up.

'My confidence always spikes after a few drinks.' I raise my eyes heavenwards on the telling, but Agaves doesn't say anything, not yet. He seems to be willing me to continue.

I tell him how relaxed Nathan was, and how he made me

laugh. I wasn't in such a good place in those days. When Nathan told me what he did for a living, I'd shrugged, having absolutely no idea what a cruciverbalist was.

'I thought he said cruciherbalist!'

Agaves laughs when I tell him this, and I'm not sure if he knows what a cruciverbalist is either. I certainly didn't back then.

'Not herbalist. Verbalist,' Nathan had yelled above the rowdy background din of the pub.

'Is that someone who speaks a lot?' I'd said, gulping back the wine, amused by the weirdo who would become my husband.

'No, silly. A cruciverbalist is someone who sets crossword puzzles.'

'Jeez. Do people do that for a living?'

I confide in Agaves that even now, I think of it as a strange profession. But it was the quirkiness, uniqueness of Nathan's job that marked him out. When I told Nathan my name was Amanda, he closed his eyes, and disappeared into his own world for a few seconds. I even suspected a petit mal fit. I giggle in the telling.

'Anyway, Nathan came up with some very strange words. Well, at the time, they sounded very strange, and I was very drunk.'

'What did he say?' Agaves is all ears.

'*A male attorney for the girl.*'

'What?' Agaves makes an exaggerated expression of confusion.

'A male attorney for the girl. Let me explain.'

I tell Agaves that Nathan had made up, on the spot, a cryptic clue for my name. *A male*, in cryptic speak, could be *a man*. I had to get him to repeat the rest of the clue above the din, asking 'A male what for the girl?'

'Attorney,' Nathan said.

'What's that?'

'Lawyer. US speak.'

'Whatever.' My brain whirred as it tried to unravel what the weirdo was getting at.

I tell Agaves that I finally twigged, slapped my hands on the counter, and had what Nathan calls an *aha* moment.

'I get it. *A-man-da...* a male DA. It's my name for fuck sake. That's bloody clever,' I'd screamed.

In the recall, I decide not to own up to the next bit, though, as I think Agaves has heard enough. Even now, I'm mortified to remember that when Nathan looked away, for just a second, I fell off the stool and slithered to the floor.

33

AMANDA

Agaves is a good listener. He seems genuinely intrigued by my relationship with Nathan. I'm not sure whether he's interested in learning about the competition, or if he's being polite. The spontaneous kiss he plants on my lips tastes like honey, and I trace a finger round my mouth. Agaves' moment of affection gives me the courage to carry on, and to be honest, it feels good to talk.

'Nathan taught me how to do the cryptic puzzles. He had the patience of a saint.'

'Maybe you can teach me,' Agaves suggests. 'A few pointers?'

'Okay. Hidden clues. These are when the answer is hidden within the words of the clue.'

'I'm listening.' Agaves nudges closer.

'Here. I'll show you.' I lift the pen and crossword grid we worked on earlier, and jot down a clue. '*Baby animal seen in musical, Fame (4).*' I push the paper towards Agaves. 'You've got two minutes.'

Agaves stares at the words, sucks the end of the pen and puffs out a sigh of exasperation.

'Remember, the answer to most cryptic clues generally relates to the first or last words in the clue. I'll help you. In this case, the answer of the whole is a *baby animal*. The four-letter answer is made up of letters beside each other. The pointer that the answer is a hidden clue is in the words *seen in*.'

I can smell Agaves' body. There's a woodland freshness about him which mingles with an earthy scent. It's hard to concentrate on anything other than his muscled thighs which are so close, yet so far. My hand lingers, only millimetres away.

'Hmmm.' Agaves eyes narrow, and then he flings the pen in the air. 'Got it!'

'Go on.'

'It's *calf*, right?'

He's like a kid, his face gleaming with pride at having impressed the teacher.

I remember this was the first lesson Nathan taught me in the art of solving. He was so patient, determined to keep my mind occupied, away from thoughts of drink. We'd sit for hours, side by side, working through examples.

I share one more clue with Agaves, reluctant for the evening to end. Now that Nathan has ghosted me, ignoring my calls, emails, voicemails, I've no one left to do the puzzles with. Until now.

'Last one then.'

I scribble one more clue on the edge of the paper. *Mixed breed among relatives, to some extent (7)*

'This time, you've got one minute tops.'

But Agaves doesn't need a minute. His face lights up the room almost straight away, as if he's won the lottery. He's that pleased.

'And?' I ask.

'*Mongrel*. It's another hidden clue. Look.' He taps a tanned, shapely forefinger against the word that he's written in a loopy scrawl.

In an instant, Agaves is up, pulling me off the sofa. Strong arms circle my waist, and his lips linger this time, as he pulls me close. I sink into him, before I manage to break free.

'Another time,' he whispers, brushing the top of my head with his mouth.

When we've said goodnight, and Agaves has closed the door behind me, I dig out my key. But before slipping it in the lock, I hover outside the entrance of Flat C. I wonder if I should have confided in Agaves, about the menacing clues appearing in the puzzles. He might help, put my mind at rest, and tell me I'm being silly. But a misplaced loyalty to Nathan keeps me quiet, although I'm not sure why. Also, I don't want Agaves thinking I'm crazy.

I turn the lock, my fingers sticky, and when I hold my hands out, they have a steady tremble. Inside, I flop against the door, exhale all the pent-up emotions. The silence greets me, but with a new restlessness.

It's as if Nathan is back. Inside. Watching me. Listening. Taking note of my every move.

He's not far away. Of that I'm certain.

Or perhaps he's just inside my head.

34

NATHAN

Nathan leans against the door of the dark, smoky pub in North London until he spots Bagheera in the corner. When she sees him, she waves, a small, hesitant gesture. Her smooth, fine hair hangs loosely round her shoulders in a soft, unthreatening style which matches her personality. A centre parting makes the hair hang like flimsy curtains, and a random finger flicks the strands aside every now and then. A small dark beauty spot tries to brighten up the plainness, but detracts rather than enhances the whole.

So unlike Amanda, his wife with the flaming locks of fire and brimstone. Wild, untamed. Nathan swallows back the image, as he approaches his colleague.

Bagheera, one of a handful of female setters who work for the *London Echo*, has become a friend. A friend of sorts. He feel he owes her. When she messages, asking if he fancies meeting up, he never lets her down. It's the least he can do.

'Hi. Been here long?' Nathan asks, planting a welcome kiss on a proffered cheek. He unravels his Oxford University monogrammed scarf. Amanda bought it for him one Christmas, saying that if he had to wear a labelled scarf, better Oxbridge pretension than Sawford Hartley University blandness.

'Nobody even knows where Sawford Hartley is! Let along heard of it.' Amanda giggled as she threaded the maroon scarf with the fancy logo round his neck, and tugged at the ends.

'*Dominus Illuminatio Mea*. The Lord is my light,' Nathan quoted, reading the monogrammed text, and taking his wife's hands in his.

'What are you on about?'

'Opening words of Psalm 27. The motto of Oxford University.' He pointed to the elaborately embroidered crest. He never takes the scarf off.

'I've just got here,' Bagheera says, breaking into his thoughts.

Nathan knows she's lying because he's been watching her. She circled the block at least twice while he sat outside in his car.

'Your usual? Sauvignon Blanc?' he asks.

'No thanks. Not tonight. I'm on a detox. Just a lime and soda, please.'

'Who the hell detoxes?' Amanda's derision springs to mind. She targeted zealots, eccentrics. Anyone different to her. 'Vegan warriors, body-is-a-temple freaks.' Then she'd deliberately pile high the fries if he suggested a fish and greens week.

'Jeez. What's a fish and greens week? You've got to be kidding me,' she whooped. Amanda lived in the 'now'. That was her life's motto.

'Live and let die, more like,' he'd tell her, but his sage suggestions fell on deaf ears.

Until events took over, and she was forced to listen.

* * *

He sits down opposite Bagheera, and as she takes dainty sips of wine, small tics of regularity, Nathan raises his beer glass.

'Cheers,' he says. 'Good to see you. It's been a while.'

'Four weeks exactly.'

'Oh, that long. Sorry. I've been really busy.' He leans back, letting the cold beer moisten his dry mouth. His tongue is furred, coated by a harsh metallic taste. 'How's the crossword setting?' he asks. 'Still trying to catch us all out?'

'Now would I try and catch you out? Pretty impossible,' she says, with a soft rippling laugh. 'How are things with you?'

Bagheera's eyes, when she widens them, are more white than iris. The limpid centres get swallowed up by swathes of white.

'Work's okay. Pretty tedious, but it pays the bills.' Nathan sets his glass down. 'What is your regular day now for setting? It's hard to tell, now we're no longer using monikers.'

'Ha ha. Where'd the fun be if I told you that? Can't you guess?' Bagheera's eyes have a hooded twinkle. 'I assume you still get through the grids in ten minutes flat.'

'I've got a rough idea. Thing is,' he continues, 'I've noticed a few random themes creeping in over the last few weeks and wonder who the culprit is?'

'Themes? What sort?' She tilts her head in mock surprise.

'This and that. Death. Alcohol.'

'That's a bit naughty,' she says. 'Must admit, I haven't noticed.'

Nathan knows she's lying. Bagheera never misses anything. Never has. He knows she's not the innocent she portrays.

But she's also stubborn. She'll not give any more away.

35

NATHAN

As he walks Bagheera back to the Tube, Nathan's mind is ticking. It's in detective mode. He fits the mould. Cruciverbalists are both felons and detectives.

Mathers, his early hero and one of the pioneers of cryptic puzzles in the twenties, gave himself the name Torquemada, after the first Spanish Inquisitor-General, burner of thousands of fifteenth-century heretics. Mathers himself became a pioneer in the art of torture. Nathan models himself on powerful, dynamic men. In his head at least.

Amanda was chuffed when Nathan changed his moniker from Hercules to Adnam shortly after they met. Adnam was his wife's name backwards, but without the extra A.

'What about the extra A,' she squealed, yo-yoing up and down. Adnama. Far more interesting. Why don't you use my full name?' She wouldn't let up.

'Adnam is perfect. You see, it's a little short, just like you.'

Whenever he sees it written down, even now, he thinks of his wife.

When he and Bagheera reach the Tube entrance, Nathan tucks

his hands into his pockets, uncomfortable at goodbyes. Unsure of what Bagheera might expect.

'Bye, Adnam.' It's as if she's been reading his thoughts. Bagheera smiles, a tiny, upturned gesture. 'Thanks. It's been fun.'

'Yes. Good to see you too, Bagheera.' He responds in kind.

She hangs back, waiting, until he leans forward and kisses her briefly on the cheek.

'Till later,' she says. But she's already walking away, her stiff skeletal body descending the stone steps towards the underground.

In Rudyard Kipling's *The Jungle Book*, Bagheera is a black panther, a friend, protector, and mentor to the man-cub Mowgli. The word Bagheera is Hindustani for panther, or leopard, although the root word 'bagh' means tiger.

If Adnam was forged from his wife's name, a forever memento of his undying love, Nathan can't help but wonder. Why Bagheera?

As he stares after her, it suddenly dawns on him. He thinks he knows why she chose the name.

36

NATHAN

It's been a week since Nathan met up with Bagheera. Since then, he's been unable to relax. His mind keeps getting pulled back to Brewer's Hill, Silver Birch and Amanda. Although he won't talk to his wife, face to face, she's an obsession that he doesn't know how to deal with.

Skulking outside Silver Birch in his car, Nathan smacks his hands on top of the dashboard and bangs his head in thumping rhythm against the steering wheel. He's watching Amanda, through the open curtains of their flat, her body framed in their upstairs window. She's like a hovering ghost. A spectre of luminescence. She walks up and down, round and round, as her head nods to a silent beat. He imagines her hum, a soft drone of melancholic memory.

When a shadow suddenly appears behind her, Nathan rears up in his seat.

'Holy shit. What the fuck.'

Hard hat weed, with his steel muscles like girders in the half-light, suddenly appears and hands Amanda what looks like a glass of *tiger prawns*. Amanda chuckled when Nathan told her that her favourite food, *tiger prawns*, could be anagrammed into her new must-have drink. *Spring water*. Nathan's mind is full of lettered maggots, the words gnawing, chewing, squirming around his head as his eyes grip the unfolding drama.

Hard hat weed is an anagram of *Edward Heath*, the prat in Flat B. Nathan loved the anagram, repeating it every time their neighbour appeared, and Amanda was within earshot. Nathan spent hours mulling over new, derogatory labels to use.

Nathan watches their neighbour follow Amanda round the room. No doubt she'd tell Nathan, if he ever asked, that the bastard had only popped in to cadge some tea bags. She was more than plausible with her little white lies.

She's reverted to form, sucked in by another guy who'll break her heart. Nathan knows Amanda will need him back, one day soon, and he's prepared to play for time. He'll wait until she's nowhere else to turn. For now, he has no idea how to quell the loathing for the competition. But he's patient. He'll work it out.

'Patience of a saint,' Amanda would say to him. Or the patience of the devil if she wanted to rile him up.

When he's had enough, Nathan starts up the car, and prepares to slide back into the night. Then, all of a sudden, he brakes. There's someone in the garden, the tangled wreck of Silver Birch. The silhouette is vague, unformed, but they're familiar. He peers through the window, until recognition hits. He knows who it is!

What the hell is Bagheera doing at this time of night, and in their front garden?

37

AMANDA

I wake up each morning, knowing I've done a terrible thing. I shiver from guilt, the bedsheet drenched in shame, but it takes a few minutes until the full horror hits.

Because of what I've done, I've been abandoned. Left to rot. The bedroom walls are grey, my life's reflection. No subtle hues. Even Nathan, 'will love you forever, want to die in your arms' has disappeared.

I check my phone. Nothing. No smiling selfies from friends or colleagues to buoy the sinking ship. Everyone has turned their back, contempt, disgust screaming through the silence. My misery, guilt, and shame eat away, but no one wants to listen. My good-time friends have scattered in the wind, seeking fresh blood to share the vodka shots, gin cocktails and champagne benders. Agaves is my only hope, but also my biggest fear. If he leaves me, there'll be no one left.

I tiptoe down the stairs to the hall foyer, the communal entrance shared by Flats B and C, the breath trapped inside my lungs. I still think of Flat C as *our* flat, Nathan's and mine, although there's no longer any sign of my husband.

Agaves must have left early, but I'm not sure. His death-rattle shower didn't wake me up this morning, but images skirted round my nightmares, of my neighbour's body entwined with my sodden nightdress. Dark hairs wove around my throat, choking out a sob which startled me awake.

I pick up the paper jammed in the basket that hangs precariously from loosened tacks. The headlines are grim. Wars. Floods. Earthquakes. Pandemics. Migrants. They mock my skinny life with its skeletal dearth of meaning. The door to Flat C squawks on its hinges as I push it open and flip the rubber door stop to one side, letting it slam as I cringe against the noise. The paper flutters in my nervous hands.

I'm feeling especially anxious today, more shaky because it's Monday. It's just another day, but Mondays were always Nathan's day to set, and from recent puzzles I'm certain it still is. He could have switched with someone else, but I've no way of checking now he's gone, disappeared without trace apart from the personal reminders he's left behind. Attached to the fridge in the kitchen is a daily laminated schedule, points numbered in my husband's calligraphic hand.

'Keep it rigid. Stick to the plan. Until you've made more progress.'

Twice I've binned the master plan but retrieved it later and now it's back in place and talks to me each morning, reminds me how far I've got to travel. Nathan didn't want me to forget, but whenever I'd scream at him to give me a break, he'd calmly say 'I'm only thinking of you.'

It took me time to realise his constant vigil, as well as being his way of looking out for me, was his way of controlling me.

But today, for once, I set the crossword aside to do this evening, because today I've set myself an important challenge. This morning I'm scheduled to work from ten till midday. Nathan said I ought to work longer hours, keep busier, but I'm not there yet. When I log off each day, it's as if I've climbed a mountain, relieved it's all over again until tomorrow. The outside world, after everything that's happened, seems a scary place, and I've small steps to make before I can face the world with confidence.

I reread the note I scribbled on my to-do list before I went to bed, the task starred with a huge red asterisk noting the difficulty and the importance. In my head, the downward slope of Brewer's Hill is like a cliff edge about to crumble into the sea, and drag me down with it. The note simply says:

Walk down the hill, away from Silver Birch, towards Crouch End.

38

AMANDA

It's almost one o'clock when I pick up the courage to leave the flat. The fresh air welcomes me, a cool dry breeze having replaced the sodden downpour. My phone beeps, so I plonk down on the garden parapet to check my messages. My faint hope that it might be from Nathan is quashed when I see the message is from EE, telling me my bill is ready to view.

Slime oozes through my jogging bottoms as I rezip the phone back into my pocket. A cat slopes past, zigzags under cars, then shoots across the road. It looks like Boffin, Beckles' cat, and I wonder where it's going, testing its nine lives to the limit. I tug up my hoodie, shuffle my hair inside. I've been procrastinating, but know I can't put it off any longer. It's now or never. I take a string of deep breaths, and prepare to step out on to Brewer's Hill.

'Amanda?'

The quiet questioning voice from behind makes me jump, and as I swivel round, I feel as if I've been caught in some illicit act, of what I'm not sure.

'Oh, hi, Tory. Yes, it's me.' My laugh gets choked by the blast of a car horn.

'Are you okay? Your pants are soaking,' she says.

Tory's umbrella is like a parasol, an eighteenth-century must-have fashion accessory with its pale tasselled fringe. She's only now putting it down, although the rain stopped at least an hour ago. She fiddles with the fastener, securing the delicate material.

'I'm fine, thanks. I sat on the wall to check my phone – a big mistake.' I wipe my hand over the damp patch. 'Hopefully a jog will help dry them out.' I begin to jiggle on the spot.

'Where are you heading? I'm on my way to Crouch End if you fancy meeting up when you're done? The Tea House, perhaps?'

Before I've time to come up with an excuse, I agree. 'Sounds good but I'll be at least half an hour.'

'Perfect.' With that Tory walks out through the gate and turns left down Brewer's Hill without so much as a backward glance.

I collapse against the fence, breathing heavily. Today's challenge, to make it down the hill, past Sefton Court, is no longer possible. I can't do it, not now. Tackling the issue of my bathmophobia will have to wait as meeting Tory has thrown my concentration. I'll have to pencil in the test, my personally set exam, for another day. I'm determined to jog past the hairpin bend, and wrestle with the vertigo, but I can't help feeling a flood of relief that I have a genuine reason to put it off.

When I decide to turn right instead, the panic lifts and I realise just how bad my fear of the downward incline, past the scene of the accident, really is. The challenge will have to wait until another day.

Instead, I head up towards the Archway Road and build speed quickly. It's the long way round, a less familiar route, but if I go fast enough, I should make Crouch End in half an hour. I'll make the descent towards my destination by another way.

39

AMANDA

My heart is racing when I arrive at the café, and through the misted window, I spot Tory in the corner. She's sitting quietly, immobile as a statue, fastened up against the wall. Even from outside, I can see a tightness round her mouth.

I push the door open, and the dry heat hits like a sauna. I pull down the zip on my sweat-drenched top and pick my way through the tightly packed space.

'Hi. Hope you've not been waiting too long.' I shake my hair side to side like a shaggy Afghan hound and retie it with a scrunchie I'd wrapped around my wrist.

'No. Perfect timing,' she says, tapping a china teapot. Dainty cups and a tea strainer are set out neatly on the table. A two-tiered cake stand challenges with its loaded contents. Massacred sandwiches, bulging with fillings, have had their crusts axed, but the sight of doughy bread, soft and spongy, takes me back to childhood birthday parties. Perhaps I'll manage one.

'Nathan and I used to come here,' I say as I pull out a wooden chair.

'Don't you just love scones and clotted cream? Here. I'll be mum.' Tory lifts the pot. Against her pale skin, her eyes are unusually dark – like coffee beans, the sort I grind.

'Please.'

She places the strainer over a cup, and with a faintly trembling hand, pours out an Earl Grey tea, tiny splashes tipping over on to the saucer.

'Oops. Sorry,' she says.

* * *

Since Tory moved into Flat A, we've never really had a proper conversation, other than swapping pleasantries about the weather and the lack of parking. Even on the day of the barbecue, before I scuttled off, we barely spoke and I've been avoiding contact ever since. Two months on and I've still no idea who she is, her background or anything about her.

She skilfully quarters the scones, adding a teaspoon of jam and a smidgeon of cream to each piece, making me think of the quartiles of the puzzle grid.

'Hmm. These are good,' she purrs, a stippled pink cat-like tongue licking off the topping.

'I think I'll stick to the sandwiches,' I say, while crunching a lump of cucumber. I'm not prepared for her opening gambit.

'Are you and Teddy going out?'

'Sorry?' A piece of bread gets stuck as I try to swallow, and I cough it back up.

'You and Teddy? He's quite the dish.' Her laugh is squeaky, reminding me of my mother's old jewellery box with the pirouetting dancer and the faulty mechanism.

'What makes you think that?' I set the heavily buttered sandwich back down on the plate.

'I'm just curious. Okay, I own up. I wanted to know if he's free.'

Christ, she wants my blessing.

'As far as I know he's single.' The cup wobbles in my hand.

'What about you?'

'I'm not long separated.'

'Me too,' she shrieks. 'I'd no idea you were on your own. I thought you were married.'

But she's lying, I'm certain. Nathan's been gone for ages now, and I'm sure Agaves would have told her. Tory slides the scone bits, like chess pieces vying for position, round her plate.

Before I reply, she carries on. 'I've just been served divorce papers.' She then picks up a fork, spears the prongs into the scone and nibbles.

'Nathan and I aren't divorcing. We're on a break, more like.' My words hit a nerve and I wonder who I'm kidding and why I feel the need to say this.

'A Ross and Rachel sort of break?' Her laugh is weirdly intense.

The subject moves on to the upkeep of Silver Birch. Plumbing issues. Missing roof tiles. The back garden. Tory outlines ideas she has of tidying up the wilderness of weeds and perhaps building a modern decking area.

'We could party in the summer. Have some fun.' Her excitement bubbles, like freshly popped champagne but I suspect fantasies over our neighbour might be fuelling her enthusiasm.

'Sounds like a plan.'

I excuse myself and head for the Ladies. By the time I reappear, she has her coat on and has already paid the bill.

'Here. Let me give you something.' I go to unzip my purse when she holds up a hand.

'Don't be silly. My treat. You can get it next time.'

Rather than walking back with Tory, I make an excuse about having something to do in Crouch End, and we say our goodbyes. I watch her cross the road and wend her way slowly up Brewer's Hill before I decide to jog back the way I came. It's a longer route, the hill doubly steep, but I can't face going up Brewer's Hill. Not today. Although coming down our road feels impossible, it's not much easier going up. Past where it all happened.

Also, I haven't much left to say to Tory. My mind thumps as I build speed, unease cranking up with every quickened step. If Tory has her sights on Teddy, any hope I might have had of the woman in Flat A becoming a new girlfriend, a late-night confidante, has been well and truly squashed.

Instead of being a new best friend, Tory is now my rival. Enemy number one.

40

AMANDA

This morning when I wake, my eyes are stuck together, and I feel sticky grit deposits along my lids. I roll on to my back, and frantically rub a ragged nail along the edges to clear my vision.

Almost immediately, I realise something's not right, but I can't remember what could have happened. My mind is locked, the combination lost. Shit. Shit. Shit.

My head throbs as I hoist myself up, but the spinning motion worsens. It's like seasickness, relentless, choppy waves washing over me. I need to heave, and as I lean over the side of the bed, my hair falls into a grey basin. I've no idea how it got there, as I must have passed out. Oh my god! I must have been drinking, got really drunk. But why? I don't keep drink in the flat. Did I go and buy some? I can't remember.

Recall is blank, and I'm scared my mind is trying to block something out. I try to rewind, go back as far as I can but there's nothing. An empty sheet of deleted memory.

I haul back the duvet and check my pants are still on. Why wouldn't they be? It's all a blur. The silence is holding tight its secrets. I crawl out, an animal from its pit, and prise open the rotting window frame. Chill air smacks my senses and I have to grip the sill, squeeze my eyes until the swaying, rolling motion passes.

My mouth hurts and a metallic tang coats my throat. I run a tongue along an inner cheek and find a ridge. A finger dips in, coats the tip in blood. The nausea washes over me again before I reach the bathroom. I brace before I check the mirror, and as if preparing to confront a cadaver, dread pumps my heart.

The image can't be real. Someone I don't know is looking back at me. Dried mascara has left a trail of caked soot across my cheekbones and my eyes are ringed like a panda's. A small bruise on my right temple completes the collage.

But it's evidence. Of a crime. A crime of self-inflicted assault. Who am I looking at? I peer. Is it me or my mother? *Hitler Woman.* Nathan's voice mocks. He said I was in danger of turning into my mother. 'Alcoholism. It's in the genes,' he ranted. But the real put down for my less-than-sober mother, was when he referred to her as Hitler Woman.

'*Hitler Woman* is an anagram of *mother-in-law*,' he laughed, and never let me forget.

My hair, thickly matted, is dull with defeat. Close up, blotchy red dry patches map my skin, but my lips are bloodless, parched, cracked like desert pavements. I could indeed be looking at my mother.

I sit on the toilet seat, my head hung over my chest, for a good fifteen minutes, too scared to leave the bathroom. A wave of fear sweeps through my being. Misery, deep and depraved, mingles with self-loathing but I'm too sad to cry. Too far down the hellhole. I can't believe what I'm starting to suspect, and I don't want to find the evidence. Did I really drink again? So much that I can't remember? I can't even remember anything about yesterday at all.

I finally haul myself up and leave the bathroom. As I pass the front door, I notice the chain hangs loose and the brass bolts are undone. Did I go out? Did someone come in? A small white envelope, 'AMANDA' neatly printed on the front, lies on the mat. My hand leans against the door as I bend to pick it up.

The note is handwritten. Loopy, fancy curls make artistry of the words. A calligraphic jingle of merriment.

Hi. Lovely to chat yesterday. Hope Mr Beckles enjoyed the leftover scones.

I know he has a sweet tooth!

Having an informal 'at home' Saturday night. Would love you to come. Bring a friend.

The more the merrier. 7 p.m.

Tory X

I set the note aside and lurch towards the lounge, which is a crime scene of telltale evidence. No crumbs of clues, but loaves of shame. Two wine bottles, one empty and one half empty, are sitting on the windowsill with corks alongside. *Ten Green Bottles Hanging on the Wall.* The nursery rhyme pierces my thoughts, and a madness mouths the lyrics. But why did I drink? I didn't buy any wine? Or did I? I bang the sides of my head with both hands to try and dislodge the memories.

My phone pings. But I've no idea where it is. It pings again. And again.

A random splattering of clothes snakes around the sofa. Jeans. T-shirt. A tartan scarf of Nathan's. I pick it up, no idea how it got there. But it's no use. Ten minutes in and I need to lie down again.

I swipe an arm across the sofa, firing crisp bags, chocolate wrappers and ripped newspapers onto the floor. Surrender sucks me down, irons me out, prepares me for the worst until exhaustion forces me to give in and close my eyes again.

My thoughts boomerang, back and forth. Flashbacks, and deep-seated trauma spark images. Hallucinatory. There's Martin Hunter, with a lecherous twisted leer. Nathan, haloed like an emoji. Then Joseph appears. Out of nowhere. He's dragging a wooden cross, a heavy leaden block across the desert, his sinking sandy feet highlighted by serrated blackened toenails. A wreath of thorns adorns his bloodied head and red oozes from his eye sockets. On the wooden cross, a lifeless corpse is skewered through the palms. Joseph mouths the words: *In the name of the Father and of the Son and of the Holy Spirit*, then turns his back and walks away. I try in vain to wake up.

Then Oliver appears. In the guise of an angel, and the image sets my heart racing until my eyelids finally spring open. Tears are streaming down my cheeks, as I come slowly back to life.

41

AMANDA

Not long after I wake for the second time, a purr and whine of a vacuum cleaner makes me sit up. The noise sounds as if it's in the flat with me, but as I realise the bump and grind of the machine is smacking against my front door, and the sound is coming from outside on the landing.

I can remember Agaves telling me he was taking the day off work and would be on a cleaning mission of our communal areas. When we talked about it, I promised to help but in my current state there's no way I can face him. It's strange I can remember further back, but yesterday is still a blank.

In horror, I realise I've missed an early Zoom lesson with the fifth form. The small clock on the bookshelf shows eleven already. I try to pull myself up from the sofa, but my limbs are leaden and a rolling motion in my head throws me back down.

I'm now starting to freak. There's something up. Even if I'd drunk two whole bottles of wine, I'd be feeling really rough. Nauseous, with a thumping headache, and a craving for litres of water and orange juice, but I'd still remember what I did the day before. I'm a seasoned pro, know the ropes, the hangover symptoms only too well. But this is different.

More like the symptoms of Mum's dementia before she died. A rogue thought is that months of sobriety have robbed my body of an ability to process the toxins, but it doesn't ring true.

I circle the lounge twenty, thirty times, to help me sober up. Just as a sudden buzz, like a fly on death row, tells me that my phone is near, the battery fading, I have a flashback. I remember dropping by Mr Beckles' house with a doggy bag of scones and sandwiches from the café in Crouch End. After I met with Tory.

I pick up my phone, which is concealed behind the two wine bottles, plug it into its charger, and notice seven missed calls from Joseph.

A sudden smack on the door makes me jump. I freeze.

'Yoo-hoo. Are you in there? It's me. Teddy.' Agaves' baritone booms like a double bass.

He knocks again, rapping with persistent rhythm.

'Sorry, I'm working. I'll pop by later,' I shriek.

'Just wanted to check you're okay.'

'Fine, thanks.'

I don't move for a few seconds, willing Agaves to move away. I can't let him see me like this. I watch as something gets slipped under the front door. It's my newspaper. Agaves must have collected it from the foyer. When I hear the slam of my neighbour's front door, I tiptoe to pick it up.

I start to cry when I notice he's drawn a little smiley face on the front with two large black kisses underneath.

42

AMANDA

I ring the school and select my excuse: an old, concocted story from a long list that I've collated over the years. Car break down. Food poisoning. A dodgy prawn. A rancid curry. A sickly neighbour. It's a long list. Nathan would stare, dumbfounded, and disorientated by my slick storytelling. Today, I opt for food poisoning.

'Are all alcoholics so devious?' Nathan would blow out loud draughts of resignation but leave me to my career-saving deceptions. But he found it hard to disguise his disapproval. Conversation would become stilted, he'd proffer one-word answers to pertinent questions and usually disappear for a couple of hours with some excuse about training for his next marathon. But I knew he needed to get away from me, uneasy at my duplicity.

I wander through the flat and look for more evidence as to yesterday's events. I'm desperate to know what happened, what threw me off the wagon. Where did the wine come from? I'm almost certain I wouldn't have bought it.

Down below I hear voices. I scoot to the window and see Agaves and Tory whispering. If they're talking in normal tones, I wouldn't know but the paranoia's been switched up to full volume.

Tory glances up and I bob behind the curtains. When I look out again, Agaves is laughing at something she's said and waves her off as she sashays down the drive and out the gate.

Joseph. I need to talk to him. To find out if he put me to bed. Did I call him? I've no idea. But he's the only person I dare ask, and the only person who is likely to know what happened. I pick up my mobile and with dry, cold fingers, press his number. He answers on the first ring.

'Joseph.'

'Amanda. Is that you? Are you okay?'

'I'm not sure.' A background noise of scraping chairs, rustling voices, makes me hesitate. Joseph must be at work in the hall. An echoing interference crackles on the line.

'Do you need to talk? I can pop by later. I'll be finished around two.'

'No, don't worry. Just wanted to say thanks.'

'What for?'

Perhaps he didn't put me to bed. Perhaps I clambered in by myself. Maybe I wasn't as far gone as I think but I just can't remember.

'For being there. That's all.'

'You're welcome.'

With that I hang up.

I decide to go out, get some fresh air and check on Mr Beckles. I dig out another carton of soup from the freezer, carrot and coriander. A sticky label tells me I cooked it last month.

Outside, the air is crisp, but spring is slowly turning into summer. Nathan would call it 'a maturing spring morning'.

'Maturing?' I'd ask.

'Maturing into summer. Brighter, warmer. New growth every-where.' Smug with his analogies, he'd smile, turn me round and kiss me full on the lips.

I inch along the wall that connects our property to Mr Beckles', my hands shaky, legs unsteady. Relieved when I reach the front door, I notice it's ajar. I nudge it open with my elbow.

'Mr Beckles. It's me.' My voice tunnels through the hall.

'Tory. Is that you?'

It takes a second to register what he's just said.

The first thing I notice as I poke my head round the living room is that it's tidy. A smell of polish chokes through the heat, the room suffocating despite the cracked windows. The curtains have been wrenched back, tied with the tassel which usually dangles to one side. An ambulance suddenly roars past, its screeching siren shrill with emergency, which startles me.

'No. It's me. Amanda.'

'Oh.' Mr Beckles' expression is blank and I'm not sure whether he's disappointed or confused.

'Has someone been in? The room is spotless,' I shout out, noticing his hearing aids discarded on the table.

'What do you say?'

I hand him his ear pods before carrying the soup through to the kitchen. The sink gleams with a wicked sparkle, and the caked grease line that usually circles the stainless steel has been erased. A single soup bowl is out, spoon alongside and there's a Post-it note attached.

Hi Amanda. Lent a hand with the cleaning. Catch up later.
  Tory X

Maybe it's the way I'm feeling, the wooziness, the anxiety, the not knowing what happened last night, but why do I get the feeling that Tory is deliberately trying to wind me up?

43

AMANDA

When I get back from Mr Beckles, the vanilla-scented air freshener, which I squirted round the flat before I left, welcomes me home, like a birthday banner in a prison cell.

But a pungent smell, like ammonia, assaults me when I enter the kitchen. I suddenly remember the cooked seabass, the bones, and the leftovers which I threw away into the food recycling bin under the sink. I yank up the window and settle the brick in place against the broken cord before opening out the pedal bin. I tug loose the black liner, and before toggling the ends, notice a torn piece of paper coated in hardened cheese.

Amanda. Enjoy. xx

The letters are in bold black ink, a child's effort at neatness. I rummage around for corks, my insides churning like rancid butter. By the kettle is a rogue elastic band which I don't remember having put there. I've no idea what it's come off. I rattle round in the drawer until I find the corkscrew but it's neatly in its place at the back of the unit. I mustn't have uncorked the wine bottles myself. Perhaps the elastic band held the note in place around one of the bottles.

My head still hasn't stopped spinning, and after I drink a load more water, my insides rebel again. I sit on a kitchen stool, stare at the note, and have another sudden flashback of creeping up the stairs clutching wine bottles tightly in both hands, like a thief with ill-gotten gains. I then remember picking up the bottles from the porch outside. Whoever left the wine must have uncorked it for me. Made the temptation impossible to resist. It must have been left by someone who knows my weakness. Who? Shit. Shit. Shit. Why would someone I know leave me wine?

I stagger into the lounge, pick up one of the bottles, and check the label. Whoever left the wine, also knew my favourite poison.

I spend the next half-hour, poking round the flat, looking for goodness knows what. More evidence of what happened. My flat is like a crime scene without the blue tape, and somewhere inside the walls, there must be clues.

Slowly, my mind pieces together more of yesterday. I remember having tea with Tory in the café. Popping in with the leftovers for Mr Beckles. And then finding the wine, which I must have drunk. Why it knocked me out so hard, I've no idea. Perhaps sobriety has really affected my body's tolerance to alcohol.

I tidy round the flat, and finally have a shower, in the hope that the hot steamy jets of water will help wash away the shame. Once I'm dressed, I decide to bite the bullet and pop in to see Agaves, having managed to avoid contact all day.

The landing outside my door, the small square, which is shared by Flats B and C, is tight, smaller than a two-person elevator shaft so with outstretched arms my fingers can skim the perimeter of the grey scuffed walls which rear up to a slanting roof light.

Standing in the tiny space, I press an ear to Agaves' door, but the only noise is from my own pulse and rasping breath.

Before I knock, the door flies open, and sends me stumbling sideways.

'Thought I heard you. Come in.' Agaves is bare-chested, a healthy infestation of thick hairs stuck like a welcome mat. He looks as if he's just showered, his hair messed up and wet.

'You must have good ears,' I say, red flames searing up my neck and face.

'I've been listening out for you, as I didn't see you earlier. Is everything okay?'

He touches my shoulder lightly, as I suspect he picks up on my less than sparkly appearance.

'I'm fine thanks. Just didn't sleep too well,' I lie. I can't tell him about last night, collapsing unconscious.

'Here, let me get dressed and I'll put the kettle on. Make yourself at home.'

Agaves leaves me in the lounge and disappears for a few minutes. Today, the room looks different. There's a distinct lack of mess and the coffee table, with a neat pile of magazines, and the smell of disinfectant, reminds me of a dental surgery.

A rustling noise and I twist. Agaves is at the top of the small set of stairs that lead into the lounge, looking down like a vicar from a pulpit.

'Coffee? Tea?' His firm square hands sweep back his damp hair. As I shrink against the feathered cushions, I poke a finger in the corner of my eye to relieve an itch, and battle back a sneeze.

'Coffee please. A little milk, no sugar.'

'Coming up.' As if reading my thoughts, he adds, 'Nice and tidy, eh?'

'Most impressed.' I find it hard not to smile, flattered that the effort might have been for my benefit.

'Oh, it wasn't me. Still not much use with a hoover. Tory popped by and lent a hand.'

44

NATHAN

Life with Amanda was exciting, unpredictable, and far from easy, but Nathan relished the challenge. Now his life has shrunk back to what it was before Amanda gave his life meaning, and energy.

He's back to his roots, which now seem as dull as the backstreet Hampstead pub that he's been coming to for years. He once slipped nicely into banter with fellow academics, but Amanda made him question everything. Especially his comradeship with the other setters from the *London Echo*.

He steps inside The Sunken Tavern. Black and white photos of writers, scholars and stars of stage and screen line the walls like award certificates. It's the first Friday of the month, a date he's kept with his work colleagues for the past ten years. His stomach churns when he inhales the stench of beer, strong-flavoured crisps, and the resident Labrador's fetid breath. The landlord, large and lardy like his pet, is at work behind the bar, and his gritty, mouldy skin gives him the appearance of a concrete relic unearthed from an archaeological dig. Hairy arms pull the tap handles with heavy exaggerated movements.

'Hi, Barry. Am I first again?' Nathan asks, as he glances round the room.

'You are, indeed, sir. Your usual?' A chesty wheeze accompanies the question.

The round table, crammed in at one end of the room, with its white plastic *reserved* sign, used to remind Nathan of top table at an Oxford college. Exclusively for the top brass. Now the toxic cleaner that oils the surface makes his nostrils recoil – from both the stench and the tackiness.

Poseidon ambles in, *Financial Times* tucked under an arm. Nathan wonders if it's a prop or a recently purchased copy. His colleague's tweed jacket, with worn elbow patches, looks as if it's been slept in.

When Amanda met Poseidon she called him a jerk. 'What a prat! "Oh, I'm god of the sea, earthquakes, storms, and horses"... la di da di da. Arsehole.' Her face mimicked and her eyelids flickered as she performed her sarcastic imitation. Moments like this always made Nathan crease; the more irreverent the skit, the harder the convulsions. He misses his wife's harpy tongue, her hissing viper truths. But it did wind him up that she included him in her belittling skits. His occupation marked him out as one of them.

'Poseidon, the sea god, was magnetic and moody,' Nathan told her, trying to justify the secret monikers.

'I know who Poseidon was. I'm not that thick,' she said, 'but he's still a total dick.'

Dragon Airy is next to appear, his Brylcreemed head before the rest of him, as he comes out of the men's toilets which leak a vinegar urinal smell through the opened door. A sweaty palm flattens one side of his hair parting, and he clicks his feet together and salutes, as if he is a member of the Gestapo.

'Evening, fellow setters. Evening, Barry.' His voice grinds like a salt cellar, its tone gritty and high-pitched.

When Amanda met Dragon Airy, she heaped further scorn.

'Dragon Airy. You've got to be kidding me? What... is he a character from *Harry Potter*?'

'Not Diagon Alley. Dragon Airy.' Drag-on-Air-y. Nathan broke the words into nursery syllables.

'Another tosspot. What did you say it was an anagram of?'

'Dorian Gray.'

'Who the heck is Dorian Gray?' she demanded, as she circled the room and let a hand flap hard against a yawning mouth. It seems like only yesterday. The memories, the good and bad times with Amanda, are never far away. They gurgle round his brain, from morning till night.

'*The Picture of Dorian Gray* was a novel by Oscar Wilde.'

'I know who Oscar Wilde is. Who the heck was Dorian Gray?'

'A handsome philanderer, his beauty portrayed in a painting which hung in a hidden attic. But as his heart grew darker, his deeds viler, the painting changed to show the ugliness beneath.'

'Whatever. These guys think they're god's gift but they're just a load of boring old farts.' When Amanda said this, Nathan humoured her. He let her rant. At the time, he suspected her insecurity was to blame for the targeted put-downs of his colleagues. But her distant voice cuts through his thoughts, breaks into present conversation, and makes him question his own opinions. Tonight, it's as if, for the first time, he's seeing his colleagues through Amanda's eyes.

Regal is last to appear. Amanda didn't mind Regal, tickled that his pseudonym spelled 'lager' backwards.

'At least he's approaching normal.' Normal meant he was younger, less eccentric and didn't say too much.

Nathan has sat at the same round table, like a séance participant, every time they meet, but tonight will be the last time. No more hand holding, chanting, back slapping, old boy chumminess.

He's convinced one of the setters is targeting Amanda through the crossword grid. Nathan can justify his own rogue clues. She's his wife. But misguided humour from one of the other setters, has really wound him up, and he needs to keep his distance. One of them is picking up on his angst, and playing a dangerous game.

He's still watching out for Amanda. Albeit from a distance.

45

NATHAN

Nathan doesn't ask his question of the setters straight away. He feels it best to play for time. Wait until the beer kicks in, and loosens tongues and inhibitions.

He flips a beer mat and lets it land on top of his glass. Then he flips two in sync, catches one in each hand, before repeating with four, six and finally eight. Three sets of hands clap at his renowned party piece.

'Okay, guys. Who's responsible for the drinking theme?' Nathan finally asks, as he stacks the beer mats into a neat pile and sets them aside.

'Sorry? You've lost me,' Dragon Airy says, kicking out his shiny black brogues, the shoelaces of which could have been pressed. He loosens his cream cravat, flattens it to match his laces.

'The drinking theme that's been in the puzzles recently?' Nathan's voice is sharp, and the others stare at him.

'I have noticed the drink clues, but we're all sworn to secrecy,' Poseidon laughs, placing a long white forefinger to his lips.

Nathan narrows his eyes, turns his attention on Regal. His

youthful cheeks blot as if by rouge, but he adds nothing to the thread. Amanda's comments ring in Nathan's ear.

'Regal's like a kid beside you old tosspots, and he looks as if he's going to cry every time he's asked a question,' Amanda said when she was introduced. But when she said he was pretty cute, Nathan notched up the loyalty for his other colleagues and reined in the smile when his wife fired her poisoned quips in their direction.

As he now looks round the table, he misses her irreligious levity. She was right. His colleagues are a bunch of weird eccentrics, and it's time for him to walk away.

He finishes his drink, sets the glass down and reknots his scarf.

'You're not off already? Or is that pretty little wife waiting for you.' Dragon Airy's voice has the timbre of a smirk but without the facial accompaniment.

'Yes. I'm off. But come on, one more chance. Which one of you is targeting Amanda? We've all seen the clues. It's time to own up.' Three sets of eyes stare at him, but no one answers. As he shoves his chair back under the table, the front door flies open, and heavy rain can be heard splattering across the pavement.

'Hope you've got a hood. Looks pretty nasty out there,' Regal says.

Nathan fastens his coat, tugs up the collar and for a second looks at each of his colleagues in turn. Amanda was right. He is a misfit. He's neither one of them, nor one of her.

After he says his goodbyes, he steps outside, and feels his trainers sponge up the water as it seeps steadily through to his socks. A glance over his shoulder and he sees the three musketeers clank their glasses. All for one. One for all. They're boisterous in their body language, merry in their connivance. Perhaps it's all in his imagination and he's getting more like Amanda. More paranoid with every passing day.

On the train back to his digs, he begins to wonder if perhaps they're all in on it. The three setters together targeting his wife. But why would they? Only Bagheera and the other setters from tonight know about Amanda. About what happened. About their marriage.

But unless it is some uncanny coincidence, someone is playing a weird game which is toying with his own sanity, and firing up his anger.

46

NATHAN

On getting back from the pub, Nathan's mind is more agitated than usual.

When he moved out of Silver Birch, he ended up in a cramped bedsit in Clapham. It was all he could afford on his own. He had intended a new start, to rebuild his life, but instead of moving on, his days and nights are consumed with memories. Thoughts of Amanda. And where it all went wrong.

He lies down as soon as he gets in and stares up at the bedsit ceiling. It is so low, it hovers over him like a coffin lid. The spare bed he brought with him is small and hard. He stretches a nostalgic hand across the empty spot where Amanda used to sleep. Fractious. Irritable. Always hot. She was like a raging fire next to him, scorching, inside and out. When she couldn't sleep, she'd stomp into the spare room, dragging a pillow like a sullen child slopping a comforter across the floor, with a soggy thumb stuck fast between her teeth.

Nathan got blamed for her insomnia. For most things in fact. He was blamed for hogging the comfort of the king-size bed, and thundering silent breakfasts, thick with accusation, followed. She screamed at him. Talked of suffocation. She couldn't breathe. She needed space, and space soon became the new 'must-have' marriage accessory.

But his thoughts always come back to the date their problems really started. It was the 10 June, their first wedding anniversary. Almost nine months ago.

Nathan suggested a romantic meal at their local Italian bistro followed by a late night snuggle up to a Netflix movie. He wanted her to himself.

'A Netflix movie? Can't we celebrate properly?' Amanda exhaled noisy puffs of frustration.

'We could go to the theatre if you fancy. Your choice of show.'

'Seriously? We can go to the theatre anytime.' She stomped around the flat, like a kid that wasn't getting its own way.

'I thought it would be nice doing something just the two of us.'

'You've got to be kidding me,' Amanda screamed. 'Let's celebrate properly. What about a garden party? A marquee perhaps. Champagne. Come on, let's go for it.' She grabbed his hands, gripping them with ferocity, and gave him her best puppy-dog eyes. He should have been stronger but whenever Amanda got something into her head, she wouldn't let it drop. Arguing was futile.

'Are you sure that's what you want?' His misgivings were weakly voiced, his only minor success being in the scuppering of a marquee. As his wife flitted round the flat, making plans with wild enthusiasm, a tightly held bottle of Chardonnay for company, he stood helplessly looking on. He remembers the constriction in his chest, a feeling of dread of what might happen if he gave in. But he did, and the dread was soon replaced by frustration, fear, regrets. And finally anger.

Nathan knows now he should have stood his ground. But Amanda got her way, and life changed forever when the 10 June came around.

47

AMANDA

It's hard being natural with Agaves, relaxed, when his closeness makes my heart race. There's an electricity in the air, but without a drink in my hand, I've no idea how to get past the awkwardness, and my thick fuzzy head isn't helping. Also the fact Tory's been round, tidying up and playing happy families, makes me even more edgy. She's everywhere I turn.

Nathan used to accuse me of using the puzzle as a means of avoiding conversation. I'd concentrate harder on solving and keep my eyes pinned on the grid when our battling moods were locked in a stubborn silent impasse. But today, when I produce the paper, the one Agaves pushed through my door earlier, it's to encourage communication and fend off uncomfortable silences.

'Voila!'

White rabbit, decoy. Avoid the enemy. Agaves watches, a mug of milky coffee in each hand, as I set the puzzle on the table and pat the sofa pad beside me. A determination to block out the thoughts of Tory, the image of the tabard sandwiching her slim breasts, makes me bold.

'Join me,' I say, bending over the paper and pursing my lips in exaggerated concentration. Agaves sets the drinks down, before picking up a single sheet of paper from the shelf.

'Voila to you too!' His sleight of hand is just as quick.

'What's that?' My pen hovers.

'Hope you don't mind,' he says sheepishly as he slips in next to me. 'I took a copy of the puzzle earlier.'

'Oh. Is that why you picked up my paper?'

'Maybe one of the reasons.' He smiles into my eyes. 'And I've got a printer in the bedroom.'

Last time I was in Agaves' flat, I paused outside his bedroom and peeked inside. The decor was black and white. White walls and black silken sheets. There's a canvas of Paris, Montmartre above the bedhead. But nowhere in my fantasies do I envisage a printer.

'Nathan used to make a copy. He's competitive. Well, a show-off more like.' I suddenly want to retract the last sentence, but Agaves isn't really listening. Rather he's like a horse out of the blocks, desperate to show his mettle.

'I've made a start. Nothing much, but I'm getting better.' He swivels the grid, holds it pinned between fingers. On display. Nathan used to throw it down, the gauntlet of victory.

Agaves' letters are untidy, scribbled, smudged. I think of *Amanda. Enjoy.* The words stuck to the wine bottles. I check the 'As'. The 'y' and 'j'. I look for loops, clues. But the only clue to my neighbour's character is in the childlike innocence of his hand. The largeness of his effort.

As I take in his grid, I feel a weight lift from my insecurities. Agave's not trying to prove he's better than me. A thrill at what he's managed so far is written large across his face. He's trying to prove his worth to me, not to knock me down. As I look more closely, I see that he has only completed the four-letter clues.

'Look.' Agaves points.

See post is dealt with (4)

The answer *spot* is filled in.

'Well done.' I look at him. 'Explain your logic.'

His body is so close, a heady scent of aftershave catching in my throat. I look away, letting my eyes slide up towards the ceiling which swirls to a vortex, as if the ancient stucco plaster is caving in.

'Are you okay?' Agaves puts a hand on my leg. Steadies the violence, and sends a shock of longing through my body.

'Sorry. I feel a bit dizzy.' I pick up the mug, hold it firm with both hands. 'I'm fine. Go on.'

'The whole clue means *see*. The words *dealt with* suggest an anagram. An anagram of *post* is *spot*.'

As pride and excitement ooze from him, I bite my lip to contain the smile.

'Next one.' He points again, his finger skimming mine and I have to swallow down the urge to grab his hand.

Lifeless rooms (4). *Flat* is faintly filled in, but there's no bold certainty about the letters.

'*Flat* can mean *lifeless*, I suppose. *Rooms*, plural, make up a *flat*.' His arm sweeps round the lounge. His face is pink under the tan and my finger yearns to stroke his cheek.

'Gold star. Well done,' I say.

He beams.

* * *

Time passes quickly as we carry on. Agaves laps up my help, listening like an eager pupil.

A coffee bar in Jamaica features the local produce (4)

'I've filled in *café* as the answer, but no idea why.' He throws up his palms and waits for me.

'It's a hidden clue. The answer is simply hidden in the clue. Have a closer look.'

He hunches over, our shoulders touching. I'm scared by the electricity that seems to flow between us and suddenly I crave a drink. As sweat tickles my neck, I start to rub a hand over my hairline and can feel the dampness.

A couple of seconds pass and he whoops.

'Got it! The letters of *café* are hidden in *Jamaica features*. Cool.'

He suddenly leans over and plants an impulsive kiss on my lips. He looks into my eyes, and gently circles my waist with his strong arms.

'I've been wanting to do that for a long time,' he says. He pushes me gently back against the cushions, and engulfs my body, his lips latching on to mine.

When I don't respond, he pulls away.

'Sorry,' he says, withdrawing his body and warmth.

'Hang on,' I whisper, and close my eyes, my body rigid. 'Wait.' I pull a tissue from my pocket, cover my nose, and suddenly sneeze an explosion of irritation.

'Bloody cushions,' I say, and throw them alongside the discarded puzzle as our laughs collide.

When he kisses me for a second time, there is no holding back. I melt into him, his muscled arms wrapping around me, and when he pins me down, I know this guy will break my heart.

* * *

Sanity pulls me back from the brink. Although Nathan left me months ago, I'm scared to jump straight in. If I'd had a few drinks, I would have gone the whole way. Spent days, maybe even weeks, waiting for a phone call that never came. Strange, but Agaves seems almost relieved. Again, it's as if he knows my thoughts.

As I straighten my clothes, he gets up, and towering over me, stretches out both his hands and pulls me towards him.

'Shall I walk you home?' he asks. We laugh together, before he once more caresses his lips against mine.

'I think I'll manage.' I wriggle, wormlike, as I tug down my T-shirt.

He walks ahead and un-snibs the front door.

'See you Saturday.'

'Saturday?'

'At Tory's. She says you've been invited too.' He raises his eyes heavenward in conspiracy.

'Oh. Yes, I'd forgotten.' That's the first lie I've told Agaves.

When he's closed the door behind me, I let out a long breath of pent-up air. I hover on the landing, and feel fear wrinkle my skin. I don't want to be alone. It's still early, and I've the evening to get through. Mention of Tory has dampened the excitement of what's just happened.

As I put my key in the lock, I glance back at the peephole in the door to Flat B, and remember why I drink.

48

NATHAN

On the morning of 10 June, almost a year ago, the sun shone in a cloudless sky dotted by the merest cotton balls of fluff, and by midday a heat haze shimmered on the garden stage.

Before the party, Nathan and Amanda had together tried to tame the garden. While Amanda added colour, bedding plants, and an array of vibrant pots, his aim was to subdue the encroaching weeds which hadn't been touched in months. While the lawn at the centre was mowed into photo-shoot strips, heavy overgrown trees, and bushes, loomed on the edges, a dark and ominous boundary.

Fifteen minutes before the guests were due, Amanda swirled down the stairs wearing a fiery-coloured skirt which danced above her knees and swirled provocatively. Her slim, shapely calves peeked out underneath and her feet were slipped into spiky heels, the tips of which sank fast into the damp earth.

'Stop fussing. I'll take them off later. How do I look?' She pirouetted like a ballet dancer, while he arranged the plastic flutes, paper plates, and rolled cutlery up in serviettes.

As Amanda drank and entertained the guests, he drifted like

flotsam on a murky seabed, lifting, carrying, and following orders like an unpaid skivvy at his own celebration.

But he was aware of Amanda's every move, the escalating drunkenness, the wildness of mood, and watched as she shimmied like a diva. He was already writing the closing script for when the guests departed. He'd undress her, gently slip off the rumpled clothes and run his hands over her smooth, delicate limbs and feel the suffocation of his desire and desperation. Amanda would fall unconscious and only rouse when the thirst of hangover screamed. Then she'd knock back pints of water, and drown in morbid regrets.

Jakub Nowak, a Polish worker who was renting Flat A that summer, and whom Amanda and Nathan hardly ever saw, was the first person to arrive at the party. A squat, swarthy guy who spoke pidgin English, he sloped into the garden with hands stuffed down cavernous pockets of ripped jeans. He hadn't been invited but had come through the entrance into the garden that led directly from the downstairs flat.

Amanda waved at Jakub enthusiastically, seemingly unconcerned by his unkempt appearance and the underpants that poked up through the band of his trousers, nor by the unbuttoned flowery shirt that displayed a heavily tattooed chest. He produced an e-cigarette and engulfed Nathan and Amanda in a dense vapour of fumes. Nathan turned the other way but despite coughing, Amanda flung her arms around Jakub and handed him a bottle of beer.

'Peace, man,' Jakub said, necking the beer through rough-edged teeth.

'Cheers! You're first to arrive.' Amanda's voice was loud, excited, and Nathan noticed she was already halfway through her first bottle of bubbly.

Cheryl, Amanda's best friend, turned up next with her pointy nose, protruding ears and mousy hair. But her insipidness was eclipsed, full moon, by her enormous bouncing bosoms and the skin-tight black scoop top which gaped to reveal the wobbling cleavage. Nathan hated her, both for her appearance and her personality, but more so because of the bond with his wife.

After they got married, Nathan encouraged Amanda to distance herself from Cheryl.

'She's a bad influence. Drinks far too much,' he told her. But he was more concerned by Cheryl's loose behaviour around men, especially after one drink too many.

When he saw Cheryl arrive, having had no idea she'd been invited, Nathan remembers his mood sinking. A feeling of doom engulfed him, as he watched her waddle across the lawn.

'Amanda.' Cheryl launched herself against Amanda, clinging on as if to a grieving widow. She whispered in his wife's ear. They whispered all day. Behind hands. Behind bushes. Downstairs. Upstairs. Their laughs colluded in female conspiracy, and Nathan imagined himself the target.

The Crossword Club, the Three Amigos, arrived together, like the supporting cast of an amateur production of *Abigail's Party*. Dragon Airy was dressed like a jungle explorer in khaki shorts, a buttoned-up pale green sleeveless shirt, and thick-rimmed glasses that hung from around his neck, dangling on a ragged piece of chewed string. He gripped a wide-brimmed bucket hat which was secured against his body by a bony elbow.

'It's not fancy dress,' Nathan said, eyebrow raised as he slapped his colleagues on the backs.

'This is how I always dress.' Dragon Airy's boom had the hollow resonance of a distant kettle drum.

Poseidon's tweed ensemble was rumpled, worn-out like an off-duty army officer's, whereas Regal had the sidekick look of an undergrad dressed in a pink Yale T-shirt and skinny jeans. But

Cheryl's eyes lit up when she spotted him, the only eligible man at the party, and Nathan heard his wife's and her friend's laughter screech through the air before they bowled over, and Amanda introduced Cheryl to Regal. The unlikely pairing soon disappeared through the basement door of Flat A and stayed there most of the afternoon.

Nathan remembers the party as an afternoon of two halves, with competing teams from different leagues playing side by side. Amanda kept checking her watch, and he guessed why. As he stole furtive glances at her, he burnt the sausages, burgers and steaks, but relished the welcome reek of melting skin. Searing pain caused a steady watery stream to flow from the corners of his eyes as he dipped scorched fingertips into a glass of melting ice.

At two o'clock precisely, Martin Hunter strolled up. At 2.30 Teddy Heath, the prat from Flat B, followed close on his heels.

That's when things began to kick off.

49

NATHAN

Martin Hunter, or 'Big Game Hunter' as Amanda called him, rolled up, shook Nathan's hand and apologised that his wife couldn't make it. Something to do with a sickly child but Nathan suspected Martin preferred to come alone, offering a variety of excuses for his wife's absences at every new event.

Nathan had no one but himself to blame for Hunter's presence. When he first met Hunter, his boss at the *London Echo*, they'd swapped idle chit-chat. Hunter told Nathan that he and his wife were looking to move to North London from south of the river and were scouting round for properties. In a rare moment of comradeship with a guy Nathan grew to loathe, he raved to Hunter about Brewer's Hill. Down the road from where he and Amanda lived, there were newly built designer flats with pristine interiors and competitive price tags. They'd just come on the market. Hunter took it all in, and moved down the road from Nathan and Amanda soon after.

The sight of Hunter now mocks Nathan, and his stupidity and naivety in trying to please his boss.

'Hi. Good to see you, Martin. Beer?' Nathan flicked off a metal top and handed a bottle to his guest.

'Thanks. Great party.' Hunter swigged from the bottle and pivoted on the spot. Hunter is one of those guys that men instinctively mistrust, with his condescending manners laced with sarcastic insincerity and a surfeit of arrogance. His swagger made Nathan constantly question how he had ever managed to hook Amanda when men like Hunter circled round her like vultures.

That afternoon, as Amanda sashayed round the garden, Nathan wasn't sure who he trusted less. Her or Hunter. After the evening of the Christmas party, when Amanda first met Hunter, and later apologised to Nathan for her flirtatious behaviour, Nathan hadn't given it much more thought. Amanda had knuckled down, cut back on the drink, and proved she meant it.

But now, with Hunter standing in front of him, and Amanda not far away, the doubts soon crept back in.

'Amanda's looking good. You're a lucky git,' Hunter said, wiping foam from his manicured moustache.

Nathan, ignoring Hunter's comment, managed a tight-lipped smile. 'Help yourself to more beer. I'll be back soon.'

He remembers the party as if it was yesterday and can still feel his wife's heady excitement as she came alive among the milling spectators. He suspected her energy was fuelled by other men's attention. Men like Hunter and the prat from Flat B, Teddy Heath.

Nathan spent a lot of time skulking indoors between wan attempts at socialising, and fanning the barbecue. From their first-floor bedroom window, he watched the spectacle unfold. A motley array of neighbours with pasty faces, bulging waistlines and insipid wives turned up and filled out the gathering. Even old Mr Beckles from next door hobbled in through a gaping hole in their adjoining fence.

As he was about to go back down, Nathan was beset by a

sudden attack of vertigo, and had to grip the radiator. At the bottom of the garden there was a wild untamed area, overgrown with thick foliage, that dropped steeply towards a stony platform several feet below. Amanda and he called it 'the jungle', an area not yet tamed or cultivated. He watched as Hunter slithered through a small opening, snagging his shirt on straggling thorns as he went. Amanda wasn't far behind. When she reached the edge of the jungle, she glanced briefly over her shoulder before she too disappeared from view.

Nathan didn't move. Instead, he began to count the seconds, which quickly morphed into minutes. Five minutes. Six minutes. Eight minutes. Twelve minutes exactly and the pair suddenly reappeared, Amanda's hand straightening her blouse and Hunter's flattening his shirt collar.

'If you punch above your weight, you need to be prepared.' Joseph's sage pronouncement, which his friend had made more than once, rang in his ears.

50

NATHAN

It was around five o'clock when the guests began to wander off.

Amanda was now flagging but was desperate to top up the waning excitement. She collapsed on to Nathan's lap where he sat next to the dying barbecue. The smell of embers and charcoal mingled with a smoky residue that clung to her hair. His lips brushed against the top of her head, and she took his hand and wove their fingers together. He remembers how dizzy she seemed as she rested her head against his chest and how he tried to prise the shot glass from her grasp. In that one fleeting moment, he would have forgiven her anything. He knew he would have to brush aside what he'd witnessed and put it down to a moment of madness, or once again to alcohol.

But as Hunter began to stroll away towards the gate, Amanda pushed her hand against Nathan's chest, and jumped up.

Her voice screeched in his ear. 'What about a cycle ride? I'll get the bike and do my party piece.' Her scream made the smattering of guests turn and watch as their hostess raced for the garden shed, Nathan a step behind. Hunter paused to see what was happening.

'What's the code again?' She fiddled frantically with the combination lock, before stepping aside and demanding Nathan hurry up.

'Our anniversary,' he said as he slowly unlocked the rickety door.

Nathan knew his wife's party piece. He'd seen it twice before, warned her. Not without a helmet. But she pushed him aside and hauled out the bike, flicked away the dust and flung her smooth tanned legs across the bar, hoisting herself up on to the hard saddle.

She circuited the garden a couple of times, whooping like a circus clown, the vodka shots like rocket fuel for her confidence, but arsenic for her balance.

Hunter smiled, raised a hand, and sauntered off. At that moment, Amanda lost concentration and careered into a flower bed. She struggled upright, but Nathan's warnings got lost in her pea-souper brain. The guests kept their eyes averted as she pushed the bike round to the front of the house, blood seeping from a gash in her shin.

Nathan managed to persuade her to sit on the stone step, lean the bike against the wall, while he cleaned and bathed the wound. Later, he remembers thinking, that if he'd given in, let her have her own way and leave with blood still oozing, the accident might never have happened. Hunter would have been strolling down the hill, and Oliver still safely locked inside.

If Nathan hoped the delay would cool his wife's determination, he was well off the mark. No sooner had he patched up her leg, than Amanda was outside on the road, the bike facing down the length of Brewer's Hill.

'Nathan. Nathan. Are you coming? Bring your phone and take a video. For Instagram. Hurry up.'

Reluctantly, he followed, switching his camera to *record* as she set off.

'Come on. Faster. Run along behind,' she yelled over her shoulder, her hair streaming wildly in the slipstream. 'Hurry up.'

She set off slowly at first, then a few seconds in, she lifted her arms and legs off the bike and stretched her limbs wide in a static star jump as she sped down the hill.

Nathan saw him first. Hunter, outside his flat, with his six-year-old son by his side. Amanda whooped when she spotted them, Hunter's hands beating in a congratulatory series of claps. She never heard the car behind as she lost control and swerved up on to the pavement. She fell into Hunter's arms, her bike a tangled mesh of metal as it smashed against the wall.

Nathan got it all on video. The moment Hunter let go of his son's hand to clap, and the moment the boy sidestepped the runaway bike and into the path of the oncoming car.

While Amanda blamed herself for the fateful events, Nathan blamed alcohol, seeing it as a chance to save his wife from herself and her addictions.

He needed her to think she was to blame, and it offered up a way for him to wrestle back control.

Getting her to give up drink would be the only way to save her, and their marriage.

51

AMANDA

I wake early. The recycling truck is thundering along outside and even from my bedroom at the back of the property, I can hear the nerve-jangling screech of the vehicle's crushing jaws. From where I'm lying, through a slit in the curtains, I see beads of rain glistening on the glass. Suddenly, reality hits, a slap in the face. It's Saturday, Tory's dinner party. A whole day of dreaded anticipation looms.

Before I took up the sober challenge, I would relish weekend parties, social gatherings and even dinner parties when I knew a drink would bolster the nerves and spike the fun. But not today. The seconds will be loud incessant clicks and I'll listen to them in my head as the hands clunk forward.

I roll reluctantly out of bed and head to the bathroom where I splash cold water over my face to wash away the thickness of sleep, the foggy dreams. My eyes in the mirror are wide, the look of shock matched by wild unkempt hair. The sink is smeared with toothpaste and a string of dental floss hangs off the side. I scrub my teeth until pink dots gather round the plughole.

Below I hear a rattle as something metal clatters to the floor. It's coming from Flat B. I put my toothbrush back in its mug, and gently drop down, folding my bare knees against the cold tiles. I ease the loose board apart, let my eye slither into the crack and watch Agaves' naked form mosey round his kitchen. I reel backwards when he glances up, stifling an expletive as I smack my head against the sink. His arm reaches into a top cupboard and lifts out a packet of cornflakes which he shakes and checks inside. As he fills a bowl, I slide the board back, and my cheeks sting with shame.

* * *

With Nathan gone, the flat is in chaos. The kitchen looks worse than the bathroom. Crumbs, stains, mushed tea bags and cartons litter the surfaces. Nathan used to get up first, make the tea, tidy up, wash, shave, shower and get dressed for whatever activity was first on the agenda. I'd run my fingers over the gleaming tops with a guilty smile and await my orders. My head would pound from Friday night excess, but Nathan pulled me close, kissed my nose and with an exasperated puff of air would hand me paracetamol.

'Take these. They should do the trick,' he'd say, snapping two sharply from the packet.

Truth is, I miss the company more than I miss Nathan. The quiet plays havoc, the silence reminding me I'm alone, but I don't miss the judgement, the tacit reprimands attached to every failing.

I rinse a mug, rubbing my finger round the stained rim, and squeeze the juice from a quarter of dried-up lemon. The acid seeps into a rag nail and I suck my finger to lick away the sharpness.

My Saturdays with Nathan were generally spent recovering from shameful hangovers. My moods followed a cyclical pattern, from suicidal recall to deep depression, anxiety and tearfulness until a dull acceptance clung to me like a terminal diagnosis. After we got married, Nathan tweaked the pattern, taking *in sickness and in health* to a whole new level. I became a challenge, a new-found hobby that obsessed his every moment, a hill that he had to conquer, no matter what it took. Nathan would pad around the flat, watchful, caring but I felt accusation in the quiet administrations.

'I'm sorry.' My voice was hoarse, quiet, the alcoholic swagger having flown. I knew it was tough on him, my misery following the same old pattern, and, in the mornings, I would thank him for his patience. A synthetic closeness was forged by my weaknesses.

'It's okay.' He'd tuck my hair behind my ears and tell me he was going nowhere. Then he'd run a hot bath for me to cleanse away the dross. 'When you're done,' he'd call through the door, 'we'll have coffee and do the puzzle. Then a walk in Highgate Woods?' It was always a rhetorical question, as the actions were already on his list.

He was a faithful carer, but I felt trapped, like a dementia patient not allowed to wander even though it was for my own good. Nathan watched my every move, and subtly his patience locked me in. The more he cared, the worse I got. I willed a scene, a verbal explosion, but Nathan carried on. A martyr to the cause.

That was, until the night with Martin Hunter. It was some weeks after the fateful afternoon, when I caused the death of his only son.

52

AMANDA

Before I can face the day, the preparations for Tory's dinner party, I open up the puzzle. I let my eyes skim across the grid, as I sip my warm lemon tonic.

For a change, I sit by the window on the edge of a dining chair, and lean against the sill. My finger roams, searching for the longest clue. Since the Martin Hunter clues, I'm on edge. The drinking clues are bad enough, irritating, but I'm now anxious, scared about finding rogue, more threatening posers.

'Sometimes a setter will include a theme that runs throughout the clues. At Christmas, or Easter or during some special event. If there is a special theme, the longest clue usually gives a hint of the subject.' Nathan's head would lean so close that I'd smell his Colgate mouth, his forest aftershave, his cleanliness, and he never once complained at my sour breath which I tried to mask with peppermints.

'Let me do it. Don't jump in.' I'd suck the pen, push him off and let the puzzle weave its magic. Nathan's beady eyes, pursed lips and shallow breathing were never far away. But the puzzle kept us sane, occupied our minds and while Nathan liked to have me close, not battling to escape, for me it was survival, a way to pass the hours until blackness gave in to the dull calm of acceptance.

Soft drink or beer with fruit (6,5)

Eleven letters. Today's longest clue. My leg jitters. Outside a horn blasts impatience, agitates my thoughts, stirs them up. I need to decide what to wear tonight at Tory's party. I wonder who'll be there and if I need to worry about the guest list. I grip the pen, feel a tremor in my hand and put the other one on top to steady the movement.

The whole clue could mean *soft* or *fruit*.

'The answer to the whole clue, as if a quick puzzle, is usually indicated by the first or last words. The bit in the middle helps you work it out.' Nathan's steady tone, toys with my thoughts. He'd repeat this simple formula when my thoughts would veer off track.

I can't think of something *soft* that matches the number of letters. Six and five. Perhaps it's a *fruit*. A type of apple? Melon? But why beer? I think of ale. Perhaps lager. Or bitter?

Then it clicks. *Soft drink* is the whole. Not just *soft*. Another word for *beer* is *bitter*. *Fruit* is *lemon*. The answer is *bitter lemon*. I fill the squares in faintly. Just in case I've got it wrong.

Twenty minutes in, my heart pulses as the ever more familiar drinking theme unfolds, and my skin begins to prickle. Since the wine was left at my door, the drinking theme seems so much worse. I can't work out the connection. I'm missing something. Nathan wouldn't have left the wine. I'm certain. He's probably still really angry, vengeful even, but leaving wine he'd guess I'd drink, wouldn't be his way. He spent too much time on trying to get me sober, I can't believe he'd will me now to fail. Targeting me with puzzle clues is more his thing. A cerebral payback to impress with ingenuity.

The clues become more and more irritating, but they're definitely Nathan's.

Wine from China? It was returned (7)

Chianti is the answer. It's an anagram of *China It*. Chianti has always been one of Nathan's wines of choice.

Fellow with a brown cap in New York? (9)

Manhattan. My favourite cocktail. Girls' night out. Every time. *Fellow* is *man. Brown cap... hat tan.* The whole is *in New York.* Nathan made the clue up shortly after we met, tutting when he heard of my downing three Manhattan cocktails in a row.

I nearly scrunch up the paper, throw it in the bin, cursing Nathan's childish vitriolic war of words. But with only a few clues left to solve, I decide to do them later. I need to get some fresh air, and give my mind a rest.

I set my pen down, breathe in through my nose, out through my mouth, and glance out of the window into the garden below. I can hear the constant traffic, with the regular honk of horns, as it crawls up Brewer's Hill towards the Archway Road. Where there is a small break in the overgrown hedge, I get a snapshot of vans and lorries skimming dangerously close to the parked cars.

Suddenly, I duck below the sill. Agaves has appeared underneath my window, his morning-matted hair stuck at angles. He's dressed in a blinding white T-shirt which clings to his muscular body, and his moulded biceps strain through the thin material. I crane my neck closer to the glass, and as he turns and disappears under the porch of Flat A, I gently undo the lever, crack the window, and lean my ear against the pane.

'Hi. I'm here to help.' His voice has a sing-song welcome, and I imagine his smiling emoji face.

'Hi. Come in. What a nice surprise.' Tory's voice climbs the outer walls and into my front lounge. I see the top of her head for just a second, and jump backwards when she looks up.

When the front door to Flat A slams shut, a sudden horn blasts out from down below and makes me jump.

53

AMANDA

I pull on my trainers, and sneak down the stairs and out the front door. I dip under the overhanging branches and scoot towards the road. I glance over my shoulder, but there's no sign of either Tory or Agaves through the window of Flat A. Images of them together set my teeth on edge.

I set off and jog up Brewer's Hill towards Highgate Woods, my feet pounding over the uneven concrete. Fear follows, catches up and floats alongside me. The cracked pavements slowly ground my movement as I zigzag round the crevices, the unevenness drawing my concentration until my jelly legs begin to set. A chill wind cools my angst and pushes the paranoia briefly to one side. On the edge of the woods, I slump on to a red bench, kick my legs out and stretch until my calf muscles scream.

A large ginger cat wanders up, circles through my legs, and a hearty purr draws my hand to run along its back. It then lies on the ground, revealing a downy stomach, but hisses when my fingers get too close.

The fresh air lifts my mood, and by the time I get back to Silver

Birch, I feel much better. Refreshed, I slip my trainers off under the porch, and tiptoe back up the stairs. Once inside the flat, I pour myself a long cold drink, and before I shower I collapse on to the sofa with the paper, and set to solve the last few clues.

I chew the end of the pen, gripping it in my teeth, and try to concentrate.

Suddenly my stomach somersaults. I read, and reread the first clue I come to. This one would definitely not have been set by Nathan. My husband has his own special equation for my name. *A Male Attorney for the Girl*. He never let me forget the clue he made up on the day we met. But today, someone has come up with a different clue for *Amanda*.

A girl, odd crazy number in addict group (7)

The girl is the whole. *Amanda. Crazy* is *mad. Number is n. Crazy* is *mad* and *n* in an anagram... *mand. In addict group... AA.*

If Nathan had set the puzzle, he would have used the old familiar clue to indicate my name. If he wanted to communicate from a distance, he'd have played true to form, habitual, unwavering. That's his personality.

The final clue, tucked into the centre of the grid, launches me to the bathroom. My head spins as I retch over the basin. This clue definitely doesn't have Nathan's stamp. Unless he's become evil, and really wants me to suffer more. I can't get my head round what's happening, except that something isn't right. Someone else has got it in for me. Who? Why? Oh my god!

I stumble back to the lounge, and grip the grid with trembling fingers.

Oil producer right for a musical? (6)

The ? tells me the whole answer is related to a musical. I went through the list of popular musicals, wracked my brain for those with six letters. I thought of *Grease*. There was an oil theme going on, but it didn't fit with the letters I'd already filled in: _i_v_r.

I know for sure I've got it right. There are no other possibilities. The answer to the clue is *Oliver*. The name of the Hunters' son who died. On 10 June.

54

AMANDA

I don't want to go to Tory's dinner party. It's not just because the crossword clues have freaked me out, but if I'm honest I don't want to go anywhere. I'd be happy never to set foot outside again. The walls of the flat are comforting, a familiar barricade providing protection against increasing paranoia of real or imagined threats. And I'm scared to see Agaves when I'm like this.

My lipstick hand wobbles, snakes a ragged line. I take a wet wipe, scrub it off and start again. Black, thick, caked mascara from an out-of-date brush clips my lashes together and I want to cry, slink deep under the duvet, and block out the world.

Agaves' voice floats up through an open window. He must be there already. The sound of his deep schmoozing makes me quiver through a mixture of fear, anticipation, and longing. My quarter-bottle of emergency vodka is singing, the noise getting louder. It's locked away in a small cabinet on the landing and although it's forbidden territory, like a minefield with a large danger-keep-out sign, I can't forget it's there.

A loud slam of a car door, the ping of an alarm and crisp excited voices filter through from outside and draw me back to the window. Below, a couple approach Flat A. The man is dressed in a penguin suit, red bow tie, and shiny brogues which gleam in the porch light. The woman – short, pear-shaped – wears a fifties waisted dress with a virginal white cardigan, and a set of choking pearls around her white pasty neck.

Tory insisted it was a casual get-together. But she's either mislead the other guests, or lied to me. It's not hard to work out which.

'Just a few friends,' she said. 'Drop by, the more the merrier and wear whatever's comfortable. Nothing fancy.'

But the sight of the arrivals tells me another story, that the hostess has given conflicting accounts of the dress code.

I rip off my jeans and flirty top, then pull out a green satin cocktail dress which clings to my curves. I slip it on over my head and let it slither to just below my knees, leaving my bare calves on show. I twirl in front of the mirror. My fiery red hair hangs fiercely over my bare shoulders and skims the merest hint of shoulder straps. Nathan called it my battle dress. It could break down enemy lines and weaken the hardest resolve, he told me.

As I switch off the bedroom light, there are three short raps, three long raps and another three short raps on the front door. My plus one has arrived.

'Coming.' I hop through the lounge, tugging on a pair of golden sandals like Cinderella preparing for the ball.

Joseph was my only option. Cheryl says he's a sleezy creep, eyes too close together and his holy smirk is more devil-like than Christ. I haven't told Joseph my whole story, why Nathan left, about Martin Hunter, nor my fantasies about Agaves. I open up about the alcohol in isolation, unwilling to talk any more about my past as I'm unsure how far the AA pact of confidentiality goes, and after all, he is Nathan's best friend.

'He's not a priest. You don't need to confess. He's there to help,'

Nathan told me once. Nathan and Joseph have been friends since uni, sharing a solid bond of friendship. It's the perceived strength of this bond that holds back my desperate need to confide.

I linger by the door, uneasy as I remember Joseph's seen me half-naked, and unconscious. More than once, he's humped me into bed, a leaden weight saturated in liquor. But more than once he might have saved my life, and that thought is never far away.

A deep breath, and I unlatch the door.

'Hi. Come in. Great to see you.' My voice is high, shaky. Joseph's uneven toes perch on the edge of his stringy leather Jesus sandals and on top he's wearing a sunny yellow shirt printed with cockatoos and palm fronds. He's certainly taken to heart my assurances of a casual dress code.

A ginger line of beard is snipped to a point below his chin, like a Van Gogh goatee, and his appearance smacks of student rebellion. His shaggy locks are tied back with a piece of string, and an ebony cross dangles from his white throat. Two buttons near his waist connect the shirt, and baggy beige shorts complete the ensemble.

'Oops. I seem to be underdressed.' But he doesn't care. That's Joseph; he's very much like Nathan in that respect. Accept me as I am or go to hell.

'Sorry. I've only found out that it's not casual from watching guests arrive.'

'No worries. I prefer being comfortable anyway.' Joseph steps into the hall and hands me two bottles of non-alcoholic wine.

'For us to share,' he says.

* * *

As Joseph rings the bell to Flat A, I feel uncomfortable standing outside Tory's front door as part of a random couple, rather than as a neighbour who lives in the same building and holds a key to the hostess's flat.

'Amanda.' Tory appears in a black full-length evening dress, thin satin shoulder straps criss-crossing sharply defined shoulder blades, and defined nipples poking through the flimsy material like wireless knobs.

'Hi. This is Joseph.' I nod towards my partner.

'Hi, Joseph. Come in.'

'Good to meet you,' he says, extending a freckled hand which envelops Tory's delicate fingers.

'Come in. You look lovely, Amanda,' she says as she leads us through.

Although Tory moved into Silver Birch in January, nearly three months ago, this is my first time inside her flat. Nathan would say you never know anyone until you've stepped over the threshold into their home.

The intersection of mine and my husband's personalities made our flat a mixture of order and chaos. Nathan lined shoes in pairs while I flung mine randomly in corners. He smoothed out bedclothes, plumped up pillows and straightened rumpled towels while I stacked dirty dishes for the morning after.

My first impression of Flat A is one of clinical cleanliness, with an unlived-in feel. A strange mix of scents, woodland pines, exotic spices, and sickly petals comes from an isolated dish of potpourri which sits atop a small table. As I breathe in, the overkill of fragrance makes me cough. Joseph roars a sneeze.

'Bless you,' Tory says.

The entrance hall is hexagonal-shaped, with black and white floor tiles which resemble a skewed chessboard. In fact, everything in sight is black or white, including the photographs that pepper the walls. A two-way bench, glossy oak, straddles the centre of the foyer, inviting guests to take a seat. It's like an art gallery, teasing us to pause and look more closely. My eyes flit from ski slopes to coastlines, boating lakes to mountain tops and come to rest at a close-up portrait. A handsome man, his arm flopped across Tory's shoulder beams with dazzling advert teeth. Sunglasses conceal his eyes and a ski hat locks in his hair, but he looks familiar. Like a movie icon, but too much is hidden for me to work out who it is. My brain whirrs with effort, jumping back and forth.

Down the hall, Tory turns and her voice echoes off the cavernous walls.

'Follow me. The dining room is this way.'

As Joseph moves ahead, I hesitate. I feel on edge. My throat is parched and my hands are clammy. I've absolutely no idea how I'm going to get through the evening without a drink.

55

AMANDA

Victoria's dining room is square, not rectangular like ours. The shape makes the room feel small, cramped and verging on the claustrophobic.

The extravagantly laid dining table, with six place settings, six wine glasses, six name cards in silver holders, and two small vases with red roses in the centre, screams formal. This is definitely anything but a casual get-together.

'A few drinks. Nibbles. Just turn up. The more the merrier,' Tory told me. Apart from Joseph, the dress code is more West-End premiere than a Highgate *at-home*. Even Agaves, who is dressed in smart shirt and muscle-hugging trousers, must have known. The sight of him makes my stomach flip. Tonight, he's more James Bond than guy next door.

'Hi, Amanda.' Agaves' eyes lose their sparkle the minute Joseph appears, and a faint tic takes up rhythm on his freshly shaved lower jaw. 'Joseph,' he says, offering a wilting hand.

'Edward. Good to see you.' For a second, I can't think who Joseph is referring to. Teddy. Agaves. Eddie. But my neighbour from Flat B is definitely not an Edward. Agaves tentatively kisses me on both cheeks, but I shiver, as he communicates familiarity by squeezing firm hands against my buttocks.

Victoria flits in and out with canapés of caviar, smoked salmon, avocado, shrimps, truffles. A long-painted fingernail works the platter. She then asks Agaves to follow her, cupping a muffled hand over her mouth while she stretches her arm out to take hold of his hand.

From the kitchen, which is void of doors, a champagne cork explodes, a single gunfire shot, and our hostess's laughter can be heard howling round the flat.

'Someone's happy,' says Joseph, his thick wet lips very close to my ear. 'Here. Let me.' He unscrews the non-alcoholic wine bottles which are like accusatory pointing fingers, and fills two glasses. 'Cheers,' he says, smashing our glasses together. Eyes look our way, and my cheeks burn.

Tory hasn't introduced us yet to the other two guests, but I already want to leave. Make my excuses. I can't let go of the thought that Tory is playing some sort of weird game of control. Agaves couldn't possibly fancy her, could he? I've gone up and over it a thousand times.

My mouth is so parched, I have trouble swallowing. Even talking is a challenge.

'Could I just have one glass?' I whisper, leaning close in to Joseph. He shakes his head, a quick but violent action which sends a straggling strand of ginger hair flopping across his eyes. He settles a large white hand on my bare shoulder, tilts my chin towards him.

'No. You can't.'

'I want to go home,' I say, shielding my mouth with a palm.

'Why? The food will be good, and we can leave straight afterwards.' His hand moves on to my thigh, but I shift in my seat until he takes it off. It's the last thing I want Agaves to see.

When Agaves returns, he looks sheepish but raises a glass and winks. Joseph's hulked frame shifts towards me at the same time, until his shoulder skims mine. Agaves' shoulders droop, until Tory reappears, and she propels him back to the table.

The small woman I saw from my window is called Rachel, pronounced Raquel. When she tells us it's spelt R-a-c-h-e-l I wonder at the phoney pronunciation and think of Del Boy's wife, the aspiring actress, in *Only Fools and Horses*. Rachel's husband, the guy in red bow tie, is called Sebastien.

'Sebastien Warner-Wilkes,' he says when Tory suggests we introduce ourselves. Sebastien stands up, circles the table in his hard squeaky shoes and shakes hands with each of us in turn.

Nathan, at this point, would be warning me not to comment. 'There's nothing wrong with double-barrelled names,' he'd say. 'Don't you dare say anything.'

But I'd made fun more than once of his pompous colleagues, asking them directly, with an intense questioner's stare, for the history of their names, enquiring with phoney intent if their family had at some time lacked male descendants and the double-barrelled surnames were a way of preserving a name that would otherwise have died out.

Nathan berated me for being facetious. I knew right well the hyphened names were for show, an attempt at artificial one-upmanship by a wife who coveted her identity and a man who was more than happy to feign aristocratic ancestry.

'Pretentious pricks,' I'd mutter when Nathan told me to zip it, although underneath I know he agreed. When I drank, I'd let rip, keep at it, winding up the audience. Only sobriety could put a lid on my wicked tongue.

Agaves catches my eye, raises a brow, and uses his topped-up fizz to swallow a laugh. My heart does a little flip, and I can't help but smile knowing we're on the same page.

'What do you do, Amanda?' Sebastien asks in a thick plummy accent as he twizzles with his disconnected bow tie.

'I'm a teacher. Maths. What about you?'

'Boring. Lawyer.' He throws an arm along the back of Rachel's chair, taking ownership of his mousy spouse. Sober, I look more closely. Drunk, I'd have joined in, played the charade of interested sycophant. Sebastien's nose is Concorde pointy, eyes verging on cross-eyed, and his eyebrows look as if they've been tattooed and shaped like a woman's.

Agaves puts a hand to his mouth and stifles a yawn, biting back another laugh. I have to look away to stop the giggles.

'And Rachel. Do you still work?' Joseph's interjection breaks the mood. His question lacks intonation, his voice having the drone of a dentist's drill. I'm suddenly aware of his heavy breath, his chair too close with its wooden edge touching mine.

'No. My wife's expecting. Aren't you, darling?' Sebastien doesn't wait for an answer, preferring the sound of his own voice.

Small talk wafts around the room, like chill air through window cracks. *Where do you work? Any holiday plans this year? Do you ski? Do you jog? Where did you meet? Been married long?*

It's like a slow-moving theatre play, when the actors are dull, and the script even duller. This is my sober perspective of the conversation round the table. Tory keeps topping up the wine glasses and smiles at me with nauseous magnanimity. When she catches my eye, her expression is one of challenge, her smile tight-lipped, with no show of teeth.

Agaves seems far away, as if he's drifted off into his own private world, but I could stretch across the table and touch his hand. Tonight though, he's off limits and I cringe when Tory's skinny fingers rest on his shoulder as she pours the wine.

When there's an awkward lull in conversation, I share my pastime.

'Crossword puzzles, eh?' Sebastien uncoils his arm, rests his elbows on the table and cups his chin. I redden, suddenly embarrassed.

'Yes. It's quite a hobby,' Agaves says, chipping in. 'She's got me hooked, and I'm an addict now myself. Amanda, though, still has to help me with the clues.'

'Oh. I didn't know you were a cruciverbalist too?' Tory hovers over us, gripping soiled plates.

'I'm not a crossword setter, if that's what you mean. It's just a hobby,' I say.

'A cruciverbalist is someone who enjoys puzzles, as well as the label for someone who sets them.' Joseph's voice makes me turn, as does the noise of his teeth tapping against his glass.

'That's not what Nathan says.' I'm the expert. This is my subject. 'He says cruciverbalists are the setters of the puzzle. Not the hobbyists who solve the clues.'

'Who's Nathan?' Rachel's gentle soprano joins the chorus.

'My ex. That's all.'

56

AMANDA

When Rachel hears I do crosswords, her face lights up while Sebastien's eyes dull. Agaves steps in, makes the next move.

'Let's play Solve the Anagram,' he suggests. 'More fun than charades.'

'What's that?' Sebastien replenishes his glass with tortoise speed. I bite my lip, as I try and quell the alcoholic envy.

'Amanda, you tell us. You're the expert.' Agaves nods in my direction. I'd marry him now if he asked me.

'Okay. I'll give you a word, or a couple of words, and one point goes to whoever makes another word or phrase from the letters first. An example.'

I hum, mouth pursed, eyes closed. '*Garden*. If you scramble the letters, what other word can you make?' I ask.

Agaves' legs stretch out under the table, and his shoe tip clips mine. He knows the answer, as he's solved it before. But my choice of anagram tells him I'm giving him a heads-up. Another wink, and he eggs me on.

'Danger,' Rachel says. Agaves claps lightly.

'One point to Rachel. Next one.' I become quiz master, expert, Jeremy Paxman smart, and fall into the role with confidence.

I can hear Joseph's feet flap up and down in his flimsy sandals, knocking my concentration, until I come up with the next clue.

'Red wine.'

'Shhh. I can't concentrate,' yaps Sebastien, looking at Joseph. But before Sebastien has a chance to think, Rachel comes up trumps. Again.

'Rewiden,' she says.

'Stupid bloody game.' Sebastien stares down his wife, and I think of Medusa, whose eyes turned her targets to stone.

'Why doesn't someone else ask a question now?' I sip my drink, momentarily forgetting its lack of bite.

'Okay, I'll go next,' Agaves says, drumming his fingers on the table. 'Famous people. I'll give you words and phrases, and you need to use the letters to come up with the name of a famous person.' His eyes are aglow, and I feel a tingle of happiness when I realise we're in it together. He's going to use phrases I taught him recently.

'*I'm a jerk, but listen*. It's a singer. That's the clue.'

Tory excuses herself from the table and disappears into the kitchen where she clatters round with plates, pans, cutlery before turning up her music playlist. Chopin polonaises, Mozart, Vivaldi, the resulting racket like cars round a Formula 1 racetrack. 'Won't be long,' she yells. But the noise is deliberate.

'*Justin Timberlake*.' Joseph whoops.

'Jeez. How did you work that out?' Sebastien's fingernails chip at his glass.

'Here's another one.' Agaves plays his audience. '*He bugs gore*. A politician this time.'

'*George Bush*. That's an easy one,' Tory says, chirping over our shoulders, as she suddenly reappears with a cafetiere of coffee and a plate of mints. 'Anyone for sugar?' she asks.

Joseph ends the game when he raises a hand, like the pupil at the back of the class that no one's noticed. 'Can I've a go? Last one, I promise. *Real fun*,' he offers. 'It's just a simple anagram. Not a person's name.'

'That's another easy one,' Tory says. She laughs as she sits down, plunging the strainer of the cafetiere through the water. She's got our attention, and we listen as she purrs the answer. '*Funeral. Real fun* is an anagram of funeral.'

* * *

Whenever I go to bed drunk, a violent tornado spins me to sleep, and the resultant amnesia is a short-lived bear hug of comfort. But sobriety causes bright lights of alertness.

Tonight, I finally crawl into bed around 11.30, but even when I close my eyes, I can't slow my thoughts. I toss and turn, left side, right side and then on to my back before I start the routine all over again. I tug at the duvet, wrap it round me like a sleeping bag, but nothing helps.

About half an hour into the futile routine, my phone pings, like a scary boo in the dark. I sit up, still my face, and take a horror selfie to unlock the screen. I scan the message with blurry eyes.

Well done! Weird night though? T X

It takes a second to work out who T is, before I twig it's from Agaves. Teddy.

I imagine him lying down below, naked, dark, dangerous. Drunk, I'd have smacked on his door, demanded attention. Sex. Men obliged, thought they ought, but duty rarely obliged more than once. While I craved closeness, love, a relationship, they'd only add me as a notch on their bedpost, put off by my brazen attitude.

Sobriety now makes me cautious, tells me how I should behave.

I plump up the pillows, straighten up, and let a shaky finger send a reply.

Thanks. Wasn't easy. Yep. Very weird! X

As I sink into fitful sleep, words, letters, swirl round my head like litter in the wind. They gust up, flail around, and refuse to settle. This morning's clues come back to haunt me.

A girl, odd crazy number in addict group (6). Amanda

Oil producer right for a musical? (6). Oliver

These aren't teasing, simplistic alcoholic bullseyes. There's threat involved. I feel it. Deep down. What? Why? Who? The questions keep coming.

My nightmares finally suck me down. Nathan's face appears, his features vague, changing, indistinct. I then see red hair, a ginger beard. A woman's fragile nose, pale lips. Finally, a full, luscious mouth with dazzling teeth.

Agaves' smile is the last thing I remember before I fall asleep.

57

AMANDA

I mooch around the flat all morning. Thoughts of last night's dinner party follow me from room to room. I can't settle. Even the puzzle is untouched. But after how close I got to Agaves the other day, it felt unsettling, and hurtful watching him with someone else. Tory. She's uneasy company, and there's a contrivance about her.

It's early afternoon when I take my chances. From the lounge, I watch Agaves outside as he bends to tie his laces. He looks up at the sky, smiles at the sun, and jogs out through the main gate. I feel jealous of his contentment, the routine of simple pleasures, which seem to make him happy.

I wonder if I was ever that content. I certainly miss my old life. The life before things went wrong with Nathan, the life before the accident, before Martin Hunter, before alcohol became an ever-present threat. But I wonder what it is I miss. The lack of fear, perhaps, before thoughts of death moved in to keep me company, and the inbuilt optimism for the future. I'm now terrified by my feelings for Agaves, and that he might not feel the same.

Joseph tells me things will get better, that it's a slow road to recovery, and he's confident I'll get there. He tells me my agoraphobia, a fear of open spaces, is a temporary symptom of my condition. I don't bother to ask if he means of my alcoholic condition or the PTSD which followed on from the accident, and the death of Oliver. But Joseph tells me what I need to hear, a mantra he repeats by rote. I've heard him with the other addicts, comforting, caring. But also suffocating.

If Nathan hadn't drawn up a battle plan, a neatly written schedule for the weeks after the 10 June, and watched me like a hawk, I'd probably have finished it all. Gone to the other side to be with Oliver. Tears still take me unaware, drenching chinks of light. When Cheryl read Nathan's action plan, points one to ten, she slapped a hand against her face.

'Christ, Amanda. You can't be serious! He is so in-your-face. Tell your bloody husband to get a life.'

Instead, I told her to back off. When I finally accepted I was an addict, I locked myself away and ignored her pleading texts. Nathan congratulated me on breaking toxic cycles, with less than subtle put-downs aimed at my one-time best friend. But I still watch Cheryl's Instagram posts, nostalgic for the fun times.

I quickly dig out my tracksuit, vest, and trainers and run a finger through the canvas gash. Trainers were on my birthday wish list, halfway up, above a slow cooker, but below a girly spa weekend. Nathan bought me books instead, not liking to be cajoled, and certainly not into sanctioning a girls' trip away. He was silent in his disapproval.

When I'm dressed, I lock up and head off along the route I know Agaves always takes. It's a male thing, the predictability, and he's not unlike Nathan in that regard. I don't aim to catch up with him, rather to catch him on his way back.

I reach the break in the iron railings that skirt Highgate Woods, and hover behind the towering chestnut tree that guards the entrance. I lean my back against the gnarled trunk and wait, count down the seconds. About twenty minutes later, just as I'm ready to abort, I see Agaves pounding towards me. I drop my eyes, fiddle with my phone.

'Amanda. What are you doing here?' Agaves slows to a walk, looks around and strolls towards me.

'Same as you, it looks like,' I reply, zipping my phone away. 'But I've got cramp and not sure I can carry on.'

'Oh. Is it really bad?' His eyes crinkle with concern as I stretch out my calves.

'No. It's easing off.' I smile. 'Thank goodness.'

A second passes, before he asks if I fancy grabbing a cold drink.

'I'm really thirsty and the café over there should be open,' he suggests.

'Yes, that would be nice. I think I'll have to knock the jogging on the head.' I grimace and rub hard at my lower leg.

'Maybe you'll let me massage that for you when we get back,' Agaves says with a wolfishly wicked grin. His expression, his bright eyes, tell me I haven't lost him. Another thing I know for sure is that I'm at the point of no return with this guy.

58

AMANDA

We sit alongside each other on a bench outside the café, and slurp noisily from cans.

'Did you enjoy the dinner party?' Agaves asks, swivelling round to face me. As his thigh touches mine, I feel heat rip through my body.

'It was fun.' I'm not sure what else to say as I don't want to sound rude and say what I really think. I've no idea what might have happened after Joseph and I left the party, and I'm scared to ask. I'm not keen to hear the details.

I said goodnight to Joseph outside the door to Tory's flat, avoiding his wet lips as they aimed for mine, and offered up a reluctant cheek instead. Joseph didn't push, and thanked me for the invitation, and with a slight over-the-shoulder wave, ambled down the path, and disappeared up Brewer's Hill.

I ran upstairs to my flat, slammed the front door, and raced across the lounge to take up sentry by the window. My senses screamed against the slightest noise, and my stomach gurgled with anxiety, but the minutes ticked steadily by. I didn't move, rigid in my vigil.

Rachel and Sebastien left after about half an hour, and then time slowed to a crawl as a sickness built in my gut. I'd almost given up, accepted the worst thing imaginable in that Agaves might spend the night with Tory, when all at once I was jolted out of the nightmare. Tory's front door opened, and Agaves appeared and hovered on the porch.

I scooted behind the curtain, inched it aside, just enough that I could see, and then craned my neck to get a better view. I didn't see Tory, but heard her laugh. It was a bit too loud, a bit too forced, until an eerie silence followed. I closed my eyes and began to count, willing the seconds to pass. Four minutes, twenty-five seconds. That was all, and then I heard Agaves say goodnight. Thank the hostess for a great evening. I clasped my hands together in relief, and finally slid away from the window.

Agaves' gentle finger brings me back to the present as it teases a stray wisp of hair behind my ear. 'Are you still with me?' he asks.

'Sorry. I was miles away.'

'Yes, the evening was fun,' he says. 'The food was good, although pretty dodgy company. Apart from yours truly, of course.' Laughter lines, tissue paper soft, crease his eyes which are dark and chocolatey smooth.

He reaches for my hands, takes them in a firm grip before he leans forward and kisses me gently on the lips. My heart begins to race. Over his shoulder the sun beams down, and I feel a rare moment of contentment, and something more. Hope. Optimism that things might be okay, and that Agaves might just be my future.

He looks startled, when I pull away, but doesn't let go of my hands.

'I did wonder about you and Tory,' I dare to say.

'She's a good hostess, but not really my type.'

My heart soars. That's all I need to hear.

'Did you find out anything else about her? What she does? Ex-husbands?' I want to close the lid on the worries that kept me up all night.

'Not sure exactly what she does, but she's separated. Getting divorced, I think that's what she said.'

59

MRS HUNTER

Mrs Hunter was more commonly referred to as Martin Hunter's wife. Her own identity had got swallowed up by her husband's controlling behaviour. She was his possession, a trophy wife, but not a gold cup on show for all to see, rather a third-rate bronze statuette that got stuffed away in a drawer.

Brewer's Hill, its horse chestnuts boxed in concrete sockets along the pavement creating an air of welcome, had seduced their little family with its faux grandeur. It had sung to her of new possibilities, a fresh start, broader horizons. It was a huge step up from their small, cramped flat south of the river.

It wasn't long till the phoney splendour of their new address matched their marriage. To the outside world, their union was one of perfection, but it was all an illusion. Mrs Hunter lived in a prison, albeit one with an exclusive post code, one with thickly constructed walls through which there was no way out. While her husband grafted to climb the corporate ladder, nailing each advance with gleaming tacks, a heavy hand kept his wife in check, and more importantly, out of sight.

Chief sub-editor at the *London Echo* newspaper, Martin Hunter had only one more rung to climb to reach his goal. To be top dog and to be in charge. It was all he'd ever dreamt of.

June the tenth. That was the date when her life changed forever, the date and its events indelibly imprinted on her mind. That afternoon, she had kept a steady vigil, waiting for Martin to return. She kept watch, her fingers poking through the slats of the window blind, as she peered out. The sun, eager to beam through the scant opening, was blocked by the barrier, but Martin insisted the blinds were kept closed. Only when she knew he wouldn't be home for some hours did she dare wind them up and unlock the view.

Oliver, their six-year-old son, was dressed in a football kit and clumping round the flat in his boots with the laces overflowing, huffing, and puffing like his father. She couldn't get him to sit still. He dribbled the football across the floor, picking it up when she told him to wait on the sofa, from where he began to bounce it up and down.

'He'll be here soon. I promise.' Her knotted acid stomach growled when she moved to clean the kitchen, buff up the granite tops as Martin had instructed. The clock clunked forward. Five o'clock. 5.10. 5.20. 5.30. She spun round when she heard Oliver tug up the blinds the whole way, as he pressed his nose to the glass. She remembers him gripping the Man U football between his tiny hands. His golden hair was shocked and tangled.

'Here. Let me.' She got a brush and dragged it through his locks, closing her eyes and inhaling her son's smell which was like nectar to a honeybee.

'He's coming!' Oliver's scream threw her backwards. 'Quick. Tie my laces. Hurry up. Hurry up.' The football rolled across the floor, and his feet jiggled as her damp hands slid around the laces.

'Sit still.' Her heart raced as the key turned in the lock.

'Daddy. Daddy. I'm ready.' He barged past and leapt into Martin's arms.

'What did I tell you about football boots? Not till we're outside the flat.' Martin gently set him down, ruffled his hair. 'Oliver. I'll not repeat myself. Remember for next time.'

Martin's face was flushed, a ruddy glow across his cheeks and his shirt was stained below the armpits, the damp encroaching like a swamp across his chest.

'Mummy. Did you forget the rules?' Martin asked as he stepped closer, took her shoulders, and dug his fingers deep. Behind him, Oliver popped the football up and down in the air, impatient to get going. The memory of his perfect face, saucer eyes and upturned golden lashes, would never leave her.

Martin whispered alcoholic fumes against her ear. 'You won't forget again. Will you?'

She nodded and winced as he pierced her bones with steel-tipped thumbs.

After they left, she hung by the window and watched as her son and husband moved towards the kerb. As she gently rolled the blind back down, she raised an arm, wiggled her fingers, and blew Oliver a kiss. He raised his tiny hand, put it to his mouth and puffed out a tiny spit of air. It was enough to melt her heart.

The bike flew out of nowhere, like a vulture swooping down for blood. It wobbled, the rider scooting across the pavement, catapulting Oliver's little feet forward. On to the road. The car hit him head on. Mrs Hunter heard the silence, that stopping of time, an eternity, from inside the flat. For a moment she thought she too had died.

* * *

It seems so long ago. Another life, another world. But Martin Hunter's wife remembers that her husband forgot to beat her up that day. He forgot to bruise her ribs and blacken her eyes.

But she can't forget the day.

It's tattooed on her soul, for all eternity.

She remembers every little detail.

60

AMANDA

We stroll back from the café and Agaves insists on walking with me, rather than running on, in deference to my phoney cramp. His stride is so long, I have to scurry, two of my steps to each of his, but I do so with the eagerness of a child to stay abreast.

'You look as if you're jogging,' he says, grabbing my hand and pulling me along. 'At least your cramp must have gone.'

I laugh when he takes both my hands and swings me round. It hits me that I've never had a relationship with anyone so physical. So perfect. A chink of realisation that maybe I never gave myself a chance to let the good guys in. I drank through insecurity, fear of rejection and my wild ways scared them off.

Cheryl said I married Nathan because he was safe and that I'd at last never need to worry, look over my shoulder at the competition. When I argued back, saying that I loved Nathan, I knew she'd hit a nerve. When she asked 'Who else would want Nathan anyway? Apart from you,' I knew I had to flush Cheryl from my life. She was the past, and Nathan was my future. Well, that was what I thought back then, and Nathan encouraged the idea with gusto.

In the early days, after he left, I missed Nathan. His caring, solid presence, and his endless patience. But I never missed him in the gut-churning way that I would miss someone like Agaves. The way I once thought I might feel about Martin Hunter before I knew him better. Before I knew he was married, and before he spiked my drink. And raped me.

As we reach Brewer's Hill, I turn towards Agaves.

'Fancy a quick coffee?' I'm worried he might make an excuse, but I have to talk to him. Properly. I've been putting it off in case what I have to tell him might scare him off. But I've no one else. Apart from Joseph, who has started to freak me out. On the night of Tory's party, my sponsor's goodnight kiss, which I managed to deflect, left a soggy imprint as his wet lips smacked against my cheek. The memory's pretty potent.

'Yes. Why not. I've no plans till this evening,' Agaves says. A sickness bites. This evening. Who with? Where? Tory? It's hard not to ask, but I manage to swallow the inquisition.

Agaves slows again, takes my hand, and pulls me along. 'You're like a kid,' he says. 'Come on. Get a move on.' He drags me along and suddenly stops, hoists me in the air and throws me over his shoulder, fireman style.

'Let me down. Shit. Let me down,' I scream. But I'm loving it. My head lollops down his back, his hot strength sizzling me into submission.

As we enter the rusting gates of Silver Birch, Agaves gently lets me go, deposits me on to the path. He begins to fiddle with a slanting post and wobbles it from side to side.

'This needs replacing. Shall I get a quote?'

When I don't answer he looks up, but my gaze is elsewhere. I'm looking at what's on the porch. I flail sideways against the wall.

'Are you okay?' Agaves takes my arm. 'Sorry. It must have been the fireman's lift. Are you feeling dizzy?'

'I'm fine.' But I'm far from fine. Our building appears to be moving, swaying, and leaning forward as if it's about to collapse and bury us. But I somehow reach the porch, flop on to the frozen concrete step, and drop my head between my legs.

Agaves bends down, his knees clicking, and a strong arm circles my shoulder and pulls me close.

'You'll be okay. Give it a minute and let me make the coffee.' He kisses the top of my head, takes my hands, and hoists me up. 'Oh, look. You've got a present. Two presents, I should say.'

I know. I've already seen them.'

On the step are two more bottles of wine, one with the cork un-stoppered. My shaky fingers unwrap the note. The same writing as on the one before.

Enjoy, Amanda. You deserve a break X

61

AMANDA

I stagger up the stairs, the stairway to heaven, or hell. Depends on the day. Agaves carries the bottles, promises to keep them, hide them if I beg. I want to cry when he says he likes a good Merlot, and won't let them go to waste. He understands, but does he? Does anyone, other than an addict, really get it? I've never owned up to Agaves about the last two bottles. I'm too ashamed.

'You want to talk about it?' he asks as he turns the lock in his front door. 'Come in and I'll put the kettle on.'

The mess inside Flat B is back. It's like a recycling centre, cartons and containers making mini mountains. But there's something comforting about the mess, as there's no sign of a woman's touch. More importantly, no sign of Tory's fastidious administrations.

Agaves busies himself in the kitchen, on my peepshow stage. I flush in shame as I listen to the rattle of crockery, cutlery, pots and pans.

My eyes alight on a neat stack of newspapers by the window. I think of Nathan, his ordered alignment of the broadsheets. From where I'm sitting, I reckon there are at least twelve editions, and a crossword grid from the *Echo* is visible on top.

Agaves, bare-footed, creeps back in with coffees and a plate of chocolate biscuits.

'It's your fault,' he says.

'What's my fault?' I give him a quizzical look.

'The puzzles. I'm hooked.' He's seen my gaze, and goes and picks up the pile and plops it on the coffee table. I'd no idea he was really hooked, even after the claims at Tory's dinner party. I know he enjoys the puzzles, but it looks like he's becoming obsessed. He doesn't really seem the type, but I'm making assumptions. If I had better things to do, would I be the puzzle nerd I've become? It's hard to say. Perhaps it's a novel way for Agaves to impress me. He seems pleased, proud, that I've spotted the pile.

When he sits down, and I've got his full attention, I start to open up. I try not to sound too cooky, weird, when I talk about the puzzles, and the random clues that seem so personal, but can't help my voice from speeding up. The last thing I want is to scare him off, yet if Agaves really is into puzzles, it might be easier to explain.

Before I've finished, Agaves pulls a paper from the Jenga pile, slides it out from somewhere near the top and sets it out. The grid is familiar. It's Saturday's puzzle with the drink theme.

My eyes are dry, scratchy, and I have to keep my fingers from dipping into the corners to find relief. Suddenly I blast a sneeze and Agaves throws the offending feather cushions over the side of the sofa.

'Sorry, I forgot. I'll need to buy new ones if you keep popping by.' Agaves chuckles, but my mind is elsewhere. I need to keep his concentration.

'Do you think I'm being paranoid?' My voice quivers, as we stare at the clues together.

'To be honest, it was only the last clue that made me wonder,' he says.

'The one about *a crazy girl?*' My coffee gurgles, ebbs, and flows.

'I worked it out. Aren't I the clever one? *Amanda.*' Agaves' finger stabs the word, thickly penned. '*A girl, odd crazy number in addict group.* That's you, isn't it?'

Inside Agaves' flat, although only a stone's throw from my own front door, my overly suspicious thoughts seem ridiculous, and my neighbour's Cheshire cat grin beams through my foolishness. I try and lighten my tone.

'It could be Nathan, having *fun*, but...' I wiggle inverted-comma fingers round the word *fun*, but pause mid-sentence.

'But? Do you think he's having fun, or having a go? You don't think it's someone else, do you? That would be very random.' Agaves slurps his coffee, and sloshes milky liquid on to his shorts. 'Shit.' He grabs a scrunched-up hankie from his pocket, and furiously wipes them down. 'I think I need to take these off.'

He hops up, scoots up the stairs towards the bedroom, and yells over his shoulder. 'No peeking though.'

Once he's out of sight, images hurtle round my brain, a race-track wet with danger. It's not his naked body, his powerful, muscled chest that's set me off. Rather, I'm staring down at the puzzle. At Agaves' workings.

Thick black marker pen has picked out words, specific numbered clues and scribbled them outside the grid. *Chianti. Manhattan. Adam's wine. Corkscrew. Martini.* And, of course, *Amanda.* Agaves has also picked up the theme, worked it out. Each word is heavily underlined, back, and forth with angry pressure.

My first thought is how has Agaves managed to solve the clues himself. He's good with short clues, but these longer ones are quite a leap up. Perhaps he really is hooked, spending longer on the grids than he's letting on, but it crosses my mind that he might have had help. Who? I've no idea.

I shiver, and finish off my coffee. The puzzle we've been looking at with Agaves' scribbled answers, the thoughts of Nathan, or someone else toying with me, winding me up, is bringing on the panic. I'm finding it hard to breathe. The paper bags. I need to get back to my own flat.

I pick up my keys and mobile, just as Agaves reappears in the doorway.

'Are you off? Already? Was it something I said?' His mouth droops.

'No, of course not.' My voice is shaky. 'I've got lots to do. Marking to catch up on. But thanks for the coffee. And biscuits.'

'Are you sure you're okay?'

'I'm fine, and the cramp is much better.' I rub a hand over a calf muscle.

'What say I walk you home?' Agaves jokes, lightens his disappointment, which makes me feel bad.

'Ha ha. You're okay. I think I'll manage. Hopefully I'll avoid the mines on the landing.'

Our giggles collide. By the door, his fingers hover above the handle, but instead of letting me out, he leans his back against the door and pulls me towards him. His body is hard, urgent and our mouths meet in a wet desperation of lips and tongues. Longing wracks my body.

Sanity pulls me back. It's not that I'm scared of giving in, jumping off the bridge, opening my heart to the possibility of something magical. There's nothing more I want to do, but it's something else.

The puzzle clues. The drinking clues, which Agaves had written down. Something isn't right. It's intuition. A sense that something sinister is afoot. I pray it's got nothing to do with

Agaves, but I need to be certain, and find the strength to play for time.

'No worries. We'll catch up properly another time,' he says, un-snibbing the latch.

'Thanks. Yes, another time,' I echo, as he closes the door behind me.

62

AMANDA

My pig snort wakes me up as a sudden bout of sleep apnoea shocks away the nightmares.

I flick the lamp, sit up in bed and check the time. It's only midnight. My head is foggy as if stuffed with cotton wool. I pinch a nostril, close my mouth, suck up the air and try to breathe, but my nasal passages are blocked. An angry itch rages on my forehead.

There's a presence in the silence. Something has woken me up. The emergency sleeping pills should have kept me fast till 3 a.m. at least. I reach for the switch again, dim the light and turn over. My nightdress is soaked but I'm too fuzzy to care. As I begin to drift off again, a sudden bang pierces the stillness.

Jolted awake, I jump out of bed, my heart thumping and slip behind the bedroom door. I peer through the crack. There's no one in sight. The nightlight on the landing casts an eerie glow, and I leave the bedroom, inching towards it. The bolts on the front door are still done up, top and bottom, and the chain is pulled across. I look through the peephole, my breathing ragged. Then I hear the noise again. It's a softer, steadier rhythm this time and it's coming from the bathroom. I've got two choices. Get out fast or confront the intruder.

I lift the baseball bat that Nathan left by the front door – an emergency weapon – and tiptoe towards the bathroom. The door is open but it's still in darkness.

'Hello? I know you're in there.' My voice sounds like that of a rookie cop on a Netflix drama, but I trip the fluorescent light switch on the wall outside and go in. It's then I remember I peeled back the floorboard earlier, and it's still askew.

* * *

When I got back from Agaves' flat earlier, I couldn't settle. Before I went to bed, I watched him in his kitchen through the slit in my bathroom floorboards, as if soaking up a porn movie. He mooched around more than usual, getting up and down, moving back and forth from the kitchen, through to the lounge, and to the bedroom. TV on, TV off. His unrest gave me hope that the imprint of our kiss, with its hard urgency, was lingering.

I slither down again now, iron myself flat against the floor and put an eye close against the loosened board. Agaves is lying on the kitchen floor, squirming, writhing, like a pregnant beast. His hand grips his stomach as he emits a keening sound like a funeral lament.

'Agaves? Agaves? Are you okay?' I push my lips through the hole and scream. When I remember his real name is Teddy, I shout again. 'Teddy. Teddy. Can you hear me?' When there's no response, I slap the board in place, rush through into the hall and rifle through the spare keys to find the one for his flat. I lift out the Donald Duck keyring, grab my mobile and battle with shaky fingers to unlock the front door.

'Teddy. Teddy.' Outside his flat, my voice bounces off the bare walls and my fist bashes on the door. I insert the key, but still no answer. The chain is pinned across and rattles in defiance. 'Shit. Shit. Shit.'

I dial 999, run through the emergency procedures. Police. Fire. Ambulance. I'm not sure where to concentrate. The operator talks in practised monotone, asks me what I've seen. Is he breathing? Is he conscious? Ten minutes they'll be here.

I race down the stairs, open the front door to outside and pummel my fists on Tory's front door.

'Tory! Tory! Are you there?' I scrunch my face against the frosted glass. 'It's me. Amanda. It's an emergency.' I bang and bang, rapping my knuckles on the wood, screeching like a banshee. A forefinger jabs at a silent bell.

A slender ghost floats into view, wafts through the hall and slowly un-snibs the door.

'It's Teddy. Something's up. He's not well but I can't get into his flat. I've called the ambulance and police, but they'll be at least ten minutes. I don't know what to do. The chain's pulled across.'

'Oh my god. What's happened? You say you can't get in?' Tory's eyes glisten, her skin oiled with cream and her hair is sticking out like straw on a scarecrow. Before I get a chance to answer, she pushes past me into the communal hall, and yanks open the downstairs cupboard and finds a long-head hammer. It's only later that I wonder how she knew it was there.

'Let's go.' She's off, her flimsy nightdress billowing on her bony frame. Her long skeletal feet gallop up the stairs. At the top, she heaves back the hammer, and as she smashes the head through the door to Agaves' apartment, the chain shoots off and clatters against the hard-wood floor.

'Where is he? Is he in the bedroom? The kitchen?'

I nod. If she wonders how I know he's in the kitchen, she doesn't ask, but races through.

* * *

My sweaty palms press against my gaping mouth and my body trembles. I'm perched on the edge of a stool and watch as Tory bends over Agaves who is letting out a steady moan, a hum of consciousness.

'Teddy. Teddy. Can you hear me? Stay awake. You must stay awake. Amanda, get a pillow for his head.' Her command sends me scooting to the bedroom.

As I pass the lounge, I notice an empty bottle of wine on the floor. A trail of purple liquid, like crime scene blood, has splayed out across the carpet. My hand smacks against a wall.

'Amanda. Hurry.'

Down below, the wail of sirens is followed by heavy footsteps charging up the stairs. I step aside to let the medics past.

'Over there. In the kitchen,' I say, my voice a trembling whisper.

Tory's head is leaning over the patient, her hair tickling Agave's face. She plants a gentle kiss against his forehead. Her slender fingers are curled through his, and her soft voice lets me know Agaves is still alive.

'He's breathing,' she says. 'He'll be okay.' She seems sure, certain. I don't know why I trust her, but I say a silent prayer of thanks.

Agaves gets stretchered down the stairs, a clear mask pumping oxygen to his lungs. Tory is close behind.

'Are you his wife?' a medic asks.

'No. His neighbour, and a close friend,' Tory says, cheeks rosy in the half-light.

I stay in Agaves' flat, too weak to follow, and wait for the police who are on their way. When the voices downstairs fade, I collapse on to the sofa and cry. Heaving sobs wrack my body, thick convulsions of despair. My head flops against a cushion, its smell of woodland pine, and of Agaves.

As the room begins to spin, I'm gripped by a choking fear. A fear of what might happen. A fear of death. The vision of Oliver, his lifeless body broken like a sparrow's, flashes in and out. In the silence, I can hear Nathan's gentle, coaxing voice, taking over as he dealt with all the mayhem. But this time, if anything happens to Agaves, I'm completely on my own.

My hand dips down and lifts a cork that's lying on the floor. I squeeze it to my nostril, inhale the heady stench of alcohol. I stand it on the coffee table, alongside the empty wine glass.

'Yoo-hoo. Anyone here?' A rap at the smashed door is followed by a deep-throated voice which heralds the solid welcoming appearance of a policeman.

'In here.' I scrub my eyes, tear back my hair and get up.

It's going to be a long night.

63

NATHAN

On the fateful afternoon of the garden party, Nathan waited for the police at the scene of Oliver's accident. A rancid stench of burning rubber had scorched the air and the smell was forever etched in his memory.

Slumped on a garden wall, a spectator at the gruesome spectacle, he watched as officers in yellow high-viz jackets wrapped blue and white ribbon round the crime scene. Muted voices buzzed their business. He remembers the pins and needles that pierced his arm as his chest constricted, but he knew he had to hold himself together. For Amanda. No one else.

Amanda was a person who didn't do quiet. Even sulking moods of silence would thunder through the air. But after the accident she didn't speak for days. She clambered into the ambulance, blood oozing from serrated limbs, stiff as a shopfront mannequin, and eerily silent. Her bike, a mangled heap of spokes and bars, exhibit number one, was cordoned off by orange bollards. Nathan stayed to sort things out, to keep an eye on the bike as he knew Amanda would want him to bring it home.

Broken white clouds drifted overhead, outline maps of countries, dogs, and other beasts. The sun popped in and out, heat and chill syncopating to bathe his skin in sweat. Police swarmed, like robotic ants, blocking off the scene.

Nathan waited. Kept an eye on the bike. He can't remember when Hunter disappeared, or where he went, but he didn't really care.

Instead, he went inside to help Martin Hunter's wife.

* * *

For the next few months, life tinkled on. Routine bound his and Amanda's household in a tough unyielding framework. He drew up lists of chores, tasks and dates, displayed like weather charts, to guide them through the storm. Amanda, with her swollen face and tatty knotted mane, lounged in acquiescence.

'Cup of tea?'

'Fish and chips tonight?'

'A walk into the village?'

His suggestions were met by fragile nods of gratitude, weak and pasty smiles, and a bird-like hand fluttering in his grip. It was all he had ever wanted. For his wife to need him. For four months she belonged to him, and his life couldn't have been more perfect. But it only took four months for Hunter to reappear and finish what he'd started.

* * *

When Nathan gets back from a wet early morning walk, Merlong, his new canine companion, shakes his body, and sprays spume across the floor. Nathan hangs up his waterproof, before gently peeling apart the sodden broadsheet. Damp dog breath mingles with the mouldy smell of soggy newspaper.

Merlong is a constant reminder that he and Amanda are no longer together.

'We can't have a pet. I'm allergic, you know that.' Amanda's voice clangs in his memory as he pats Merlong on his nobbled pate, flicking a finger every so often behind his pet's healthy ear.

Amanda had a way of turning arguments around so that it was always his fault.

'It's either a pet or me. Your choice,' she'd announce, flouncing off before he could respond.

Nathan sits down at his rickety desk, turns on the reading lamp, and shines the blinding light on to the crossword grid. He smiles down at Merlong, whose steady thud of tail smacking against the cold tiles talks to him of loyalty. His pet understands him better than Amanda did. Or ever wanted to. He's still tickled with the name, *Merlong.*

Merlong, an anagram of *mongrel.*

64

NATHAN

Nathan licks his fingertip, rubs it across the dried nib of his biro, and shakes the barrel. He decides to write the answers to today's puzzle on a separate pad, unwilling to disintegrate the already sodden grid. He's no idea who today's setter might be, but it doesn't stop him trying to work it out. He knows the different setters' quirks, tricks and methods. It usually doesn't take him too long.

Cut of meat, bet it's pronounced? (5)

Nathan's seen the clue before, remembers using it to teach Amanda.

'What's a "sound-alike" clue?' Amanda had asked, immersing herself more intently in the daily puzzles when the agoraphobia kicked in. After the accident, from June to October, she honed her hobby, until she raced ahead and began to pip him with the more simplistic solving. Often he'd let her win, her victory gleam worth all the false defeats.

He broke the clues down, with painstaking instruction on how to find the answers.

'A sound-alike clue is where the answer is a word that sounds like the meaning of another word. *Cut of meat, bet it's pronounced?*

(5). The answer is *steak*. But when you *pronounce* this, it sounds like another word meaning *bet... stake*.'

'How do I know if the answer is *steak* or *stake*?' Her nose would wrinkle with little dents of concentration.

'*Bet it's pronounced...* the *pronounced* tells you that the word meaning *bet* is the sound-alike word. Not the answer. The answer here is *steak... cut of meat*. There are different sound-alike indicators. You'll get to learn them as you go along.'

'Okay. I've got one for you. *A country, cold it's said.* Five letters.' She threw her pen in the air, caught it, swizzled it in her fingers and locked her eyes on his.

'Hmm.' He hummed, pursed his lips, played along. 'Go on. What is it?'

'Can't you guess? *Chile*.'

As he gets further into the puzzle, he spots a mixture of clue types. As he concentrates and his mind gets immersed in the challenge, Merlong finally falls asleep. Soon the pet is whimpering, barking gently, and every now and then his body twitches.

But Nathan blocks out the noise, and ten minutes in he spots it. The random clue, the one that's out of sync. The editor maybe missed it, or let it go. But the setters know the rules. No swear words. No mild suggestions. Nothing sexual. And nothing linked to violence. The rules are lengthy, stringent.

Violent crime, 5th October perhaps? Eats mushy pear (4,4)

It's not the clue itself, but the date: *5th October*. That's when his wife slept with Martin Hunter. Amanda pleaded rape, but Nathan didn't care. After that day, she was on her own.

Amanda met Hunter for a drink that day. Her hysteria, when she returned to their flat, collapsed over the threshold, was tinged with an opaque but definite hue of guilt. Nathan sensed deceit, another drunken lie. Amanda's words were laced with alcoholic chicanery. When she exploded, choking on rancid bile, he stood and watched, arms limp by his side.

'I've been date raped,' she screamed. 'Don't you understand?'

He really didn't care. He covered his ears and simply asked, 'It wasn't by Martin Hunter by any chance?'

Date rape is the answer to the clue in front of him.

The *?* (question mark) indicates some sort of wordplay. There is no direct synonym for *5th October*, so Nathan knows the answer is the single word *date*. *Rape* is an anagram of *pear*. *Mushy* is an indicator of an anagram.

As Nathan sets down his pen, Merlong drags himself up, a weak tail swishing across the floor. Nathan pats his lap and, with two hands, hoists up the dog and offers the animal his face. He grimaces when a fat wet tongue slathers across his skin.

The clue is no coincidence, he's convinced. Someone, other than himself, is targeting Amanda. Perhaps Martin Hunter hasn't let up. Perhaps the bastard has used his position as boss and overseer to the *London Echo* crossword setters, and found a colleague to filter through his hatred.

If it's not Hunter, then who the hell is it?

65

AMANDA

Once the police have cordoned off Agaves' flat, and told me I need to go back to my own place, get some rest, I reluctantly obey orders.

I'm now prowling round the lounge like a caged animal. I've opened all the curtains, and thrown wide the windows. My mind is churning and I know I won't be able to sleep. I've no idea what's going on, as Tory won't pick up when I call, and Agaves hasn't got his phone with him. The hospital keep telling me to try again in the morning, with casual assurances that my neighbour is still alive.

By the time I reluctantly fall into bed, plump up my pillows, smack the feathers into shape, it's nearly 5 a.m. Eerie hallucinations cloud my half-consciousness. It was only when the police officer asked me if I knew what had happened, that I twigged, and things began to click into place. My sodden tear-stained face and choking sobs, stopped the officer from pushing me.

I didn't know how much to tell him, as I somehow felt to blame for what had happened. He asked about the spilt wine, the broken bottle, and I shrugged my shoulders. I told him I'd heard a noise through the paper thin divisions between our flats, at no time owning up to the peep show in my bathroom. If I told him the wine was meant for me, and I'd handed it across, the officer might have put two and two together and come up with the wrong answer. He might have thought I'd deliberately drugged my neighbour. But guilt that Agaves might have died because of me is hard to shake.

Someone is out to get me, that much is clear, and Agaves has got caught up in the crossfire. Whoever left the wine yesterday afternoon, and the time before, must have drugged the contents. There's no other explanation. I hadn't been blind drunk through heavy drinking as I'd suspected. I'd been poisoned by something stronger. Something much more sinister.

The wine, Agaves' collapse, the menacing crossword clues. I know there's a connection, but what is it? I try to count back how many weeks ago since the puzzles became personal. Four? Maybe five? Maybe even longer. I've lost count and need to check back. If Nathan is hell-bent on taunting me, punishing me, I need to track him down. Get him to stop now he's hit his mark.

A link between the drugged wine and the crossword puzzles might be tenuous at best. Perhaps there's no connection, but I don't really believe this. The only setters I've met are the odd bunch of eccentrics whom Nathan seems to worship, and whom I've met only a couple of times. The last time was at the garden party.

Then there is Bagheera, a female setter Nathan talks about, but someone he's never introduced.

But what's the motive? Has anyone a motive for anything? Nathan might be vengeful, wanting to punish me, but I can't believe he'd go to such lengths. To drug and try and poison me. It doesn't ring true with all I know about my husband.

Finally, I conjure up the evil mask of Martin Hunter. He's got motive to hate me, for what happened to Oliver. He spiked my drink once before, raped me. It's likely he can't let me forget. There's also his wife. Someone else I've never met.

Oliver's mother.

66

AMANDA

I'm up three hours later, drenched in sweat, and finally manage to get through on my mobile to the ward where Agaves is recuperating. Visiting hours start at 11 a.m.

I pop out briefly, pick up a box of truffles from the corner shop, and a six-pack of beer as welcome-home presents for Agaves. I put them by the front door, before I dig out a carton of home-made chicken soup meant for Mr Beckles, and leave it to defrost. Then I call an Uber, and set off for the hospital.

When I finally locate Agaves, third floor up, bed in the far corner of Ward 10, I breathe more easily. He's sitting up in bed, and his smile warms my heart.

'I'm really sorry,' is the first thing I say.

'What for? It's not your fault. I think I need to give up wine,' he quips. 'And, jeez, you look worse than I feel. Are you okay?'

'The wine was meant for me,' I say. 'I think it was drugged.'

'So I gather. The police were here early, told me the wine was laced with Rohypnol. The date rape drug.'

I hover by the bed.

'Pull a chair up,' he says, 'unless you're in a rush.'

As I drag a plastic chair nearer to the bed, he jokes, tries to make light of what has happened.

'Quite a relief to hear the wine was drugged. I thought I'd become a lightweight,' he jests. A throaty laugh makes him cough, and I reach for a jug by his bed and pour some water into a flimsy cup, as he pulls himself up. 'Any idea who left it?' His chocolate eyes are ringed with charcoal, his wavy hair like a flattened pancake. My fingers twitch to touch it.

'I don't know,' I reply, shocked to hear the truth.

He takes my hand, links our fingers, and asks me to give him a kiss. I lean across, close my eyes and melt into his warmth. When an old lady in the next bed tuts, we reluctantly untangle, and giggle.

'When are you coming home?' I ask.

'Later today.'

'So soon. That's great. Shall I call you a taxi? I'm still not comfortable driving, but I'll order you a cab if you let me know what time.'

'No need. Tory's already offered to pick me up.'

I leave shortly after the announcement that Tory got there first, and hope Agaves didn't pick up on my unease and irritation.

I'm now back by the window, waiting anxiously for them to get home. When they finally appear, Tory reminds me of Florence Nightingale as she floats through the gate gripping a small overnight bag, and walking with the reverential tread of a mourner.

My heart misses a beat when I see Agaves moving with an uncharacteristic stoop. As he dips out of sight under the porch,

Tory waves up. She's seen me. My arm raises like a remote-controlled prosthetic.

I listen to the front door downstairs open and close, and soon muffled voices join footsteps on the stairs. I slump into a chair when I hear them go into Agaves' flat and close the door.

I make myself tea. Flick through a magazine. Nibble at a biscuit, but I can't settle, knowing Agaves and Tory are down below. I finally give in and head for the bathroom.

I promised myself not to look through the floorboard again, to fight the impulse. But who am I kidding? It's an obsession, like all my others. I'm an addict driven by compulsion. I slip into the bathroom, my cotton socks a mere whisper across the floor, and with damp fingers, inch the board aside. I go rigid as the gap widens and a grating noise screams rebuke in my ear.

I never owned up to the police about how I knew my neighbour was in trouble. I recounted a crash, a loud moaning sound, and then a lack of response when I banged on his front door. The loosened floorboard is still my guilty secret, my company when there's no one else around.

Below me in the kitchen, I see the crown of Tory's head bobbing about like a buoy in water. She moves steadily up and down the galley, her hands flapping with saintly endeavour.

'Teddy, I've put the kettle on,' she yells and flicks a switch.

She reaches up to grip the long stainless-steel handles of an end cupboard and throws it wide open. Her hand dips inside and roams through the mugs, her fingers caressing their surfaces. She lifts out a black one and reads the letters painted on the shiny surface. I know what it says. *I love you to the moon and back.* I washed it up once but didn't dare ask where it had come from. Seeing it again adds to my doubts about how well I know Agaves.

Tory puts it back, tucks it in behind the other mugs which she neatly rearranges. She then lifts out two plain white ones and drops in the tea bags.

'Thanks.' Agaves' voice is muffled as it seeps through from the lounge, bubbling up as if from under water. I imagine him on the sofa, bare toes curled.

'Won't be long,' Tory calls back as she lifts the lid on a small saucepan and stirs a tomato-coloured sauce. 'I'm just putting the pasta on.'

When the tea is ready, milk two sugars for Agaves and black for Tory, she moves towards the door. But when she stops, I run my tongue over dry lips. Her neck stretches out and her eyes scroll up towards the ceiling. Towards the gap.

As I flail backwards, I bang my head against the basin.

'Fuck.' I rub furiously at my scalp.

When I look back down again, she has gone.

67

MRS HUNTER

The football kit still lies strewn across Oliver's bed, on top of the Man U duvet cover. She balls the shirt, stuffs it to her nostrils, squeezes out the scent. It smells of boy. Musty, with a heady scent of innocence. She doesn't think she'll ever clear his things away. She keeps a bedroom for him, just as he would have wanted.

She kneels below the silver-framed picture of Oliver, and flattens her palms together, fingers pointing heavenward. An incense burner emits a thick woodland scent and behind the shrine, is a mirror which runs the full length of the wall. She doesn't recognise the woman who stares back at her with her cracked, swollen lips and an estuary of broken veins. Saucer eyes, like those of a fevered dementor, reflect decay and despair. Peace, hope and happiness have flown, her soul an empty shell. A crusty finger makes the *Signum Crucis*: father, son, and the holy spirit.

She uses a fragile hand to push herself up and as she looks out the window, she says a silent prayer of remembrance. She drapes the football shirt across her chest in a masochistic ritual and stares out at the street below.

* * *

On that fateful day, she watched Amanda wobble like a unicycle clown down Brewer's Hill and stared aghast as the rider lost control and catapulted over the handlebars. Amanda's flailing arms and legs, extended starfish style, suddenly flew off in all directions.

Mrs Hunter had parted her hands, ready to clap, like those of her husband which were slapping together like a performing seal. When Oliver stepped out into the road, her hands recoiled and flew to her mouth. She watched as her son's body catapulted into the air, and landed back down on the tarmac. Flattened. She thought it was all part of the show. Soon her little hero would get up and take a bow. He so loved the circus. The stacked, mangled metal was all part of the act, part of the extravaganza.

Martin never came back inside, and she stiffened from the wait. As the clock ticked louder, her limbs turned to stone, like solidified lava.

Sometime later, a knock crashed against the door, but she had no idea who would be calling. Martin had a key, and Amanda had left in an ambulance with a blue flashing light on top. Only Oliver was unaccounted for, but he would rap gently. He must be waiting down below, and now she'd have to take him to the park.

Through the door she remembers someone shouting, but she couldn't be certain if it was all in her head and that she was hearing voices.

'Yoo-hoo. Are you in there? Please open up.' She'd no idea who it could be, but the banging persisted. 'Are you in there? It's Nathan. You need to let me in.'

She remembers feeling cold, the violent shivering as her body turned to ice, and she remembers turning up the thermostat before she opened the door, determined to send the intruder away.

She wanted to put on her coat and go and join Oliver, keep him company outside where the sky looked brighter. He would warm her up. But she remembers a long persistent scream, chilling in its intensity, and not realising at first the screech was hers.

When Nathan came inside, she pummelled against his chest, right fist, left fist, then right again as if he were a boxer's dummy. He was hard and solid like a punchbag as he silently absorbed the pain. He put the kettle on, made her tea. Sweet tea, so sweet it cloyed her teeth, set the nerves on edge. Her spoon clattered round the cup in frenzied rhythm.

'Come,' he said. She wasn't sure what he meant, where he wanted to take her. To the park? To identify the body? To the funeral parlour? She had no idea.

Clinging to Nathan's arm, she slithered down the stairwell outside the flat, and thought of school when her father would drag her reluctantly through the imposing metal gates and dump her, floppy like a rag doll, with tears rolling down her cheeks, by the classroom door.

Outside, she clambered into a waiting ambulance and said goodbye to Oliver. She kissed her son's frozen body, combed his wavy hair, and promised that they would be together soon. She needed to pop back inside and choose his favourite kit, but she wouldn't be long. She staggered out of the van and watched a man in uniform zip up the black bag.

'See you soon.' She blew a kiss, a gentle zephyr of farewell and went back inside to find his clothes. But instead, locked herself inside.

One month later, Martin packed his bags and left.

68

AMANDA

Before I met Nathan, my single life was fraught with guilt, alcoholic-induced guilt following on from too many drunken evenings.

The morning-after guilt would be accompanied by a throbbing head, sweaty palms and masochistic memories of the night before. Regrets would fester, cling to me until evening came around, and recall would slowly fade. The guilt, regrets at lost opportunities to behave and sell my worth through sobriety, soon got scrubbed away like caked make-up, using wipes of self-justification. I'd do better next time, I'd say to myself, as I buried the remorse under vacuous promises for tomorrow. But rather than change, clean up my act, I would begin the cycle all over again.

When Oliver died, although it was a devastating tragedy, it was declared an accident. But I blamed myself, and misplaced guilt still smothers me when I think back. I can't shake the thought that it was all my fault.

Then there came along a different type of guilt. The Martin Hunter guilt.

It was quite some time after the accident that Nathan finally went back to work, leaving me puzzles, magazines and books, on the bedside table as if for an invalided patient. I mumbled from below the bedclothes, egging on the silence, and willing him to leave. He would kiss my forehead, squish my bundled form, and say he'd call, which he did hourly until I switched my phone to mute.

The kitchenette became a convict's cell, days marked off in black felt-tip on a chart fastened to the wall. Big, bold strokes marked my progress, a memorial to the battle. Lest I forget. A plague to remember the fallen. The black lines were meant as a record of progress but felt more accusatory than celebratory.

'Another day. Well done, you!' Nathan's praise was overzealous when he got home, but I couldn't remember seeing him so happy. It was as if my incarceration had set him free, fired up his zest for life. As I struggled, Nathan hummed with new-found meaning.

It was three months on from the fateful garden party that I decided to help my own recovery and lay to rest some ghosts. It was the first Friday of the month, the night when the newspaper setters met, and Nathan hadn't been for ages.

'You should go. Have a few pints with the guys and enjoy yourself,' I said.

'It's no big deal. If you'd rather I came home, I'll put it off. It's always pretty boring.'

'Go and have some fun, I'll be fine.' I knew he'd still use me as an excuse to leave early, so I took a deep breath and told him I was also going out. 'I'm meeting Cheryl tonight.'

'Oh. You didn't' tell me. Where are you meeting?' he asked. I knew I stood accused, guilty before my husband's jury, as he automatically assumed it would be the pub. But cussedness kept me from saying any more, and irritation and stubbornness made me unwilling to explain myself. I could never tell him where I was really going, or he'd have locked me in.

'Not sure yet. It'll be like parole, getting out for good behaviour,' I joked. 'Seriously, you don't need to worry.'

But I saw the doubts cross his features: the puckered brow, the tight drawn lips and the tiny tic that pulsed in his neck.

'Okay. Whatever,' he said, pecking me on the cheek as he reluctantly left the flat.

69

AMANDA

I decided not to drive. I'd only been behind the wheel twice since the fateful day in June, my confidence still at an all-time low. Although driving would have cut the risks, trim the fraying threads of temptation where drink was concerned, I craved fresh air, exercise to calm my racing heart.

Looking back, I should have driven. The threat of criminal repercussions if I succumbed to a glass or two might have been enough of a deterrent. But I'll never know.

'I can pick you up,' Martin Hunter said, his voice brusque through the crackling static. It was hard to tell if he was surprised by my call, his tone uncharacteristically flat, unemotional.

'I'd prefer to meet you there if that's okay. I'll walk, it's not far.'

'Sure. What time?'

When I reached the pub, I sat on a bench outside the entrance, twenty minutes early. My throat was parched, my stomach gurgling from anxiety. I shivered, glossed my lips, teased my hair, and tried to relax.

When his Mercedes turned into the car park, I got up.

The last four months had left their mark on Martin Hunter. His eyes had lost their sparkle, the flirtatious crinkles now deep ridges of hardened permanence, the weathered troughs of a saddened life.

'Hi. What a nice surprise.' He leant across and kissed me on the cheek, petrol cologne catching in my throat.

'Hi, Martin. Thanks for coming.'

I wasn't after his forgiveness but wanted to tell him how sorry I was. I needed to look him in the eye, for him to feel my over-whelming sadness and regret, and know that'd I do anything to turn back the clock. As well as wanting to tell Martin Hunter, face to face, how sorry I was, the evening was meant as a first step at wresting back control of my life and prove I had the strength to beat the demons. That was the plan. I believed I'd moved on enough to not forget the pitfalls. How wrong I was.

'One drink? We've catching up to do.' In the brightly lit pub, Martin's question tinkled, a merry clink of orchestral triangle. But I should have taken more note of his shuttered smile and hooded expression.

It only takes a second for your life to change, 'turn on a sixpence' as my mother used to say, but my goal that evening was to prove I was ready to make my own decisions and regain my independence. Nathan. Joseph. The AA groups. Everyone telling me what to do, who I was. My weaknesses had been building up others' self-esteem, but not mine.

When I'd call on Joseph, he gained points with God and it fed his new-found purpose in life, that of helping others. Where Nathan was concerned, my misery seemed to rebuild a flagging ego. He grew in confidence as he fussed and nurtured. I knew I had to move forward and escape this bond of dependency. The night I met up with Hunter was meant to be the start.

'Why not? One drink can't hurt,' I replied when he asked if I'd like a drink. I was confident I'd have no more. I'd learnt my lesson. That night was all about showing Martin my regret, and for him to understand my sadness at Oliver's death, and my commitment to recovery.

I wasn't after forgiveness. I just needed to tell him I was sorry.

70

AMANDA

After accepting the drink, I've no recollection of what happened next except that several hours later I woke up in the front seat of Hunter's car. A thunderous bang against the driver's-side window from outside the car smashed me out of a coma.

'Nathan?' I looked to the person in the driver's seat alongside me. After I said my husband's name, I waited for a response, but none came. I knew something was wrong as he didn't look himself. At this point, I'd no idea I was speaking to anyone other than Nathan. The black shoulder bag on the floor, as well as the white lace knickers by my feet were familiar as was the flimsy bra wound around the gear stick like a cup-final-day flag stuck to an aerial.

'Where are we?' My sticky eyes, glued from sleep, peered out into the black shadows of the night. I saw the familiar tall, over-powering trees that lined the street. The driver's window was cracked, and the whistle of wind, like air through toothless gums, hissed through the gap.

'Where are we?' I repeated when I got no response.

Slowly, I bent over and tweezered my pants between icy fingers and slipped them back on. Then I unwound the bra and shoved it into my shoulder bag. I didn't need an answer to my question. I knew where we were. The car was parked halfway down Brewer's Hill where the road bends in a serpentine chicane: parked near the scene of my worst nightmares. Where I came off my bike. Where Oliver died.

Outside, a man's gargantuan body suddenly appeared out of nowhere. After smashing his fists against the driver's-side window, he moved round to the bonnet of Hunter's car. The guy smashed boxer's fists against the metal, screaming obscenities.

'Bugger off, you filthy scum. Get the fuck out of here before I call the police.' The man glowered from Martin to me and back again. He was dressed in striped pyjamas like an escaped psychiatric patient. He moved round to Hunter's side of the car, and with almighty effort began to shake the vehicle. This time his voice was drowned out by the revving of the engine and he was forced to step backwards on to the pavement. Hunter then turned up the demister and let a blast of cool air drown out further noise, and flood the car with an icy blast.

At this point the irate resident, disgusted by what he must have witnessed, walked away, making an obscene gesture in our direction as he went.

'I'll drive you closer to your flat if you like.' As he spoke, Hunter's fingers tapped up and down on the steering wheel, as if playing scales on a keyboard.

The clock on the dashboard showed 3.30 a.m. It was only at this point that my mind began to clear, and I realised who the driver was.

'Martin? Oh my god!' I dragged my skirt down, fumbled with the buttons of my blouse.

Martin's face was buckled in the shadows, thickened contours rippling along one cheek. He looked like a gargoyle, repulsive and grotesque.

'How long have we been here? What happened?' For a moment I thought I might be dreaming, having another nightmare. I pinched myself but nothing changed. My voice shook but sped up as it tore through the silence.

'A few hours. I let you sleep it off.'

'Sleep what off?' My wild eyes stared at him.

'I didn't want to take you home until you'd sobered up. You'll thank me in the morning.'

Nathan. No. No. No. What would I tell him? I had no idea what had happened. I'm certain I had only one small drink. A tiny glass of wine. Or did I have another? I promised myself I wouldn't. I couldn't have fallen off the wagon so quickly, please God no.

Martin's hands gripped the wheel and the dark matted hairs straggling up the backs looked so familiar, and it was then I remembered his fingers, with their neatly clipped nails, toying with the buttons on my blouse. As he snapped my bra off, whisking it through a sleeve, I had heard a victory whoop.

'You don't need to walk. I'll drive you back,' he said, as I flung open the car door and gagged gurgling filth through an open grate. I lurched from the car and leant a supporting hand against a lamppost.

'I'll walk.' I slammed the door so hard it sounded like a crack of thunder.

My legs were weak, and I had to stop every few yards to catch my breath. Nearby an owl hooted in the darkness, a steady mocking accompaniment to my progress. I staggered up Brewer's Hill, past the scene of Oliver's accident where I paused, and sat on the wall for a few moments.

Hunter cruised past in his Mercedes, like a punter eyeing up prostitutes. When the car finally disappeared from view, I inched on up towards the gates of Silver Birch, hugging my bag against my chest, and once outside I looked up at the clear night sky, with its quilt of twinkling stars, and prayed.

But my prayers came too late. I felt Nathan's gaze as he looked out from our upstairs window, like a ship's captain looking out to sea at the approaching storm. I slipped my key in the front door and walked slowly up the stairs towards the entrance of our flat.

One thing I knew for certain. Nathan would never believe I'd been raped by Martin Hunter.

71

AMANDA

It's two days since Agaves got back from the hospital. Tory has been up and down the stairs, and I've seen her from my window coming and going with overflowing bags of shopping.

Down below, through the bathroom crack, I can hear her bustling around. It could be my imagination, but her voice seems to get louder when she's in the kitchen. Not louder because the loosened board helps me hear better, but louder as if she's deliberately ratcheting up the decibels. She wants me to know she's there, taking charge. Also I think she's trying to warn me off, as she wants Agaves to herself.

I log off from lessons around lunchtime, and at the same moment as I close down my laptop, I hear Tory yell goodbye to Agaves through his front door, and scurry on down the stairs. When the front door slams, I wait a bit, to be sure she's not coming back.

A few minutes later, I'm outside on the landing with a small cardboard box containing the chicken soup, truffles and six-pack of beer I bought for Agaves' return from the hospital. Before I rap, I glance over my shoulder. Shit. I can hear Tory's front door open, and close, and I'm just about to scuttle back into Flat C, when I pick up the sound of her feet crunching across the driveway and away from the building.

My fingers hover, before I finally knock. Once. Twice. My hand is raised, about to try again when the door opens and Agaves' haggard, smiling face appears.

'Amanda. I thought you'd forgotten me.'

'Hi. How are you feeling?'

'Come in. It's great to see you. Come in.'

'These are for you,' I say, handing over the cardboard box. 'Sorry, I should have brought them round sooner, but I know Tory's been looking after you, and I wanted to see you on your own.'

Agaves takes the presents, sets them on the floor, and pulls me towards him. He pushes the door closed behind us, and smothers me with his strong arms.

'I've missed you,' he says. 'I was worried why you hadn't been round.'

'Sorry,' I say. 'I wanted to.'

'Better late than never. I've missed you,' he repeats.

'I've missed you too.' More than I could have imagined possible.

He holds me tightly, as if he's scared to let me go. Heat, sweat, and longing twist our bodies together. We kiss for what seems like an eternity, before he hoists me up, forces my legs to wrap around his body and carries me towards the bedroom. Neither of us speak, and instead let our bodies do the talking.

Making love with Agaves is everything I thought it would be. For the first time in as long as I can remember, my mind releases, and all the worries get nudged to one side. When it's over, I lie in the crook of his arm, anchored by his warmth and strength.

The first time I was in Agaves' flat, I peeked into his bedroom, and remember my relief at noticing the lack of a woman's touch. There's little in the room. A chest of drawers, a wardrobe and two bedside tables. A couple of bland black and white pictures hang over the bedhead, but nothing else adorns the room. The only difference this time, is how tidy the room is.

There are no clothes out, no mess anywhere. I remember socks on the floor, a couple of T-shirts, shorts, strewn across the bed. It's as if it's been unslept in. Or perhaps he tidied it, hoping I'd come round. But I can't help myself. When he finally gets out of bed, I pull the duvet round my chest, and ask.

'Your room's really tidy. Were you expecting me?'

My stomach knots before he replies. I know what he's going to say, but he doesn't hesitate, or lie.

'Oh, that's Tory. Ha ha. You know I'm not this neat. She's been round the house again, cleaning and tidying since I came home. Fussing like my mother.'

I laugh. A forced tinny sound. But before I think of what to say, he disappears into the bathroom and turns on the shower.

72

AMANDA

There's no awkwardness after what we've done. A post-coital contentment has wound itself around us, no hint of shame or regret. There's no edginess about Agaves. His hair sticks out at weird angles and his bare feet slop freely across the wooden floorboards.

I feel warm inside. His relaxed manner helps soothe my concerns about Tory. His flippant manner when he mentions her, gives me confidence that she's not a love rival. Not in Agaves' eyes anyway.

But she still makes me nervous. There's something contrived about her, that I can't share with Agaves without sounding jealous, bitchy. I keep checking my watch every few minutes, expecting her to return.

'You're not rushing off, I hope.' Agaves looks concerned when he thinks I might be going.

'No. I've no plans,' I say, smiling to put his mind at rest.

'What say we do the puzzle? Have you done today's yet?' he asks, picking up the paper from the coffee table and turning to the back page.

'Not yet.'

'That's not like you?' He raises a quizzical eyebrow.

'To be honest, I haven't done the puzzle for a couple of days. I've sort of lost heart.'

'Oh. Why's that?' Agaves sits down beside me, shoves up close, pouts his lips for a kiss, and rummages down the side of the sofa for a pen. 'Look what I've found.' He wiggles the biro.

'Tory didn't attack the sofas then,' I say, and we both laugh.

'Okay, let's give it a go. See if you can get your heart back.'

As Agaves dips his head in concentration, my eyes are drawn to the fine moist line which coats his neck. My hand itches to stray, to trace the contours of his throat, and weave my fingers through his hair. A moment of fear creeps in. He's so perfect. Too perfect. I spot the cardboard box by the door with the pack of beers inside, and crave a drink. The beer is calling to me. When Agaves sees where I'm looking, he puts an arm round me, as if he can read my thoughts.

'Come on. I need your help.' He taps the pen on the paper, and starts to read aloud the clues.

Side by side, our thoughts unite, and for a brief while, my worries are forgotten.

* * *

Agaves isn't competitive like Nathan. He's quick though, his mind sharper than I imagined. Assumptions about muscled men with small IQs are well off the mark where my neighbour is concerned. He reminds me of myself when I first caught up with Nathan in speed of working. Agaves is weirdly thrilled when he solves a clue before me.

'What about this one?' Agaves reads the question slowly.

'*Take steps to provide tea for three (3-3-3).*'

'Easy-peasy,' I say. '*Take steps* is likely to be a dance. And *tea for three* is probably *cha* three times. *Cha* is crossword speak for tea. Tea originated in China and the word for tea in Chinese is *cha*.'

'*Cha-cha-cha*. Yo!' Agaves tosses the pen in the air and fails to catch it as it catapults over his shoulder. When he's picked it up, we carry on. Twenty minutes in and, like a body massage, I feel the knots loosen through seamless concentration.

Then, my skin starts to prickle. Goosebumps dot my arms when Agaves points to four down. I get the answer straightaway.

State Victoria's location (9)

'Have you got it?' he asks. He leans back against the cushions, no need to concentrate as he's also solved the clue.

'Not yet,' I lie. It's the word *Victoria* that brings me back down to earth. Our neighbour, Victoria, Tory, seems to be following me around. I wonder if I'm going crazy, as it's just a random clue.

'The answer is *Australia*,' Agaves announces as he fills in the squares, each of his letters capitalised with thick jagged lines. '*Victoria* is a *state*, and the *location* of the state is *Australia*. How cool is that?' He blushes when he adds, 'Okay. I worked it out from the letters already filled in. I already had the three *As* from other clues.'

When Agaves pops off to make some coffee, I check the remaining clues. There are three left. My eyes blur, and I blink rapidly to try and clear my vision. I suddenly can't swallow, as if my throat has swollen through anaphylactic shock.

'Amanda? Are you okay?' Agaves has reappeared, he sets the coffees down, and puts a hand on my shoulders. 'Jeez. You're shaking. What is it?'

I don't know where to start. But I have to talk to him. I take a deep breath, not sure where to start, when suddenly a door downstairs bangs, an almighty thwack like thunder.

Tory must be back.

73

AMANDA

I've no idea where to start, but Agaves is looking at me, concern etched on his features. I don't want him to think I'm crazy, scare him off, but I need to trust him. He'll need to trust me if we've got any chance of a future together.

'Look at these last three clues. I know we've both picked up random drinking clues before, yes, probably Nathan having fun, but the clues are getting more pointed. More sinister. And to be honest, it's starting to freak me out.'

The clues I need to show him, I've seen before. The setter is repeating clues. It often happens, but these specific ones stand out, and they've appeared so recently.

'Go on. Show me.'

'*A metal bundle of twigs for a tree (6,5)* – twenty down. I won't go through the workings, but the answer is *silver birch*.'

'That's where we live,' he says.

'Correct. Then look at this one. It's not the first time I've picked it out. *Oil producer right for a musical? (6).*' I swallow hard as I read the words.

'What's the answer?' Agaves mind is ticking, but he's not there yet.

'*Oliver*. The answer is *Oliver*.' I try to blink away the tears.

'Here. It's okay.' He takes out a crumpled handkerchief, and gently dabs my eyes.

'Oliver. It's the name of the boy that died.' I don't use the word 'killed'. It wasn't manslaughter, premeditated murder. It was an accident, even though I still feel responsible.

'What's the last clue?' Agaves finger settles on the blank spaces along the bottom.

'*Mishap caused by stress – I'd go into it (8)* The answer is *accident*.' My voice is hoarse, my mouth dry.

I knit my fingers together, hold my hands up against my mouth, and look at Agaves. He doesn't seem to know what to say. I want him to feel my fear, share it with me, understand, but he looks blank, as if he's lost for words.

'Come here. Don't cry,' is all he says. 'It'll be okay.' He hugs me to him, and I let the floodgates open. Tears stream down my cheeks, and his fingers roll over my face to wipe them away.

Agaves is wrong though, because one thing's for sure, it won't be okay, and I don't know how to make him understand. The nightmare of what happened with Oliver is never going to go away.

'If you think it's Nathan setting the clues, and not some weird coincidence, why don't you talk to him?'

'He never picks up. I gave up ages ago when he ghosted me.'

'Why don't you try again? Listen, I'll come with you. You need to get him to stop if it's upsetting you this much,' he says.

'Without sounding completely kooky, I'm not certain it's only Nathan playing with me. The *Oliver* clue is pretty specific, yet I can't imagine Nathan being that mean.' I pause for breath, and wonder if I believe what I'm saying. I'm no longer sure. Did I ever really know Nathan? Properly. Maybe he's harbouring his anger, not prepared to let it go.

'You think there's someone else involved?' Agaves widens his eyes, and the way he asks the question, light of tone, almost flippantly, makes me wonder if he's making fun.

'I sort of get the drinking clues. They've got Nathan's stamp all over them. He blames alcohol for everything that happened, and the failure of our marriage. When I see a drinking clue, I think he's trying to communicate, let me know he's still around. Does that make sense?' I'm scared to look at Agaves, hear his answer.

'Yes. I can see why you'd think it's him. But someone else as well? I think you definitely need to talk to Nathan.'

Agaves kisses me, a soft caress across my lips, and I know it's time for me to stop talking.

Suddenly, a clattering noise at the door, makes us pull apart.

'Hello? Hello? Anyone at home?' Tory's voice screams through the letter box.

Neither of us move. Agaves bites his top lip with his whitened bottom row of teeth, and pulls a face. I frantically rub the back of my hand across my tear-stained cheeks, but Agaves' horror face makes me giggle.

'We'd better let her in,' he whispers. 'Otherwise, she'll never go away.'

'I'll go back to my flat, and leave you to entertain her. Or for her to entertain you.' The lightness in my voice is at odds with my thoughts.

When Agaves goes to open the door, I scoot to the bathroom, throw some water over my face, and prepare to face the enemy.

I needn't have worried. Tory goes straight through the kitchen, and the kettle is whistling to the boil as I sneak out.

74

AMANDA

Agaves is right. I need to speak to Nathan.

I can't concentrate on anything. Somehow I bluff my way through this morning's private tutoring, mooch around the kitchen, chop up past-their-sell-by-date vegetables for soup, and dope myself up with caffeine.

I'm not sure whether Agaves just wants to keep me happy, and if he's humouring me by saying I should contact Nathan. Agaves says he's more than happy to come along. I pour a long glass of cold fizzy water, which gushes over the top and puddles on the floor. My hands shake as if I'm hungover. I get my mobile, and stare at the blank screen. The answers to yesterday's clues – *Oliver*, *accident* and *silver birch* – keep flashing through my thoughts, and it's hard to concentrate on anything else.

Agaves is right. I need to speak to Nathan. Face to face and find out what's going on. Also, it's time to tell him that we're over. I'm moving on, met someone else. I don't need to say who, but suspect it won't take Nathan long to join up the dots.

My fingers jiggle down my contact list, and I realise how long it's been since I've spoken to Nathan. I used to click recent calls, and Nathan's number would be at the top. Now, like my husband, the number has disappeared, and needs locating. I can't even remember the number by heart, and that tells me how long it's been.

I wander through the flat, picking things up, putting them down again, and run a finger across rogue dust trails that coat the furniture. The mess screams rebuke, and frustration at the images of Tory's saintly cleansing of my neighbour's flat gnaws away. But my mind is in a worse state than the flat, and suddenly I press 'call' on my mobile. I stiffen as I wait for it to connect.

But there's nothing. Nathan's number is not even going to messaging. It is no longer in use. I try several times, but still nothing. I want to hurl my phone across the room. Nathan has taken ghosting to the next level.

I've only one option. I need to contact Joseph, plead with him to tell Nathan it's urgent, and that I need to speak with him. They'll still be in touch, I'm certain. When I get back from Mr Beckles, I'll call my sponsor. As well as getting Nathan to stop the pointed, vindictive crossword clues, I need to start sorting out my life.

Any possible future I might have had with Nathan is over.

75

AMANDA

Mr Beckles' front door is bobbing back and forth in the wind and an old boot has been stuffed between the frame and the door to stop it banging. I gingerly descend the steps, which are covered in a viscous slimy green coating, until I reach the bottom of the stairwell where rancid air has collected in a concentrated pocket. At least the pile of scavenged rubbish has been bagged, the sacks neatly stashed beside the bin, but an uneasiness accompanies the sight.

The soup pan shakes in my hands. I'm so on edge now that I've decided to make contact with Nathan. I step into Beckles' hallway, and feel a sense of suffocation. I need to get back as soon as possible, and phone Joseph. Thoughts of what lies ahead wash over me in a wave of panic. I halt my step, close my eyes and set my free hand against a wall, and breathe deeply. Like Nathan taught me.

Mr Beckles voice, shaky and indistinct, brings me back.

'Is that you? Tory?' The question is faint, but there's no mistaking what he's said.

'Hi, Mr Beckles. It's only me, Amanda,' I say, my tone crisp, as I enter the lounge.

Mr Beckles is slouched in the armchair, head slumped on to his chest and his body is contorted like a ventriloquist's dummy. A gentle, but steady whistle escapes his sagging lips.

'Amanda,' he repeats. 'Can you help me sit up straighter. I've slid down.'

I set the pan to one side, plump up his cushion, and steady his movement with both hands as he raises himself up.

'I'll be back in a minute. Let me put your soup on.'

Before I've reached the kitchen, toxic fumes from an abrasive cleaner catch in my throat, and a wracking cough convulses my body. I can't breathe. I nearly turn and run out of the house, desperate for fresh air, feeling I'm about to choke to death. Instead, I head for Beckles' cooker, set the saucepan containing the chicken and sweetcorn soup on the hob, before lunging for the window. I frantically twizzle at the latch on the wooden frame, and yank at the window until it opens. Instead of holding fast, it catapults downwards and smacks like a blast of cannon fire.

I manage to lodge the window open using a random brick by the back door, and hold my mouth close to the gap as I greedily inhale the fresh air.

The kitchen is spotless. The draining board and sink have been scoured, and nothing sits on the surfaces. The engrained finger-marks which were smeared across the pale green cupboards doors, have disappeared. All the dirt has been scrubbed away. I peer closely at the surface of the old rickety table jammed in the corner, and there's no familiar trail of grease.

Tory has been here before me. Why is she playing the role of caring, thoughtful neighbour to Mr Beckles? There are plenty of needy people in the neighbourhood. Her obsession with Agaves, and my neuroses, tell me she's doing it to get under my skin. But why? What's it going to achieve, proving that she's a bloody saint?

Mr Beckles doesn't mention Tory, although a couple of times

he's called out her name when I arrive, as if he's expecting her. The place has definitely been much tidier recently, as if she's upped her visits, but why the secrecy? Maybe Mr Beckles likes to keep us both, two for the price of one, but it's odd he doesn't talk about her.

When the soup is heated, I pour it into a clean bowl that is already sitting out beside the cooker. Even with two hands, I'm scared of spilling any.

'Mr Beckles. Here's your soup.' His rheumy eyes light up when I appear, and his bony fingers tug at his pyjama top before he flattens down his wayward threads of hair. I lift the tea towel which he keeps near, and tie it round his neck.

'Smells good,' he says. He lifts the spoon, his hand a steady tremor, and slips it into the soup.

'Let me help you.' I bend, but he shoos me away.

'It's nice and tidy in here, and the kitchen is spotless,' I begin.

Beckles slurps tiny mouthfuls, leaving a fine trail of yellowy broth on the tea towel. Without looking up, he says, 'Victoria, your neighbour, was here earlier.'

'Oh. You should tell me when she's coming, and I could come on another day.' I shouldn't snap, it's not his fault, but I don't know why he doesn't tell me.

Beckles ignores me, carries on eating, and ten minutes later, he proudly plops the spoon in an empty plate, running a slithery tongue round his gums.

'That was very tasty,' he says. 'You're a good cook. You'll make some man very happy.'

'A pleasure.' I lift the plate, wheel back his eating tray, and get up.

As I head for the kitchen, desperate to get away, and back into the safe confines of my own flat, Beckles starts talking.

'Maybe you'll have children one day too.' His voice is faint, but I pick it up. I turn round, poke my face back into the lounge.

'What's that?'

'Maybe you'll have children as well, one day,' he repeats.

'As well as who?' My heart thrashes in my ribcage, a pulse throbs against my temple, and I think I'm going to blackout.

'Victoria. It's really sad though, don't you think?'

I know what he's going to say. It's all starting to make sense. I need to sit down. My legs are like jelly, and I can't halt a sick swaying motion that has taken hold.

Beckles is looking at me. Waiting for my response. I could walk away, say goodbye, that I'll see him soon, but I don't. I ask the question anyway.

'What's sad? What's Victoria sad about?'

'She lost her little boy. Didn't you know? Oliver, I think she said his name was.'

My legs buckle, as the soup bowl flies out of my hand and splinters into tiny pieces across the hallway.

76

AMANDA

I manage to get home. I don't know how. After I cleared away the broken crockery, rinsed through the pan, I hurried up the slimy stairs, away from Beckles' basement, until I reached the drive of Silver Birch.

As I creep up the path, I keep my eyes averted from Flat A. The front window is open, pushed wide, and I can hear music as it drifts out from inside. It's a melancholic chant, not unlike a funeral dirge.

I manage to get the key into the main entrance to Flats B and C, and turn the lock. My hands are thick with sweat, and soon I'm shooting up the stairs. I turn my ankle halfway up, bite down against a searing pain, but manage to hobble to the top.

At least Agaves isn't working from home. I can't face him with what I've just discovered. Not yet. A sick suspicion crosses my mind that he might already know. Maybe Tory confided in him, and he doesn't want to upset me further. My mind is skittering all over the place.

When I get inside, after bolting the door, top and bottom, and pulling the chain across, I collapse on to the sofa. My ankle is screaming, and I watch it swell. I shuffle to the kitchen to get some ice, and by the window, my hands grip the sink as a wave of vertigo makes the room swim. Tory. Mrs Hunter. Oliver's mother. The lady in Flat A. The Woman in the Window, my love rival for Agaves. They're the same person. A multitude of people, all rolled into one.

Somewhere down below a door slams, and makes me jump. Through the window, I watch a bony tree creak from the effort of staying upright. As squalls of wind increase, its skeletal limbs flounce against the force. That's me. I've no idea how I'll stay upright, on the straight and narrow. I feel I'm being battered from all angles.

Why didn't I know who Tory was? But then again, who should have told me? Why did Tory never say? A dreadful thought occurs, that she might have moved into Silver Birch because it's where I live. But why? My suppositions are too horrific to contemplate.

Before the accident I knew the Hunters lived down the road in one of the newbuild flats, but I can't remember ever meeting Mrs Hunter in person. I caught sight of her occasionally, from a distance, with her short, cropped hair and rounded shoulders, but I didn't dare catch her eye.

Tory's hair is long now, shoulder length, and smooth, and she walks with a tall straight gait. I can't believe it is the same person. How did I never twig?

Nathan sorted out the aftermath of the accident, and all the shit that followed. I never spoke to Mrs Hunter. I never went to see her, or tried to explain. Nathan apologised on my behalf, told her it was a sad, unfortunate accident, and conveyed, as best he could, how sorry I was.

I took the coward's way out, guilt keeping me well away. My one mistake was to trust Martin Hunter, and to try and make amends through him. All I wanted, was to apologise.

* * *

It's midnight. I'm in bed, lying on my back and staring up at the ceiling which never seems to still. It circles inwards, a merry-go-round of movement, dizzying in its speed as my thoughts race to keep up.

Elsewhere Silver Birch is quiet, its voice muted as if by duct tape, its laboured breath wheezing through blocked nostrils. Even the pipes have quietened. Outside the wind has worn itself out and ghostly shapes smile through the window as a branch taps rhythmically against the pane.

I heard Agaves get back from work. It was after eight. He knocked on my door, but I didn't answer. When he texted me half an hour later, I told him we'd catch up tomorrow. I'd a migraine and was already in bed.

Perhaps I should have let him in. Instead, I slip out from under the duvet and sleepwalk across the darkened room, towards the small cabinet on the landing. My dry fingers fiddle with the key, and click it open. I reach in and lift out the small vodka bottle.

I've no options left. I'm desperate for the company, and for something to anaesthetise the horror.

77

AMANDA

I don't want to wake up, but I can't get back to sleep. My head is thumping, my mouth parched, and I'm desperate for liquid to quench the thirst. My eyes are dry, gritty, and it's hard to focus, but as I look round the bedroom, I realise what has happened.

The morning after a heavy drinking session, holds its own unique set of clues. I know the ropes. Unlike a perfectly constructed crossword puzzle, no ambiguity in answers, the random pointers as to how the previous night unfolded are pretty indistinct.

The vodka bottle, the telltale evidence singing from my dressing table, is linked to the last thing I remember. Twisting off the red cap, and the first swig play clearly in my head, but the rest is a blank.

My jeans are neatly folded, laid flat across the bedroom chair, and my Harvard T-shirt hangs loosely across the back. Blue furry slippers, nestle underneath. My head is plonked atop a pile of pillows, and below the edge of the bed I can just make out the rim of a grey plastic bowl. Towels arranged around it provide a splatter guard.

The scene tells me what I don't want to know. It also tells me someone helped me into bed, tidied up my clothes, and set the basin out in case I threw up in the night. These are things I never did when I got drunk. Too much drink and I'd fall into bed, more often than not fully clothed.

I pull myself out of bed, wearing only my bra and pants, and stagger towards the kitchen. A sudden rap at the door, and I freeze. Agaves. Was he with me last night? It's unlikely. I remember hearing him come back from work, and then a blank.

'Amanda. Are you okay? It's only me. I know you're in there.' Agaves' voice is kind, gentle, but it frightens me. Why am I frightened? My mind is squirming as if it's being eaten up by maggots. Then it starts to come back to me. Yesterday. Mr Beckles, Tory, Oliver. Oh my god.

I don't reply to Agaves. My legs give way, and I slither to the ground. The floor is cold, and even the rug that covers the tiles feels like an Arctic icesheet. I lean my back against the wall, willing Agaves to leave. I cover my eyes with both hands to block out the light and to calm the waves of nausea.

'I'll pop by later. Text me you're okay. Please.' Agaves' mouth must be close to the door because it sounds so loud he could be in the flat with me.

Agaves hovers, before his tread slowly dissipates like a steady decrescendo until the front door slams, the sound an empty thump. The ensuing silence coaxes me into the lounge, and despite the heat from the sun on the window, I swivel the thermostat on the wall to its highest setting. I glance out through the pane, and watch Agaves disappear out the gate as he makes his way to the Tube, taking the warmth and comfort with him.

A couple of minutes pass, before I wrap my dressing gown tightly round me, and head to the front door. The chain isn't on.

The bolts not secured. But the door is locked. If I'd locked up, I'd have left the key in the door. It's a habit.

In a drunken stupor, I must have phoned Joseph, and he came round and helped me into bed. I look at my face in the hall mirror. My eyes are red, swollen. No doubt I cried on his shoulder. Again.

I usually scuttle down the stairs to collect the paper, scared Agaves might catch sight of me with my wild morning hair, and rush back up again before he might appear. But today, I grip the banister, and move slowly. I've a weird feeling that Tory might be watching, waiting for me. Perhaps she's outside our front door. My mind is still in nightmare mode, and questions are starting to mount.

As I grab the paper from the mat, the idea that Tory might have moved into Flat A to be near me, keep an eye on my movements, is really freaking me out. The questions won't let up. Why would she do that? Has she got a plan? Could it be coincidence? But I can't kid myself any longer.

The most likely answer is that she's out for revenge for the death of Oliver. And I'm the target.

78

AMANDA

I don't delay in phoning Joseph. Although I'm uneasy talking to him, especially after what happened last night, I need to see him. Talk to him about Nathan, and find out how I can get in contact. Joseph is my only hope, as Nathan has deleted himself from Facebook, Messenger, and taken down his Instagram account. I have no other option but to meet up with my sponsor, and plead for his help.

Joseph tells me to come to the hall where the AA group meets. I walk up Brewer's Hill, and soon I'm pushing through the large swing doors that lead into the large, cavernous space. There isn't another meeting for a couple of days, and there's no one about. Joseph is sitting in one corner reading, and he stands up when he sees me, sets the book down and stretches out both arms as I approach.

'Amanda. I'm glad you called. I've been worried,' he says, taking both my hands in his. His own are dry, chapped, and his knuckles are bright red, in contrast to his white and freckled skin.

'You're freezing,' he says. My hands are shaky, and bloodless like the rest of me. 'Let me make you a hot cup of something.'

'No thanks. I'm okay. I just need to talk.'

'About last night?' Joseph's voice is calm, caring, but his eyes twinkle. They're slightly glassy, faraway.

'I'm really sorry,' I say. 'I feel so ashamed.'

'Don't beat yourself up,' he says. 'Here, take a seat and tell me all about it.'

He pulls a chair up very close to his, and I subtly move it back before I sit down.

'I need to get hold of Nathan. He's ghosted me and he must have changed his phone number.' Joseph looks surprised, as he's expecting me to talk about last night, and what made me fall off the wagon.

'Oh.' Joseph sits back, retracts his long legs, and crosses his feet at the ankles.

'Could you let me have his number, or maybe persuade him to call me?' My voice quivers, but I hold his gaze.

'Probably best I get him to call you. I'd rather not give you his number until I've spoken to him.' Joseph runs a thick tongue around his wet lips, and his fingers graze up and down over his ginger beard.

'That's fine. But it's really urgent. We haven't spoken for months, and I need to move on.'

'No worries. I'm seeing him for a drink in a couple of days. Can it wait till then?'

'Yes. I'm really grateful.'

Joseph leans his arm across, and touches me on the shoulder. I stiffen and feel my teeth grate against each other. I know he's trying to make me feel better, lend comfort as is his vocation, but it's hard to forget that he's seen me semi-naked.

I picture the folded jeans, the carefully hung T-shirt, my fluffy slippers side by side. And the duvet tightly tucked around me.

'I'm there for you, Amanda. I understand. I'm only glad that you call and let me help. How's the hangover now?' He takes his hand away, rubs both his palms down the length of his heavy thighs, and puffs out a thick stench of air. The smell is familiar. Too familiar. It's a mix of rotting eggs, and cheap instant coffee.

'It's getting better, thanks.' I get up, and stretch out my neck and shoulders, tipping my head from side to side.

'Anytime you want to talk. I'm here. And if you fancy catching a meal sometime, let me know. Perhaps we could talk about something other than our addictions.' He laughs rather loudly.

'Sounds like a plan,' I say, unable to own up that there's nothing I'd like to do less. But I need to keep him on board until I've got through to Nathan. Joseph is my best, probably my only hope, to make contact with my husband.

At the door, Joseph opens his arms wide and offers me the *addict hug*. He coined the phrase, encouraging his group to find comfort in one another. To let them know they're not alone.

As his arms engulf my body, I close my eyes, count to ten. I finally break away, but not before I feel his hand slide across my bottom and squeeze my flesh.

79

NATHAN

Nathan and Joseph sidle into the corner of the pub, a stone's throw from Nathan's bedsit. The pub is cramped, pretty dingy, but it allows pets in the dark stone-floored back room that leads directly out into the garden. Nathan refuses to leave Merlong alone, and insists on taking him everywhere with him.

As Joseph orders drinks at the bar, Nathan is surprised when his friend orders two pints of beer, rather than one for him and a soft drink for himself. When Joseph sits back down, Nathan asks, 'Are you back on the booze?'

'I'll only have the one. I've managed it a few times recently, and think I might have it cracked. To become a social drinker, that is.' Joseph licks the foam off the beer, and takes a large swig.

'Well done. I'm most impressed,' Nathan says, popping his own finger in his glass and offering the moistened tip for Merlong to lick.

Ten minutes of small talk, and Nathan picks up that Joseph has something he wants to talk about.

'What's up? You don't seem yourself?' Nathan asks.

'It's Amanda. She's not in a good way.'

'Oh. What's up?'

'She's back on the booze. She really wants to talk to you.'

Nathan tickles Merlong's ear, and takes a moment to answer.

'Not getting on so well without me then? What does she want to talk about?' Nathan finds it hard to contain his mirth. He knew she'd come back, tail between her legs. She still needs him.

'I'm not really sure, except that she doesn't seem to be coping. I had to go round a couple of nights ago. Somehow she managed to phone me, but she'd drunk half a bottle of vodka.'

'Shit. You're joking me. I'm really sorry you've got caught up in all this. What state was she in?' Nathan jiggles with Merlong's metal choke chain, unsure if he really wants to hear.

'Pretty dreadful. I had to hoist her into bed, and wait until I was sure she was going to be all right. I was scared she might be sick, maybe choke, as she was so out of it.' Joseph takes another long swig of his beer, staring into the glass afterwards, looking at how little he's got left.

Nathan has known all along that Joseph isn't really an alcoholic, but he plays along with his friend's pretence. He knows Joseph uses the line of addiction to give him more credence with the AA group that he runs. It's easier to get them to listen, to trust him, if they think he's one of them. Joseph thinks he's playing Nathan like a card sharp.

But Nathan still trusts his friend to keep an eye on Amanda. He and Joseph go back a long way. Through thick and thin, they've weathered a few storms, and Joseph has been nothing if not loyal. Yet, as he listens to Joseph take ownership of his wife's problems, he feels a growing sense of irritation. Joseph is taking too much of a personal interest in his Amanda's well-being, and Nathan is getting images of Joseph undressing Amanda, putting her to bed. The images are becoming more sordid each time he thinks about it.

'Also,' Joseph continues, 'Amanda mentioned something about the crossword puzzles. She thinks you're setting loaded clues directed at her.'

Nathan suspects this is why Amanda is so desperate to get hold of him. His clues have maybe hit their mark, especially the drinking ones. Maybe they'll bring her back to him, after all. He finds communicating through the grid quite therapeutic, and sort of lets him have the last word.

'Okay. I'll own up. I have been sending a few personally targeted clues, but surely she's not that worried? It's just a bit of fun.'

'At first it didn't bother her, and she says she took it on the chin. But now it's really getting to her. She says the clues are no longer fun, and pretty cruel to be honest. That's why she wants to talk to you. Get you to stop, or help her find out who's doing it, and get them to stop.'

Merlong suddenly sits bolt upright, and his drooling mouth drops open as a thick panting tongue appears when Nathan gets up to head for the men's room.

'Won't be long, keep an eye on Merlong,' he says. 'Like you do Amanda.'

'Ha ha. Will do.' Joseph laughs, as he tries to placate the whimpering mongrel with a heavy hand.

But Nathan doesn't laugh.

80

AMANDA

It's nearly seven when I finally open the door to Agaves. I've showered, washed my hair, and tried to scrub away the horror of yesterday. The hangover is now manageable, but not the memory of learning that Tory is Martin Hunter's wife. Finding this out was what tipped me over the edge, and back to the bottle.

Meeting Joseph hasn't helped. Although my thoughts are skewed, with crazy notions as to why Tory might have moved into Flat A and not given any hint that she was Oliver's mother, I no longer want Joseph as my sponsor. I need to find someone new, but will have to wait till he's spoken to Nathan. I desperately need to talk to my husband, and Joseph is the only person I know who can put me back in touch.

I take a deep breath after I hear Agaves' solid rap before I open the front door. I need to lighten up, or he'll run a mile.

'Hi.' A sheepish Agaves appears in the doorway, his fist gripping a heart-shaped helium balloon. In his other hand he holds a bunch of flowers, reds, yellows, whites and purples wrapped in cellophane. A little card pokes out the top, stuck to a metal spike.

'The card was in case you didn't open the door,' he says, quick to read my thoughts. 'I was going to push it underneath if you were avoiding me.' He gives a tentative grin, like a child, unsure of what's coming next.

'Sorry, I've not been in a good way. Come in.'

He steps into the hallway, releases the string on the balloon and lets it float up into the corner.

'What does it say on the balloon?' My eyes squint upwards.

'*For a special girl.* The best I could find.' He blushes. 'I've missed you.'

He sets the flowers down, and reaches for me, circles my waist with his firm hands, and for a minute I give in, close my eyes, and lean against his chest. I want to stay this way for ever. His kiss is urgent, and sends sparks of longing through my body.

When I pull away, his eyes cloud over with doubt.

'Can we talk?' I say.

'Sounds serious. Should I be worried?' He releases his hold and follows me through to the lounge.

'A lot has happened since yesterday, and I'm really struggling.'

'Okay. I'm all ears. Bring it on.' Agaves sits down, settling uneasily at one end of the sofa.

I don't know where to start, but my words pour out like water from a burst pipe. I start with the puzzle thing again. I've collated the grids from the last few weeks, in date order. Agaves watches quietly as I spread them out, fanning the evidence in logical order.

'The puzzle the other day was only the tip of the iceberg. The clues we went through. Look here. There are so many clues linked to drink, places I've visited, small seemingly insignificant events linked to my life. And to Nathan's. At first, I thought it was a coincidence, but soon twigged it was probably Nathan having fun at my expense.'

Agaves stiffens, a steady tic throbbing in his jaw. 'You really think all these clues are aimed at you? There's an awful lot of them.' His eyes widen, but I feel his scepticism. It's in his voice, his expression.

'Yes, I do.' I point at the date rape clue. 'Look at this one. It appeared the first time shortly after the wine appeared on the doorstep.'

'You think there's a link between the clue and whoever left the wine? The wine was laced with Rohypnol, the date rape drug. It's what landed me in hospital.'

'Yes, and was obviously meant for me.'

'Do you think Nathan's capable of something like this?' Agaves' hair flops over his eyes as he crunches his brow in concentration. His finger trails along the grids.

'I did at first. But as I said I'm starting to suspect someone else is involved.' I hang my head in my hands, battle back the tears. It's as if I'm going round and round the same circle. Agaves leans across, kisses me on the lips.

'What say you put the kettle on? Maybe camomile tea instead of coffee,' he says. 'I think there's more to come?'

I've no idea how much to tell him, but now I've started, I don't want to stop. I need Agaves to understand, and help me work out what to do.

81

AMANDA

'You can't be serious?' Agaves' face is a picture when I tell him about Tory. 'She's Martin Hunter's wife? The guy who raped you?'

'Yes. Mr Beckles told me yesterday that Tory was Oliver's mother. Oliver was the boy who died. The boy whose death I caused.'

'Holy shit. She's never said, and I'd absolutely no idea. What a coincidence!' Agaves slurps his tea, swilling it round in his mouth.

'I'm not so sure.'

'You think it's not a coincidence that she's living here?'

'I'm starting not to. It's just a feeling that she's got it in for me. She's everywhere I turn. Not to mention the fact that she won't leave you alone.' I can't help the snap in my voice.

'I've told you. She's not my type. Do you think I'd be here if she was?'

Agaves isn't really picking up on all my fears. Tory has sucked him in with her female wiles. He might not fancy her, but that's not stopping her from chipping away at the possibility of something more. Agaves' straightforward honesty is what I love, but Tory's not naive. She's manipulative, and will use his decency to inveigle further into his life. I'm not even certain if she really fancies him, or is trying to coax him away from me, and douse any chance I might have of happiness.

'Seriously, Amanda. Don't worry about Tory. It's likely to be one huge coincidence. She probably doesn't want to confront you. She seems pretty decent.'

I can't say any more. I need to keep Agaves on side. If I carry on with the neurotic summations, he might not be so keen. His warmth, enthusiasm, and eagerness to be with me should make my heart soar. But he makes me even more confused. He thinks Tory incapable of subterfuge, but I'm not taken in by her scheming. She's got an agenda, and it looks as if I'll have to find out what it is on my own.

'By the way, have you managed to get in touch with Nathan? You wanted to talk to him, about the clues.'

'Joseph is going to chase him, get him to call me.' When I say Joseph's name, Agaves stiffens. I know he doesn't like Joseph, his closeness to me, so I don't expand. Now certainly isn't the time to bring up what happened last night. I can't tell Agaves about the vodka, about Joseph putting me to bed, and my wish to ditch my sponsor. I think Agaves has heard enough.

'Great. Let me know when you see Nathan, and if you want me to come with you.'

'Will do. Now let me put those flowers in a vase. Thanks, Agaves.'

'Sorry? Algarve?' Agaves raises a questioning eyebrow.

'Sorry, I meant Teddy.' I let out a nervous giggle.

'I've often wondered why you and Nathan called me Algarve. I heard the pair of you a couple of times when you thought I couldn't hear, or wasn't listening. Is it because I'm hot?'

Agaves has his anxious face on, the crumpled forehead, the tightened jaw. There's an uncertainty, a childlikeness about his expression. I want to forget everything, and run away with him. We could keep each other safe.

'It was a nickname Nathan and I used. Agaves. Not Algarve.'

I tell him of Nathan's and my word games, anagramming people's names, or attributes.

'What is Agaves an anagram of?' he asks.

'Savage.' It sounds ridiculous in the telling, and I want to blame Nathan, but I was the one who made it up.

'You think I'm a savage?'

'No. Nathan was jealous, called you a savage, and I came up with the anagram. Agaves is the name of a prickly plant, and of a honey-flavoured syrup.'

'Come here you. Enough of the wisecracks. All a bit weird for me. What say you stick to Teddy, bin the gloopy syrup label.'

He nudges me down on to the sofa, and lies alongside. His breath is warm, and the smell of him calms my senses. He's just so perfect, and if anything goes wrong, there'll be no way back. I swallow back the fears, and let his fingers roam my hungry body.

Teddy. He's all I've ever wanted.

82

AMANDA

By the time Teddy has gone, I'm exhausted. For a brief moment, when we were together, nothing seemed so bad.

I know Teddy is concerned about my worries, but more concerned for how they make me feel, how they get me down, rather than the reality itself. Until I have the proof that Nathan could be that vindictive, enough to try to poison me, or until I find out who is, I'll not have Teddy's full attention. Convincing him that Tory is a stealthy stalker out for revenge, will be harder still to prove.

I turn off all the lights, and nearly forgo brushing my teeth, I'm that tired. Recently, I've forgotten all about the loose board in the bathroom, which I slotted firmly into place after Tory glanced up at the ceiling in Teddy's kitchen. She might have heard me yelp when I banged my head. I can't be sure.

Keeping the gap sealed has blocked out temptation to spy on Teddy, but it's also helped shut out the thoughts that Tory might know the board is loose. She might have spotted the slit, and is holding her suspicions close to her chest until the moment's right. Until she decides to reveal my sneaky secret.

My stomach is full of acid, and my breath is unpleasant, a bad taste sticking to my gums. I give in, head for the bathroom, brush my teeth and gargle with a minty mouthwash. As I wipe the edges of my mouth with the towel, I look down. One last time can't hurt. I'm too tired to argue with myself, and give in to the addict trait of an urgent need to act.

I switch off the main light, hunker down, and slowly ease the damp slat apart, millimetre by millimetre, until a tiny triangular gap lets through a chink of light from down below.

Teddy is wandering round the kitchen. His sculpted feet are bare, and his strong muscled legs threaded with their dark jungle hairs, are barely covered by boxer shorts that leave nothing to the imagination. After what we've just done, I smother a giggle. My eyes are dry and blurry, but it's hard to tear them away from his body. It takes me a second to spot the mobile pressed against his ear.

'Sorry, I can't tomorrow night. Another time.' He's speaking quietly, firmly, in a work-like tone of efficiency. He pads to the window, looks out into the dark. I wonder who he's talking to. As the conversation carries on, I'm not sure I want to listen. I bite my lip, draw blood from a burgeoning cold sore in one corner, and lick the smear away.

Teddy nods, replies to whatever is being said with single words, short phrases: *yes, no, maybe, when I'm free. I promise.* Then out of the blue, I hear his voice more clearly.

'Amanda? Why do you ask?' Teddy stops prowling, leans his back against the sink, and his right foot taps up and down.

I know who's on the line! She'll have been watching us. From outside her flat, down below my lounge. She'll have been looking up, and seen our silhouettes in the window. I remember that I didn't shut the curtains tight when Teddy suggested that we should. I laughed, saying no one could see us from this far up.

But Tory could! From inside the grounds of Silver Birch, near the fence by the tree, you can see up into Flat C. Nathan insisted we put curtains up, as the window had been uncovered when we moved in. He proved to me, by standing by the tree, that anyone could spy on us. It's all coming back. OH MY GOD! Tory has been watching us. Watching me.

I tuck my ear close against the hole, turn my eye away, and listen. I start to fill in the other person's questions. The gaps in the conversation. I imagine the dulcet, sickly sweet, cajoling tones. Teddy believes Tory's sincerity. He's not unlike Nathan, easily taken in by flirtatious flattery, and unthreatening offers of friendship. Tory wants Teddy for herself. She'll do everything she can to prise him away. I'm not sure if she's genuinely fallen for his dark good looks, or if she's got it in for me. It's likely a combination of both.

'No, she's fine. No worries,' Teddy continues. 'The drink? I think she's doing well.' I can hear a steady drumming noise, and slip my eye back in the slot. He's tapping the fingers of his free hand on the worktop. 'What's that?' he asks.

He suddenly goes rigid, and stops moving. He's listening intently to what's being said.

'Nathan? How do you know? Did he tell you he wants to come home. Back to Amanda?'

Nathan? Tory? What's she saying? What's she got to do with my husband. My mind rewinds.

After the accident, Nathan helped Mrs Hunter. I remember him telling me he felt guilty, as he'd been the one who'd encouraged the Hunters to move to Brewer's Hill. If he hadn't told them about the flats, they would have lived somewhere else. Oliver wouldn't have died. That was the connection with Tory Hunter. But Nathan didn't mention her much after the first few weeks. I assumed he never saw her again. At the time, although I regretted everything that happened, I didn't give her that much thought. I had enough battles of my own.

That was months ago. Another lifetime. Unless they've kept in touch.

As I slip the board back in place, the acid in my stomach refluxes into my throat. As I lie slumped on the cold tiles, one question is going round and round.

If Nathan and Tory are still in touch, I need to find out why.

83

NATHAN

Nathan stares at the screen of his mobile. He's been picking it up, putting it down all day. Every time he goes to ring Amanda, he feels an overwhelming surge of anger.

Ghosting his wife has definitely helped ease the torture, and not speaking to her, seeing her, has helped bury the lurid memories, albeit in a shallow grave.

Since meeting Joseph in the pub, the images are coming back. Stronger. More vivid. He has enjoyed teasing Amanda with his loaded crossword clues, mild recompense for her drunken infidelity, but the silent admonishment has definitely wound her up, and helped him through the worst. Although irritation with someone else targeting his wife is really starting to piss him off.

Finally, he keys in the call. She picks up on the second ring.

'Amanda. It's me. Nathan.'

Nathan slips his car up on to the kerb, directly across the road from Silver Birch. He's recently taken to driving up to Highgate, and cruising past their home. Watching for sightings of his wife. It's a masochistic hobby, but helps him keep in touch. He's toyed with calling in, catching Amanda unawares, and maybe even coming back. But not yet. Amanda needs to plead, beg forgiveness, show more desperation. He's a patient guy.

Meeting with Joseph has fed his hope. Joseph recounted Amanda's desperation, her relapsing into drink, and how badly she's coping on her own. Tonic to his ears.

He can see Amanda through the window, standing to the right, then padding up and down. She stops, midway, when she hears the phone. He watches her pick it up, put it to her ear. Her silhouette shines like the star of a West End stage, lit by a floor lamp whose drooping attachment circles a halo beam around her head.

'Nathan? Is that really you? Oh my god. I'm so glad to hear your voice.' Her relief sizzles through the airwaves, burning in his ears.

'Who else?' He takes his time, watching her every move. 'Joseph tells me you wanted to talk. What can I do for you?'

Amanda is slugging from a glass, and a feeble cough swallows up her words. She puts the phone on loudspeaker, sets it on the sill, and her hands wrench her straggling hair up into a topknot. He slouches low, worried that she'll spot his car, and breathes more easily when he remembers he changed it after he left. He pulls his baseball cap over his eyes, just in case.

'Nathan, can we meet? I really need to talk to you.' The pleading, helpless tone, makes him nostalgic. Sad for what they had.

'When did you have in mind?' he asks.

'As soon as possible. Tomorrow? Please say you can.'

'I don't think I've got anything in my diary for tomorrow.' His voice carries the hint of a laugh. Amanda would berate him for meticulous date keeping, rigid routines, and lack of spontaneity. It would drive her crazy. Since they split, he's been more lax in keeping up a schedule.

'Brilliant. Where?'

'What say the Boatyard Pub in Shoreditch? You remember where that is?'

Nathan had already planned the venue. It would help him keep the upper hand if he had to mention Justin Blakemore, and the Friday night trysts Amanda had shared with the adulterer in the very same pub. Amanda never twigged that Nathan knew. He might need to tell her if he weakens in resolve. The memory of her wantonness will help smother the desire to have her back too soon. Before she's done full penance.

'I'll be there. Seven o'clock?' He can hear the relief in her tone.

'Suits me. Bye, Amanda. Till tomorrow.'

Nathan disconnects and watches her stretch her arms wide, and unclench balled-up fists. But then she lifts her phone again, taps the screen, and puts it to her ear.

He jerks up from his slouch position in the driver's seat, and bangs his knee against the steering wheel. He wonders who she's talking to, but can guess. From hints Joseph made, he suspects it's the savage bastard in Flat A.

Edward Heath.

84

AMANDA

I decide not to tell Teddy that I'm going to meet Nathan tonight. It's something I need to do on my own.

I've no classes today, so spend the day separating Nathan's and my possessions, neatening the lines of division. He didn't take anything with him other than his clothes, but it's therapeutic to box his books, gadgets and random shoes he left behind.

As I work, my mind is skittish, anxious, veering off in all directions. The calming effect from concentrated organisation is fragile, dissipating when I let my mind wander from the task at hand. As I stack and separate our possessions, dust coats my throat and fear tags me like a stalker.

Sunday is the anniversary of when Nathan and I first met. May the third, three years ago. I wonder if Nathan remembers the date and if he'll mention it tonight. Perhaps he's long forgotten. There's so much I need to talk about. The puzzles. The threats. Tory, and most important, about Teddy. I've no idea how Nathan will react. He's been gone so long, perhaps he's already found someone else. But tonight, I'll be asking for a divorce.

* * *

I arrive ten minutes late at the Boatyard Pub. I stand outside, sick with nerves. I remember meeting Nathan, thinking it was such a coincidence that the guy who'd given me a paper bag on the London Eye should have turned up a few days later in place of Justin, my married lover. Strange, but I never heard from Justin again.

I put it down to fate. I never told Nathan I recognised him from the capsule of the London Eye, nor about Justin. As I hover, I feel the guilt pile up. I was never really truthful, perhaps less than fair on Nathan. Fate threw us together, and he was my saviour. But not my soulmate. We've come full circle, and now it's time to go our separate ways.

My heart races as I push the leaden door ajar. I pop my head round before the rest of me. It's dark, dusty, and the Friday night crowd is already buzzing. I see a man sitting in the same corner where I sat when Nathan walked in the night we met. He's swivelling on a stool, his rucksack placed on the one adjacent. The man's hair is long, straggling over his shoulder. I look round the room, but there's no one else sitting on their own, and there's no sign of Nathan amongst the rowdy guys around the bar.

Slowly, I walk up towards the counter. The man turns, he's so familiar, but so strange.

'Nathan?' I ask. I know it's him, but he's so unrecognisable. His hair is lank, greasy, and a greying beard coats his chin. His eyes are black ringed, and his skin darker than I remember, yellowy in the half light.

'Amanda.' He stands up, comes close and kisses me on each cheek. He smells of beer, neglect, defeat. I swallow back the shock. 'I've bought you a drink. Bitter lemon. Okay?' he asks.

'Thanks. Perfect.' I put my bag on the ground, climb up on to the old familiar stool, plant my feet atop the metal bar. 'It's good to see you. Thanks for coming, Nathan.' What else can I say?

It's been so long, it's hard to know where to start. We make small talk, like two strangers who've only met. No banter. No flirtation. More like business colleagues discussing office politics. When I've had enough, I bite the bullet.

'Nathan, I need to talk to you.'

He keeps sipping his beer, not moving it away from his lips. 'Go on,' he says.

'The crossword puzzles. Is it you who's sending me coded messages?' It sounds so flippant, unimportant, unthreatening when I ask him face to face.

'What do you think?' A twinkle in his eyes gets dimmed by hooded lids.

'I guessed the alcohol clues were yours. They were too familiar.'

'Okay. Guilty as charged. A pretty novel way for payback, don't you think?'

'At first I thought so, but it got pretty irritating.'

'Did you expect me to do nothing?' His eyes narrow, and his voice deepens.

'Is it you with the more recent threatening clues. Date rape. Funeral... Oliver.' My voice tapers away with the last word.

'No. Can't take the blame for those.' Nathan smiles, a beam of relief that he's not to blame, or a beam of satisfaction that the clues have really wound me up. I'm not sure which.

'Who's doing it then?' I swivel right round until I'm facing him, and up close. 'You must know.'

'I've got my suspicions. But can't be certain.'

'Who?'

'I suspect it's Bagheera. She's pretty cute, clever with words. I meet her now and then, and perhaps she fancies me. Likes having a go at my wife. Who knows?'

I fight the urge to throw my drink in his face. His explanation rings false. Why would some random female go to all the trouble? It's hard to see a random setter target a colleague's wife. Also, looking at Nathan, his unkempt, unattractive appearance, makes his suggestion feel unlikely.

'Who the hell is Bagheera? How does she know so much about me? About Oliver. You wouldn't have written that clue, not on the heels of the date rape clue. You're not that mean.' His bland expression makes me wonder if I ever knew him at all.

'Bagheera? She's Mrs Hunter. Oliver's mother. I think she's got plenty of reason to have it in for you.'

85

AMANDA

I slide off the stool, tell Nathan I'll be back, and head for the Ladies'.

I battle through the sweaty bodies, reeling from side to side, scared I'm going to throw up. The rowdy drinkers pump up the noise, and I can't think straight. Inside the cubicle, I slam and lock the door, and collapse onto the toilet seat.

Oh my god! Tory is the crossword setter. She never told Teddy or I what she did for a living. Nor that she knew Nathan. All this time, she's been toying with me, taunting me. Did she move to Silver Birch to be near me? Why? Why so close? Is it all about revenge? It must be, or why all the secrecy?

The questions won't stop. I hold my hands against my temples, push them tight, to stop the flow of terror. I count down from one hundred. Like I've been taught to fight a panic attack. I breathe in through one nostril, out through my mouth, and repeat as I say the numbers.

I'm desperate to get home, see Teddy. Tell him what I've found out, but I can't. Not yet. In case Nathan disappears again, I might only get tonight to talk divorce. Also, he might fill me in on Tory's state of mind. What she might be capable of. Nathan knows her. Do they still talk about what happened, the day Oliver died? Do they discuss me? My part in it.

By the basins, I throw cold water over my face until it stings. Handful after handful. When a young girl walks in, she keeps her eyes averted, in embarrassment. I look mad, slightly deranged, there's no doubt.

When I get back, Nathan has ordered me another bitter lemon, and a beer for himself. He's looks much more relaxed than I feel, and it crosses my mind that he might be enjoying my agitation. The thought spurs me on. I climb back on to the stool, and thank him for the drink.

'Did you know Tory lives in Silver Birch, in Flat A?' I ask, wanting to find out how much he knows.

'Silver Birch? No, Bagheera moved out from Brewer's Hill a while back. That's what she told me. Somewhere close by, was all she said.' Nathan sets his glass down, cracks his knuckles on both hands, and fiddles with a beer mat.

He didn't know! He cracks his knuckles when he's under pressure, or when he's been caught out. Tory never told him. She's been torturing me on her own. They're not in on it together. I'm certain. If they were that close, she'd have told him where she lived.

Relief washes over me that Nathan didn't know. His only crime has been to taunt me with drinking clues, to make me feel guilty, and to wrest back a measure of control for all the hurt.

'Nathan. Can we talk about us?' I finally get up my nerve.

'What about us?' Nathan has rounded up several beer mats from along the counter, and begins to flick them onto the alternate beer glasses. He doesn't look at me as he plies his party piece.

'I'd like a divorce,' I say. I feel blood drain from my face.

'Shouldn't it be me saying that?' Nathan's face contorts.

Sadness. Anger. Humiliation. Regret. The cause could be any of them. 'You've met someone else, haven't you?'

'Yes.'

'It's that savage in Flat B, isn't it?' He hisses the words.

'Teddy and I've become close. After you left, not before. You and I have no future, Nathan. I've said I'm sorry, but I can't keep saying it.'

'Whatever.' He stands up. He looks shrunken in height as well as in appearance. His shoulders have lost their upright confidence, stooped in defeat. 'It's been good to see you, Amanda. I'll be back in touch.'

He doesn't kiss me, but turns and walks away, his rucksack hanging sadly off his shoulder.

I want to ask when I'll hear from him again, but he moves with speed. We've so much more to talk about. Tears stream down my cheeks. It's the end of a chapter, but not the end of our story.

The Nathan I married, the guy I knew so well, is unlikely to give up without a fight.

86

AMANDA

I don't go and see Teddy when I get back. It's late, and I'm in no fit state to tell him about my meeting with Nathan. But tomorrow, I'll tell him everything. Exhausted, I fall into bed, but toss and turn, until I finally slip away.

But my fears get rolled into disjointed nightmares which are becoming more and more vivid. I keep seeing the wine. The bloody red wine left on the doorstep, the wine that knocked me out, and nearly killed Teddy. A shadowy figure appears in my sleep, but I can't make them out.

Then Joseph appears, his thick fingers busy with my buttons. Even in my sleep, I can feel his heavy breathing as he drools like a rabid pit bull. His eyes are red, bloodshot as he leers over me and holds me down. A hand sweeps back my hair, as he undoes his trouser belt. Nathan stands in the corner watching, his arms crossed, expressionless. Next I conjure up Tory, dressed in a nurse's uniform, with a small white cap perched like a saintly mitre atop her pale, wispy hair. Then something else. Nathan comes up to her, takes her hand, cups her chin, and kisses her, his eyes glowering at me over her shoulder.

In the dream, Tory and Nathan know each other well. Not as passing acquaintances. They go way back. Before the accident. Before Martin Hunter. Nathan knew Bagheera as a setter, long before the accident. Nathan didn't only help Martin Hunter's wife because of guilt at what had happened, but because he knew her as a friend. A colleague. Maybe even as a lover.

I toss and turn, desperately try to wake up, but I can't. Recall of the accident flashes up macabre images. Images of Nathan, and Tory. I killed her son. Perhaps they talk, share motives for revenge. Or perhaps Nathan eggs her on, the pair like Bonnie and Clyde; coupled in crime.

A squeal of an animal outside finally wakes me up. Drenched in sweat, I sit bolt upright, and cover my ears. But I can't block out the noise. A long, piercing screech of pain carries on, as the prey won't give in. The night-time fox is out again, hungry, and determined.

When silence returns, I know the deadly deed is done.

87

AMANDA

It's Saturday, 2 May. Teddy sends me an early text, asking what time he should come round. I need to get up early, get moving, because tonight I've got a date. The first romantic date I've had in as long as I can remember. I should be happy, radiant, at last having got a chance to get things right. But unease won't let up.

I stumble out of bed, throw on leggings and a jumper, and brace for what's to come. Tonight, I need to talk to Teddy, and get him to really understand. I want him to help me make decisions on how to deal with what I've discovered. But I'll need to pick my moment, because I also want to tell him I've asked Nathan for a divorce.

I clock watch all day. I think of Nathan, with his love of written lists to organise events, times neatly penned against each task. A sadness follows me around the kitchen as I chop vegetables, potatoes, and pare down the fattened lamb. Tomorrow is 3 May, the anniversary of the day Nathan and I met. Not the encounter in the London Eye, but the time Nathan walked into the Boatyard Pub and introduced himself as *A Male Attorney for the Girl*. My male attorney. That was when he coined the cryptic clue against my name. *Amanda.*

By two o'clock, the casserole is in the oven. I set the timer. Three hours, and I put a tick against my hastily scribbled list. Although I know Teddy is a meat man, I still asked what he'd like for supper. I smiled when he told me again that he's not into vegetarian stuff. Red meat all the way. Hard not to compare my lover's tastes with Nathan's. The oily fish salads, the avocado mixes, fruit cocktails spoke to me like medicine, as Nathan obsessed to keep me healthy.

Nathan made me doubt I could survive alone, and made me think I couldn't live without him. In the sober light of day, after so long apart, I realise it was all a smokescreen. Nathan depended on me, more than I did on him. Controlling me was his way to cope.

By 6.30, I'm ready for my guest. As ready as I'll ever be. I've no idea how I'll eat, my stomach shrunken to nothing, and I can't remember when I last entertained a guy without a glass of wine. I perch on the edge of the sofa, and count down the minutes: 6.40. 6.50. 6.55. Then a rap at the door lets me know the wait is over. Five minutes early gives me hope that Teddy has been counting down as well.

I don't want to spoil the perfection of the evening. I smile, laugh, share small talk, as we eat. When the meal is over, I make the coffee, set the cups on a table by the sofa. Teddy is already sitting, and stretches out an arm to pull me down beside him. On top of him. Under him. It's all we both want, to consummate our longing. The meal has been the foreplay to our desperation. But I can't give in. Not yet.

I hover, and listen to my shaky voice.

'Yesterday, I met with Nathan.' It feels like I've dropped a bombshell.

'Oh. Is that's what's been bothering you,' Teddy says. 'Come and tell me all about it.' He pats the space beside him, and with a single hand pulls me down.

I tell him how Nathan has changed.

'I hardly recognised him,' I say. 'He was gaunt, unkempt, and had lost a lot of weight.'

I drag my story out, like a comedian unwilling to get to the punch line.

'I've asked for a divorce,' I say. I bite my lip, scared to look at Teddy, see fear, hesitation, or shock that it might be on his account. A few seconds pass, it feels like hours, before he speaks.

'I'm sorry. For Nathan, not for me though.' His mouth finds mine, and I nearly give in. Live for the perfection of the moment.

'There's something else.' I struggle upright, inch apart.

'Jeez. What now?' Teddy's eyes lose their sparkle.

'It's Tory. You know she's Oliver's mother, but I found out from Nathan that she's also a crossword setter at the *Echo*. She goes under the pseudonym of Bagheera.'

'Wow. I'd no idea. She never talks about what she does, and I've sort of given up asking.'

'Yes, I suspect she doesn't want me to know.'

'Why?' he asks.

'Because I'm certain she's the one sending the malicious clues through the grids.'

'You think she's out for revenge?'

I can feel Teddy's mind working, as his brow furrows, and he clasps his hands together.

'Yes, I do. And I'm frightened,' I simply say.

But I'm more than frightened. I'm terrified. Petrified. The terror is eating me up, with the belief that someone is out to get me.

Teddy doesn't really understand, but he listens. Lets me talk. And talk. And talk.

For now it'll have to do.

88

AMANDA

When I finally fall silent, Teddy looks at me, and asks if he can get a word in.

'You're not a setter too, are you?' I joke with him and try to lighten the mood, but he doesn't laugh. Instead, he circles me with strong arms. I stiffen when I hear an exaggerated intake of breath.

'I love you Amanda. That's all.' He kisses my crown, lets his lips linger, and wraps me up in warmth. 'Now if you'll be quiet, I need to show you just how much.'

He lifts me up, wraps my legs around his waist, and carries me into the bedroom where he throws me onto the bed.

'Now let me show you what a savage I really am.' We laugh together. My Agaves. My savage.

What follows is a perfect moment in time. A climax after years of getting things so wrong. Maybe it is that simple. All the years I tried so hard to get it right, fuelling my insecurities with drink, trying to create an illusion of someone very special. And here he is. Teddy, my perfect knight in shining armour. With our bodies entwined, I close my eyes, shut out the world, which for a brief period, seems to stop spinning on its axis.

Teddy is the first to get up. He tells me he's going to sleep in his own flat tonight as he's leaving early in the morning to drive to Brighton to see his mother.

'I don't want to wake you. There'll be plenty more times,' he says, pulling his jeans back on and slipping his T-shirt over his head.

I tug the duvet round me, reluctant to let him go. I don't want the moment to end. I'm used to men leaving, unwilling to face the morning after. But not Teddy. I know he'll be back. It's just that I don't want him to go. He sits beside me, takes my hands, lifts them to his lips.

'I'll text when I leave in the morning, and again when I leave Brighton, and will definitely pop in for a goodnight kiss when I get home. I promise. Will you miss me?'

'Yes, I'll miss you.' He's no idea how much.

After we say goodbye, and I close the door after him, I peek through the spyhole and watch my lover fade away. A day suddenly seems like a very long time. I wander back into the lounge. Through the window a full moon, with a grinning pull of madness, beams into the room.

Too quickly, my mind takes up from where it left off before Teddy arrived. Tory, Nathan, all the fears. Teddy promises he'll help sort things out, get me through, but I know he doesn't feel the gravity. He's trusting of people, and I'm not sure he believes there's anything sinister afoot.

Teddy says he'll never leave me.

But then so did Nathan.

MAY THE THIRD

89

AMANDA

I'm up at the crack of dawn. After I hear Teddy leave, I get up, sleep no longer possible.

In the kitchen I chop up the leftover lamb casserole into tiny mouthfuls and fill a small airtight container. I then cut up some bread and decide to set off early to look in on Mr Beckles. He doesn't mind what time I call, because for him the days roll into evenings in twenty-four hours of sameness and solitude. He never knows what time it is, although I've noticed he's started wearing his watch again.

'I'm going to try and get some fresh air soon, see if I can get up the steps and reach the road.' He's been more positive recently, a new determination coinciding with the brighter weather, as he potters round his flat using his hands to grip the furniture for support.

If he's not awake, I'll do some cleaning, tidy round and leave the food in the fridge because today I won't linger in case Nathan remembers the date and turns up. Today is 3 May.

It's quiet outside, early Sunday traffic sparse, no snake-like queue snarling up and down the road. By the front door, I glance through Tory's downstairs window, through the opened curtains which tell me she's likely to be at home.

I can almost hear the palpitations of my heart as I tiptoe down the path, and I tug my jacket tight against the early morning chill. I dip through the gap in our front hedge and disturb a pair of pigeons pecking at a bloody morsel on the ground. Behind me there's a grating sound as a window creaks ajar, and I move faster until I'm out of sight. I glance back through the thorny thicket and can just make out Tory's face behind the glass as her hand pushes out the frame.

I hang close to the wall that circles Mr Beckles property and slip down the stairwell to his front door, let myself in and tiptoe through to the kitchen. As I busy myself, I can hear Beckles's heavy snore coming from close by. The rhythm gets interrupted by a sharp intake of breath and a nasal splutter every few seconds.

I poke my head into the bedroom which is next to the lounge. Beckles is on his back, the blanket heaped on the floor but he's not in his pyjamas, dressed rather in grey trousers and a chequered shirt, and his ivory-topped walking stick is propped up against the radiator. I gently slip off his shoes and set them on the floor.

The room is spotless. A smell of polish cloys with synthetic odours, and I feel my chest constrict. Tory's been in again. The silent competition is like a statement, as if she doesn't want me to forget that she's nearby.

I leave the casserole in the fridge for when I come back, and leave the bread out on a separate plate in case Mr Beckles manages to get into the kitchen.

I creep back up our driveway, gently retracing my steps across the gravel path. Silver Birch is slumbering, a gently beating behemoth, but Tory's window is now wide open, inviting in the daylight. The emptiness of Teddy's flat with its large front expanse of silent glass makes the property feel like a ghost ship, adrift at sea. My gaze wanders towards the roof, patches of missing tiles like an unfinished quilt, and notice a steady drip of water from an unfastened gutter is sliding down the walls from some thirty feet above.

Inside, I pick up the paper and scuttle back upstairs. The grand staircase, the landing, and the towering ceilings echo like a rumbling stomach and I hoot like an owl, listening to the noisy vibrations.

I'm scared of opening up the puzzle. I'm all over the place, and know I should give myself a break. Maybe wait till Teddy's back, and we can do it together. But I can't. I'm curious, now I know Tory is a setter. Teddy was surprised when I told him, but he was doubtful that Tory is targeting me with clues. He's more suspicious of Nathan. Tory's done her innocent sell on my lover, that's for sure.

Before I attack the clues, I tidy round the flat. Try and clear my head. I keep checking my mobile for Teddy's texts. And Nathan's. I'm desperate to hear from him, so that we can discuss moving on. But I know he'll make me wait. Think about things. He might even fight to get me back.

Although Teddy has sent greetings from Brighton with emojis of sun, parasols and smiling faces, he seems so far away.

I'm sick with anxiety, and my stomach is in knots.

At ten o'clock I take a break and collapse into the armchair in the corner, tucking my feet under my folded legs and scrunch my hair into its familiar looping topknot. I turn to the back page of the newspaper, forgoing the temptation to read the headlines, fold it in half and then half again, a smile twitching as I sharpen the origami creases. I lift the pen, squiggle the nib till the ink flows, and begin the hop around the crossword grid.

Slowly, steadily, a theme takes shape. A theme of the sort which Nathan assured me would be banned by the editor. Random clues could escape the ban, slip through the net, but not a series with connected meaning. I unfurl my legs, plant my feet on the hardwood, and swish my hand round my neck, across my brow. Damp coats my fingers. The room begins to move as the walls advance. It's as if I'm being sucked into a black hole. The coffee gurgles in my gut, like pig swill.

'Oh my god.' I stare at the clues. The indisputable, unequivocable answers. The equations of perfection. Several I've seen recently, but in isolation. Today, they're all lumped together.

One across: *A metal bundle of twigs for a tree (6,5) Silver birch*

Two across: *Two fools one country for murder (13) Assassination*

Five down: *Old Bob finds amusement at home but not here presumably? (14) Slaughterhouse*

Eight across: *Accelerator or choke (8) Throttle*

Ten down: *Undertaking final tax demand (5,5) Death duties*

Twenty down: *A killer, one not known to accept money (9) Strangler*

Violence is a taboo subject for the setters yet today's theme has a surfeit of clues relating to murder and death.

The first clue, one across, stands out in its random individuality. *Silver birch*. It has nothing to do with death, but everything to do with me.

Downstairs a door slams, a thunder crack that makes me jump. Tory must have left the building and now I'm totally alone.

90

AMANDA

I carry on. My hands are shaking, and can't keep a grip on the pen. Coffee is making me overly alert, and spiking the paranoia.

It's 11.50 by the time I'm through with solving. I've ringed four clues with thick black scribbled circles.

Four across: *Ice-cream dessert, we hear, for the Sabbath (6) Sunday*

Thirteen down: *Japanese play at the scheduled hour – twelve! (8) Noontime*

Twenty-two across: *Tim Hardy makes a date (3,5) May Third*

Twenty-eight across: *A male attorney for the girl (6) Amanda*

Holy shit. The time suddenly seems important. It's nearly twelve o'clock. Noontime!

My bare feet slither across the floor, the wooden surface chilled like an ice rink. I tug the front door safety chain across, rattle it making sure it's in place, then bolt the locks top and bottom. Through the frosted spyhole the distorted landing is empty. But a door suddenly opens and closes in the hall below, the noise followed by a slow steady tread of footsteps which gets louder until someone stops outside my door.

I push my back against the wall, blood pumping through my

veins, a throbbing in my temple. I can't breathe. Seconds pass in what seems like an eternity.

A sudden rap against the door and my body stiffens. Oh my god. I've no idea what to do. I see my mobile on the sideboard across the room, the screen flickering.

'Amanda. Are you in there? It's only me.' A familiar voice booms through the silence. I hesitate, uncertain whether I've correctly identified the caller. 'Amanda. Are you there?'

I swivel round, peer through the spyhole again, my eye coming face to face with the person on the other side, whose bulging eye meets my own. Relief floods out like a burst dam as my trembling fingers unlock the door. It's only Joseph.

'I wasn't sure if you were at home. Can I come in?' Joseph's smile, bright, sunny, fills me with relief.

'Yes, do. Am I glad to see you! Come in. Come in.' I take his arm and pull him through, slamming the door behind.

Trapped air from my lungs explodes, like a burst cloud releasing its laden content.

As Joseph lumbers through the lounge, I start to wonder why he's come.

I check my watch. It's exactly midday. It's an odd time for Joseph to have turned up, especially on a Sunday.

'I've just finished running an AA meeting, and thought I'd check in,' he says, when I ask. Joseph plonks himself down on one of the dining chairs, and leans his elbow on the windowsill.

'Oh. Did Nathan put you up to it?'

'Put me up to what?' Joseph looks surprised, but although he's relaxed, unthreatening, I feel uneasy. His random appearance has thrown me off-kilter.

'Coming round to see me,' I reply.

'He likes me to keep an eye on you. I own up, I told him about your recent relapse, and he was concerned.' He speaks clearly, but his words feel contrived. As if they've been planned. I wonder why he's called today. When I met Nathan on Friday, he never mentioned Joseph.

My relief that it's Joseph, and not someone else who knocked, is slowly ebbing away. Who was I scared of seeing when I opened the door? Nathan? Tory? I expected someone related to the puzzle, today's specific clues. I've no idea what's going on, but as Joseph slouches, heavy but at ease, I start to panic. I'm missing something.

Suddenly a cheery tune jingles from my phone. It flashes from across the room, and I dash to pick it up.

It's Teddy. I swipe it on, put the phone tight to my ear, and move towards the door.

'Hi. Teddy.' My voice is a whisper, and as Teddy's talks, I mime 'just a mo' at Joseph. He winks, does a thumbs up with both hands, as I duck out towards the bathroom.

'Teddy, Teddy. Where are you? I need you to get back. Have you checked the crossword?' My voice races, the words coming out in a breathless rant.

'Yes. I've seen the clues. You're right. Something's going on. I googled answers to several when I picked up a theme.'

'How soon can you get here? Hurry. Please.'

'Are you alone? Keep the door closed. Just in case. I'm leaving now.'

'No. I'm not.'

'Is it Nathan?'

'No. It's...'

A loud bang and a heavy rattle on the handle shake the bathroom door, and my phone crashes to the ground before I can finish my sentence.

'Coffee's ready.' Joseph's voice cracks through the door like thunder. 'Are you okay in there?'

'Coming.' My voice is hoarse, and quivering. 'Just a minute.'

When I pick up my phone, Teddy has gone. My fingertip stabs a message.

It's Joseph. He's here. I've no idea why, but he came at midday. Please hurry! X

I flush the toilet, then glance in the mirror. My face has the haunted look of death, my expression wild and demented, and I find it hard to focus.

91

AMANDA

When I reappear, Joseph has moved to the sofa. He's turned the music on, and he looks so relaxed, I wonder what I'm scared of. Maybe because he's more relaxed than usual, too at ease. Perhaps it's all a big coincidence. The clues. Joseph's midday appearance.

But when he taps the empty space beside him, I decline, opting for the window seat.

He lifts a mug to his lips and nods towards the coffee table.

'I've left yours there,' he says.

'Thanks.'

While I sip my drink, there's a lull in conversation. Joseph seems content. I'm willing him to get up, tell me he's got to go, but he doesn't seem in any hurry.

I think back to Martin Hunter. To the evening when he raped me. I'm not sure when I realised something was wrong. At what point did I realise? Since then, I've not been so trusting, less willing to take people at their word. Now my leaden limbs and acid breath are instinctual things that accompany my unease.

I've nothing concrete as to why I shouldn't trust my sponsor, but something's not right. Things don't stack. Joseph may have saved my life on more than one occasion, but turning up today, unbidden on May third? It's weird. The puzzle clues. The timing of his visit. Everything is skewed.

'You're probably wondering why I popped round.' Joseph's voice breaks into my thoughts. His voice has an unfamiliar lisp as he speaks, and I notice for the first time, a black gap in his mouth where a tooth has chipped in half. His smile is unusually wide, showing a rare expanse of gum. Perhaps that's why I've never seen the gap before.

'Yes, I am actually.'

'Nathan asked me to come. He told me about his little joke.'

'What little joke?'

'Today's little joke in the puzzle,' he says.

Joseph's eyes are darker than I remember, the red lashes hooding a blackness.

'You saw the clues? Oh. Was it just a joke?' I take a slug of tepid coffee, the tartness biting.

'Yes. All a joke. Nathan told me he's been toying with you for weeks in the clues. Did you notice?'

'I guessed it was him.' A mild relief washes over me, breaks through my fuzzy thoughts. It's going to be okay. It's all a big joke! I laugh, a forced blast of canned merriment.

'Drink up. I've brought some chocolate croissants. Your favourites.' Joseph rustles a brown paper bag and pulls out a couple of pastries and hands me one. I take a bite, wash it down with the last of the milky liquid.

I suppose I didn't expect Nathan to take things lying down. He's proud. A fighter. When things have settled down, and we've both moved on, we'll laugh about this. His novel payback scheme.

I feel bizarrely happy. The balm in hearing that it's been one big joke, sends me into a mood of delirium.

'Come. Dance with me,' I command, stretching out my arms

towards Joseph as I get up. I begin to twirl, gyrating my hips in wild excitement and sudden frenzy. Months of angst unravel, as I spin like a whirling dervish.

I haul Joseph to his feet and use his hand to spin me round. And round. And round.

I sing along to 'Back to Black', slurring like Amy Winehouse did on stage and kick my pumps in the air. Joseph's face is blank, emotionless, as if he's been expecting the weird behaviour. I see the croissant on the floor, the flaky pastry like dead silver birch leaves, floating on the floor. They're hovering centimetres off the ground. The room starts to spin, and I can't keep up the pace. Weird images appear in front of me, and I start to hallucinate. The images come in waves.

Then, Martin Hunter's face appears. His leer, as his hairy hands rip off my blouse, whip out my bra. Dull realisation of what is happening comes too late, as my legs give way, and I collapse to the floor.

Joseph is hovering over me, his stare hard, stony, unwavering. Like Martin Hunter's. Joseph is waiting, but for what? What does he want?

He moves to shut the curtains and block out the daylight.

It's then he takes his jumper off. His belt. His trousers, and bends over my crumpled form, a white freckled hand clamping across my mouth.

'Today's the day. I've been patient. This is payback for Nathan.' His voice hisses, spit splattering across my face. But before he can do anything more, I raise my head, jam my fingers down my throat and throw up. My insides explode in rancid projectile spurts.

'You bitch!' Joseph catapults backwards and lunges towards the bathroom. I hear the hiss of the shower before it springs to life and floods the silence. I hear the water, but I can't move.

I'm leaden, drowsy, losing control, until I dissipate to nothing. To oblivion.

92

NATHAN

It's one o'clock. May the third. It's been a long time coming. Nathan has been patient, but the date has finally arrived.

He's eager to know how Joseph is getting on, and feverish to know how Amanda coped when she solved the clues. She'll have done the puzzle, he's certain, as she's an early-morning solver. Like himself. Also, she'll have seen the clues before so he's confident that solving will have been quick.

After his wife's announcement about divorce, any doubts he had about the loaded clues, his plans, were wiped without trace. Oh to have been a fly on the wall when she worked out the answers! *May the third. Midday. Amanda. Silver birch. Assassination.* Brilliant if he's honest. No room for doubt, no ambiguity. Today is about more than petty payback.

Nathan told Joseph of his plan some time ago. The clues. His friend scratched his head, but soon picked up the theme, when Nathan showed him a draft grid with the full list of clues that were to appear on May the third.

'Slaughterhouse. Death duties. Throttle. What the heck?' Joseph read through the answers one by one. He was mildly shocked, amused, but had no idea that it was anything other than a ruse.

'What do you think? It's pretty clever, eh?' Nathan wandered round the room as Joseph's pebble eyes devoured the words. 'The puzzle will freak her out by the time she's finished.' Nathan laughed as he spoke.

'Oh, I see. Smart.'

But Nathan knew Joseph didn't really see. Other than believing Nathan wanted to bug his wife, toy with her increasing paranoia, Joseph never got the bigger picture. Nathan's plan was so much more than just a bit of fun.

'A game of words. You guys. I'm afraid I've never caught the bug,' Joseph said.

'Would you do me a favour?' Nathan asked.

'Go on.'

'Pop round to Amanda's on Sunday, May the third at midday. Let me know if she's seen the clues. I'd love to see her face when she's worked out the answers. But you'll have to do it for me. I haven't seen her for so long, I'm not sure this would be the time to make an appearance. She probably wouldn't let me in.'

Joseph didn't realise then that his next words would seal his own fate.

'Sure. Why not? Anything for a mate.'

As the minutes tick slowly by Nathan thinks of Joseph, and how none of the addict group know that their saviour is not an alcoholic. Nathan doubts they'd care, too wrapped up in their own tormented worlds. Joseph is clever. He keeps his real afflictions secreted under a cloak of holiness, his humble encouraging persona that of someone who has battled the demons and emerged victorious. The circle of pale tortured faces in the AA group confesses, and Joseph listens like a priest who lurks behind a latticed divide, a hand toying inside his trousers.

Nathan twigged, a while back, that Joseph is a sex addict, keeping his libidinous compulsions concealed under the victory cape of sobriety. He consoles the group, acts as their admired and trusted leader, and in the motley company manages to keep his lurid thoughts in check. But Amanda has posed a challenge, a personal Everest Joseph will never manage to climb. Not without a little help.

Since Nathan walked out on Amanda, he's seen more of his best friend than he has for years. He wonders now at how easily he handed across a key to Flat C to Joseph, and begged for his friend's help. But Nathan had no one else to turn to. The doubts came later, when he listened to Joseph's agitated accounts of the state he'd find Amanda in. How he undressed her, helped her into bed, and tucked the duvet round her.

Nathan knows his May the third plan got Joseph thinking. He watched Joseph's thoughts race ahead when he heard what Nathan had in mind. Nathan guessed Joseph would be only too keen to help. And he was right.

Today, Nathan will find out for sure if Joseph is a loyal friend, or a cheating bastard.

93

JOSEPH

The first time Amanda phoned Joseph for help, it was after midnight. He was on his way to bed, but as she cried down the phone, blubbering incoherently, he knew he should go over. He pulled on jeans and a hoodie and grabbed his coat.

'I'll be there in ten. Hang on. I'm on my way.'

As he slipped into the night, he felt a strange sense of excitement. It felt good to be needed, and Amanda trusted him. So did Nathan. They treated him like part of their family, and he wouldn't let them down.

Outside the entrance of Silver Birch, he rang the buzzer of Flat C, but there was no answer. He took out his set of keys and opened the mortice lock to the downstairs entrance. He hurried up the main stairs to the landing, and rapped gently at the entrance to Amanda's flat. When there was no reply, he let himself in.

Amanda was slumped across the sofa, lying on her front, a guttural snore piping out a steady rhythm. He turned her over, but she didn't wake. He stroked her hair, pulled it back off her face, and sat for ages, just looking at her. As the minutes ticked by, he felt himself getting aroused. He caressed her damp shoulders, exposed in a flimsy cotton top, and found himself planting a kiss on her forehead. He decided to lift her into the bedroom, tuck the duvet round her so that she wouldn't fall. As he went to hoist her up, she suddenly opened her eyes.

'Joseph. Joseph. My saviour. I'm sorry. I'm such a mess.' She tried to fling her arms around him, but they flailed in the air before she slumped backwards and fell asleep again.

'It's okay. I'm here. I'm going to help you into bed,' he said, but he was talking to himself. Amanda was letting out a slow steady snore and her face was already turned away from him.

After he'd set her on the bed, he slipped her leggings off, and had to quell the temptation to let his hand roam across her flesh. A couple of times her eyes opened and closed, she'd mumble something incoherent, but never seemed to focus.

When he was confident that she would be okay, he didn't linger. He was scared of what he might do. Instead he went to the bathroom, full of lustful images, and ejaculated over the toilet bowl.

Humiliation shadowed him for days, along with vivid images of Amanda's naked body, but at least she didn't seem to remember anything about that night, other than she'd drunk too much and collapsed. Her own disgust at having fallen off the wagon stopped her from wanting to discuss her failure, and she somehow managed to pick herself up the next day and begin the sober challenge all over again.

Joseph's shame soon turned to fear. Fear, and excitement that Amanda might phone again, sob, and plead for him to come round. Thinking about her became an obsession. He had no idea how to cope, and get over his infatuation.

When Nathan shared the story of how Martin Hunter had raped Amanda using Rohypnol, Joseph had purchased the drug on the dark web. He laced bottles of wine, guessing Amanda would be tempted to drink them, and left them on the porch at Silver Birch. That evening, when he called her number and she didn't reply, he went round and let himself in. At first he panicked that he'd laced the wine with too much Rohypnol. Amanda was out cold, but her breathing was steady, rhythmical. He undressed her, caressed her skin, until he found release. But he didn't rape her. Instead he tucked her up, and skulked away.

The second time that Joseph left wine on Amanda's doorstep, and Teddy ended up in hospital, Joseph knew he'd gone too far. It was a risk he couldn't repeat. He then had no idea how he would manage. That was until Nathan asked him to do one more favour.

The week of the vodka incident, Joseph filled Nathan in on how his wife had fallen off the wagon. Again.

'Oh. She's been doing so well, something must have set her off,' Nathan said when he met with Joseph. 'You say she'd drunk nearly half a bottle of vodka. Did you go round?'

'Yes. She rang, but by the time I turned up, she was three sheets to the wind, and out for the count. I managed to haul her into bed but she didn't wake up.'

'You're a good friend, and it helps knowing you're there for her.' Nathan patted Joseph on the back. 'Thanks, mate,' he said.

Nathan's trust was what kept Joseph true, hauled him back from the brink of temptation.

That was until Nathan came up with his May the third plan, and asked Joseph for his help.

94

TEDDY

Teddy checks, then rechecks the date. Yes, it is May third and it's the Sabbath, Sunday. He's been at the puzzle for two hours. Thirteen down, he's sure the answer is *noontime*, but he's no idea how the clue explains the answer. But it's the final clue, *A male attorney for the girl* that makes him sit up. *Amanda.*

Amanda was right. Someone is toying with her, but today, the clues are specific. Loaded. At first Teddy felt a prick of smugness that he was figuring out the clues quickly but this was quashed when he realised there could be a plan.

A premeditated murder laid out in clues.

It's only ten o'clock, and he can hear his mother in the kitchen preparing Sunday lunch, rattling plates and pans.

But he has to leave. He stuffs his clothes back into the small overnight bag and hurries downstairs.

From the hall, he watches his mum and hears her gentle whistle.

'Mum. I have to go.'

'Now?' She stares at him.

'I'm really sorry, but it's an emergency.'

'It's a girl, isn't it?' His mother sighs, but she knows his mind is elsewhere. It has been since he arrived.

'Sort of. But she's in danger. I need to get back.'

As Teddy closes the door, he can hear his mother's gentle sobs, and promises he'll make it up to her.

* * *

The satnav shows two hours and twenty minutes back from Brighton to Highgate. A23, M23, M25 and then the North Circular. He can be there by 12.30. He starts the engine, pulls out of the residents' car park, and waves up at his mother who is watching from her first floor flat. Next month, God willing, he'll bring Amanda to meet her.

As he gets up speed, he prays he'll get back to Highgate in time. To save his girlfriend's life.

95

TEDDY

The traffic back is so bad, it's nearly two o'clock by the time Teddy reaches Brewer's Hill. He parks at an angle outside Silver Birch and leaps out of the car. He glances up at Amanda's front windows and sees the curtains are drawn. He checks his mobile but there's been nothing, no calls or texts, nothing since Amanda told him Joseph was at the flat. He's tried continuously to get through, but it goes straight to messaging.

As he approaches the entrance there's a spooky stillness enveloping the property. The fine feathered branches of the silver birch are swaying in the breeze, talking to him in an eerie whisper. His damp fingers struggle with the lock, but once inside, the unadorned grey walls join the conversation with empty mocking echoes.

Death chases him up the stairs with relentless determination as his legs buckle and his feet stumble on the risers. His neck creaks as he glances back down at the empty foyer. He can feel death up ahead, past the landing and behind the door which quivers on flimsy hinges. Although its presence is all around, schmoozing like a foggy spectre, he doesn't know where it's hiding or what he's going to find.

Outside Flat C, he pushes his ear against the door.

'Amanda. Amanda. Are you there?' His voice is unsteady, hollow.

The door is ajar, the safety chain hanging loose, and it groans as he sets a palm against the flaky wooden surface and squeezes it wide. Silence moans in the hallway, a thick suffocating atmosphere wrapping itself around his body, making him convulse as if from cold. His weakened legs and leaden feet hold him back, and with colossal effort he inches towards the lounge. His ears are pricked for the slightest sound of breathing, or perhaps a ragged snore, but the silence thunders on.

The lounge is empty, but remnants of life hang in the air like Christmas tinsel not yet packed away. The stench of death beckons from somewhere else, and he follows the decaying scent. His stomach lurches when he reaches the bedroom, the fear of what lies inside causing bile to bubble. He peeks through the crack, like an actor in the wings, at the tragedian scene, but an eternity passes before he acts and follows the lines that the script demands.

He didn't expect two bodies, his worst nightmare torturing him with images of only one. The torsos are aligned differently, but blood covers each in different places and in varying amounts as if someone has swished a paintbrush over the flesh. Limbs are randomly angled on the body that is sprawled across the floor, one arm jutting upwards like a mast on a sailing boat, the other directed towards the wall like a tiller adrift from its casing. But his eyes sweep across the grotesque form as he steps over the carnage to reach the body on the bed. A red slimy baseball bat lies alongside it on the pillow.

'Amanda? Can you hear me? Talk to me.' He stares down at his girlfriend's ashen face and dares to touch her cheek. Blood soon seals his fingers, spreading through his hair and smearing the screen of his mobile which slithers like a slippery fish in his hand. He manages to tap in the numbers and croak into the handset through a faulty connection.

'Please, sir. Can you repeat yourself?' A distant voice booms in his ear. 'The line's very unclear. Take your time.'

He coughs, clears his throat, and spits out the mucus. 'I need an ambulance, and the police. Silver Birch, Brewer's Hill, Highgate.'

'Okay, sir. What's the problem?'

'There's blood everywhere. Two bodies. I think they've been murdered.'

96

NATHAN

Nathan cruises back to Clapham. The sun sparkles in the sky, an early summer omen that good things are on the horizon. At last, it's time to move on, the months of meticulous planning having come to fruition, the addicts punished for their sins.

As he nears Clapham, he turns the music down and scrolls through the contacts on his phone. He presses dial and lifts the mobile to his ear, but the call goes straight to voicemail.

'Hi, Tory. It's Nathan,' he says. 'Just wondered if you fancy dinner in the week. My treat. I'm happy to drive up or maybe meet in the centre. Covent Garden, perhaps? Anyway, call me.'

Today, he's ready for a new start. This time next year he'll celebrate May third as being the first day of the rest of his life. A new start, a rebirth. Gone is the fizzy water. Bring on the champagne.

It feels good when a plan comes to fruition. Joseph got what he deserved.

When Nathan entered the flat at 1.30, Joseph was already astride his wife's unconscious body. Joseph didn't hear him come in and had no warning when the baseball bat cracked open his skull.

Nathan then gently put the blood-splattered instrument into Amanda's hand and swung her limp and sleeping arm against Joseph's already shattered head, smacking it back and forth.

He checked her pulse: still gently beating. He didn't want her dead of course, but he needed her to feel the punishment. Go through the pain. Her eyes shot open when he lifted her arm, but they instantly snapped shut again.

When she eventually does wake up, she'll plead self-defence. The scene spoke for itself, a macabre Shakespearean tragedy.

Outside, he pulled his hat down over his thick cheap sunglasses and moved towards the gate. He glanced up and down Brewer's Hill and when he was sure there was no one about, he scuttled across the road towards his car.

Not only had Joseph lusted over Amanda, drugged her, but he'd lied to Nathan. Joseph had no idea he'd been caught out. Nathan guessed what he'd been up to, but it took time to catch him out. Until one evening he finally got his chance.

Joseph phoned Nathan, saying that Amanda had been in touch, and was begging him to come round. She sounded in a bad way.

'Can you go round? Please,' Nathan asked. 'Call me once you've seen her, let me know she's okay.'

'Will do. I'm on my way now.'

But Nathan didn't hang around for Joseph's call. He drove up and waited outside Silver Birch until he saw Joseph leave some time later. As Joseph skulked off into the darkness, Nathan called his friend instead.

'Joseph. It's me, Nathan. Is Amanda okay? I've been worried.' Nathan could see Joseph stop under a streetlight to take the call.

'Yes. I've just been round. She was out cold on the sofa, so I left her there, and got the duvet from the bedroom and tucked i round. I checked her breathing, but she seems fine. I'll check in again tomorrow.'

'Thanks, Joseph. I owe you one.' And with that Nathan swiped the phone off.

When Joseph rounded the bend out of sight, Nathan got out of the car and headed across the road his old flat. He crept up the stairs and rapped gently on the door. When there was no answer, he used his key and let himself in.

He saw the empty wine bottles on the windowsill but there was no sign of Amanda on the sofa. Instead, he found her in the bedroom sprawled half naked across the bed, the duvet in a heap on the floor. She was dressed only in her pants, with a flimsy T-shirt on top which exposed a bare breast.

Joseph had lied. Although Nathan didn't believe that Joseph had crossed the line to rape, he guessed he would, sometime soon. And he couldn't let that happen.

He never let on to Joseph that he'd called round that night. Instead, he covered his wife up and bided his time.

Until today. May third.

97

AMANDA

The white fluorescent strip light flickers on and off. But it steadies once my eyelids stay open.

A warm hand is wrapped around my fingers and a soft voice is coaxing me awake.

'Amanda? Can you hear me?'

Teddy's head is close, his mouth puffing gentle words.

'Where am I?' I can't remember. My neck is tight, locked as I try to move. 'What happened?'

Although the images won't come, a terror grips my body. I'm drenched in sweat, and yet I'm shivering.

'You're safe. It's all over. You're going to be okay.'

A clock by the door shows it's 9 a.m.

'What day is it?' It's all a haze. May third pops into my conscious.

'Monday. You've been out cold since yesterday afternoon.'

'It's not May third, is it?' Teddy takes my other hand, his sturdy presence so close I can hear his heartbeat. Or perhaps it's mine.

'No. It's the fourth. The third is over and you're safe.'

'What happened? I can't remember.' My voice is hoarse, my

throat dry and scratchy. I close my eyes again and sink back into the pillows. Teddy's voice is like a teacher's, steady yet soothing as it recounts a story. It's fiction, something not real, about villains and heroes. As I slip into darkness, hazy images, hallucinations, faces, voices, screams, make my body convulse. My eyes twitch behind their shutters as Teddy's voice drones on. I can't make sense of what he's saying.

* * *

When I come round again, the ward is quiet, and there's no sign of Teddy. A nurse is plumping up my pillows, encouraging me to sit up and she then hands me a glass of water. But instead of accepting, my eyes are drawn to the door at the far end of the room. Someone is coming in. They look familiar but it takes a moment to connect.

It's a woman dressed in a pastel-coloured flowery dress which floats below her knees, giving hint of pale matchstick legs. Her feet are encased in cream ballet pumps. Her willowy body is what draws recognition, with its teenage chest poking through the flimsy cloth. I remember the day in the garden with Teddy, the day I first met Tory. It was also the day I fell in love in love with Teddy. Agaves.

'Amanda. How are you? I've just heard. It's so dreadful.' She hovers, her body stiff, uncomfortable. She pulls up a seat. 'Here. For you. I didn't know what else to bring,' she says, setting down a basket filled with grapes and berry fruits on to the bedside cabinet.

I remember Tory was away yesterday. She'd gone to Cambridge for the day. I wonder if she did the crossword puzzle. The one on May third. Perhaps she never saw it.

'I know.' As I exhale bottled-up tension, my words get carried along.

'Sorry?' she asks. 'What do you know?'

'That you're a crossword setter. That you're Oliver's mother.' My head is thick like frozen stew, a mush of thoughts that won't warm up, but somehow, I remember what it was she's been keeping hidden all this time.

'Oh. I should have said, but...' Her answer floats unfinished.

'Did you deliberately move to Silver Birch after Oliver died? To be near me?'

'When Martin and I split, I wanted to stay nearby and be near to where it all happened. I need to be close to Oliver. The flat below yours came on the market, and I didn't hesitate. It wasn't planned.'

My silence eggs her on.

'Okay. So, I was angry. Furious. But Nathan told me I had to let it go. That it wasn't your fault.'

'Nathan said that? That it wasn't my fault?'

'Yes. He really helped me out after it all happened,' Tory says.

'He always made me feel it was my fault.' A sharp pain shoots up my side, like an electric shock. I squeeze my eyes, willing it to subside, and grip the sheets till my knuckles whiten. I gently lift my nightdress, inspect the bruises. Tory grits her teeth in sympathy, sucks in a noisy breath.

'That looks really sore. Shall I get the nurse?'

'It's okay. It'll pass.' My fingers release the bedding as the pain subsides. 'Sorry. Where were we?'

'Nathan was only trying to help you. By making you think you were to blame, he hoped it might encourage you to get dry. Battle the drink once and for all.'

'What do you mean?' I can't make sense of it. Nathan tried to help me come to terms with what I'd done. How my drunken prank had knocked Oliver into the road. Nathan talked me through it. Day after day. Telling me it would get better, that I'd learn to deal with the guilt, until one day I'd let it go. Although he told me it was an accident, and it could have happened to anyone, I know he blamed me, and the drink. I soon believed it had been my fault and that my salvation would be to get dry. Nathan took over with a sense of victory and began the quest to save my soul.

'He showed me a video of the day of the accident. He filmed you as you careered down the road,' Tory says.

'Go on.'

The fear is back. The self-loathing. The terror. The shame of what I did. Oliver would have been alive if I hadn't been so drunk, had kept control. I often think it might have been fairer if I'd been the car driver. Taken all the blame.

'Martin was to blame.'

'Martin? How was he to blame?'

'The video that Nathan took showed Martin letting go of Oliver's hand as you sped down the hill towards them. Martin was clapping, cheering you on. When he spotted you coming, he ran towards the kerb, and out on to the road.' Tory's eyes glass over. 'He completely forgot Oliver, and didn't notice when Oliver stepped out from behind him.'

I put my hand over Tory's, but she slips her fingers free. 'If Martin had kept hold of Oliver's hand, our son would still be alive.'

Tory's cheeks are wet, but the tears flow silently. Like her hurt and searing grief, they've been tightly locked away.

She doesn't linger, and once she's said her piece, she gets up.

'Bye, Amanda. Take care,' she says.

'Thanks for coming,' I reply. But she's already halfway towards the door.

* * *

Once Tory has gone, and I'm alone again, the dread returns. So many unanswered questions. Why did Nathan never show me the video? What if Teddy hadn't done the puzzle yesterday, and come back for me? Would I have died? Who knows what Joseph might have done. Did Teddy kill him in self-defence? Or to save me. Or could I have overpowered Joseph before the drugs knocked me out?

It's all a blur.

98

AMANDA

When I came out of hospital, I moved in with Teddy.

Flat B is cosy, homely after the hospital, but it's only a temporary haven from the rumbling volcano.

The crime scene above us in Flat C swamps my mind, with constant images of death and cadavers. I feel I'm on the edge of quicksand, dark menaces reaching out to pull me under and suck the air from my lungs.

Each morning, around four, the hot water pipes in the building fire up, and the death-throe rattles continue to shriek, not letting me forget that we're in a shared building. The flimsy partitioning that encases the skeleton of Silver Birch, with its broken ribs and delicate trellis of fragile bones, can't block out the noise. The din is louder in Teddy's flat than mine yet it still doesn't shut out the voices that filter through to me from the grave.

It's been two weeks since Joseph's murder, and the police still haven't made any arrests.

'I wish I knew where the police have got to in their investigations,' I say to Teddy, who constantly edges round me, checking every few minutes that I'm okay, drowning me in kindness, coffees and takeaways.

'It's a bit odd that they haven't been back to ask more questions,' he says. 'It's over a week since we gave our statements.'

I'm lying with my back against Teddy's chest, his arms anchoring my body, listening to the comfort of his heartbeat. When I don't reply, he carries on.

'Don't you think so? We must be pretty near the top of their suspect list. You were with Joseph when he died, and I was the one who called it in.' He won't let it drop. His attempts to keep me calm, soothe the fears, can't hide his own concerns. When he talks like this, it makes me worse. Not because I'm scared of the police finding evidence to implicate Teddy or me, but because it's a reminder that the murderer is still at large. Perhaps with unfinished business.

'I agree, but maybe they've got other leads.' I sound unsure, but can't think of another explanation why the police haven't been back.

Teddy tells me I can stay with him as long as I want. I've nowhere else to go, and I love being here, but I constantly fret that he had no choice but to ask me to stay. I watch him sleeping. I stare at his perfect head, the thick, unkempt curls and let my fingers tease the strands. In his sleep he gently takes my hand, tucks it round his chest and slumbers on. But I can't sleep. The fear has got a stranglehold, it won't let up, and I replay the bloody images over and over in my head. Day and night.

Fear crawls over my skin, like a poisonous spider. I wander from room to room, tidying, dusting, scrubbing, shining windows in the small hours, my ears pricked for the slightest sound.

Nathan texts regularly to check I'm okay. He tells me the police have been questioning him but they've nothing concrete to pin his way. When I tell Teddy that Nathan's been in touch, he snaps.

'It's got to have been Nathan who killed Joseph. Who else could it have been?'

I don't want to believe what he's saying. That I could have married a murderer. Deep down I'm scared that Teddy might blame me for everything.

'There's no evidence,' I say, my voice shaky with uncertainty.

'That's how murderers get away with it. They're clever, cover their tracks.'

Nathan's clever, that's for sure. But murder? It's my worst nightmare.

Teddy has taken annual leave to look after me, but in three days' time he has to go back to the office, and he'll take the security blanket of his presence with him. He keeps asking, 'Will you be okay on your own? I don't like leaving you.'

'I'll be fine.'

But I know I'm lying.

99

AMANDA

Tonight, I'm nestling against Teddy's chest, my bottom snuggled between his legs, and his arms are draped loosely around my shoulders. I flick through channels on the television, scroll through the viewing options. It's a routine that teases with homeliness.

'Nathan used to hog the controller, grabbing it back if I managed to get hold of it,' I say, flicking back and forth.

'I'm not surprised. Aren't you going to pick anything?' Teddy is laughing, as his fingers fiddle with my hair.

'Okay. What do you fancy?'

I'm not a romcom viewer, preferring wholesome crime dramas, but on Netflix I have to skip through Teddy's dark recommendation list of action movies involving hitmen and drug barons.

Teddy, before I moved in, told me he was into psychological thrillers, the more twisted and gruesome the better. But this last week, after everything that's happened, we've been watching reruns of *Friends*; *Only Fools and Horses*; *Keeping Up Appearances*. All things light and breezy. But my laughter is forced, and I've lost all concentration.

Then my finger stops as I point the controller at the screen.

'What about *Inspector Morse*? Have you watched it?'

'No, but that's fine. I've seen *Endeavour* but never *Morse*. Now give me the controller and stop flicking.' Teddy's hand swoops in and snatches the remote from me.

'"The Settling of the Sun". Nineteen eighty-eight. That'll do.' I read the title of the episode, and its date of release.

'Right. No talking,' Teddy whispers before brushing his lips over the top of my head. A second passes as the credits roll before I dare to speak and break the mood.

'Did you know Morse was a fan of crossword puzzles?'

'No, I didn't. Now shhh. Please!'

* * *

Halfway through, I pull myself up and nudge Teddy in the ribs.

'Ouch. What's that for?'

'Stop. Can you rewind that bit? Replay it.'

'What? What is it you want to know?'

'Just replay that last bit.'

Chief Inspector Morse's crisp, concise voice speaks to me.

'*It's all clues, isn't it? Crosswords are far more exotic and exciting than police work. Most murders don't require solving because they haven't been planned.*'

'We never showed the police a copy of the crossword puzzle for May the third. It's evidence of sorts, don't you think?' I crane my neck to look at Teddy.

'No. We didn't,' Teddy says, but he's not really concentrating, as he keeps the remote pointing at the screen.

'Don't you think the clues are evidence of premeditated murder?' I swivel round, knock the remote out of his hand. 'The clues prove that it wasn't a random, spur of the moment action.'

'What are you saying? That we take the puzzle to the police?' Teddy looks at me with cynicism.

But then Teddy doesn't know Nathan like I do. My husband has a brilliant mind. He can manipulate words, phrases, even more than people. He shared with the world his calculating murder plan with reckless arrogance. Circumstantial evidence at best, the police will say, but not for me. It's been staring me in the face all along.

'Are you certain it was Nathan who set that puzzle? Could it not have been Tory?'

I swallow my excitement when he mentions Tory, wriggle off the sofa, and go and rifle through the pile of newspapers stacked in the corner.

Ten minutes later, I wave the May the third puzzle in the air. It might not be a victory flag, but I need to show it to the police. The *London Echo* will be forced to reveal who the setter was for the day of the murder when the police contact them.

100

AMANDA

At first DCI Dartington curls his lips in a supercilious manner, lounging like a lion in the midday sun as he listens with half-closed lids to the flight of fancy that is Teddy's and my concoction. The theory that my husband committed cold-blooded premeditated murder and left a trail in the daily crossword puzzle is going to take quite a sales pitch.

'What am I looking at?' Dartington's sarcasm, laced with mild interest and a generous scoop of arrogance, makes me more determined than ever to prove that we're right. Dartington peers at the puzzle grid before turning the newspaper over in his thick hairy hands and back again.

'The clues. The answers.' I'm breathless, desperate for him to grasp our conjecture. Teddy sits up close, holding my hand, nodding, adding calm confirmation to my certainties.

'You say your husband set these clues? Are you certain it was him?'

I can't be 100 per cent certain, even at this point, that it wasn't Tory. Nathan owned up, when I met him, that Tory had also been playing with the grids. Hatred towards me might have given her motive for murder, but not for Joseph's. It doesn't make sense that she would have killed him and left me alive and breathing. Logic, instinct, points firmly towards Nathan.

'Yes. Nathan was the setter of the clues. He goes under the name of Adnam. My nickname is Manda, and he uses this backwards as his pseudonym.' My cheeks sizzle. Nicknames. The weird game that tied Nathan and I together like school chums, sniggering behind hands at the belittling monikers.

'So, what are the clues that suggest your husband might have come up with a premeditated murder plan? Show me.' Dartington turns the grid my way, locks his hands behind his head and stretches his long legs out under the table.

I should have expected scepticism. This isn't a Morse detective series when the far-fetched made-for-TV drama leads to compulsive viewing. This is real life, and the anticipated incredulity is the reason I didn't approach the police much earlier on. Even when I blacked out through drug-infused wine and Teddy nearly died, I never bothered to mention the puzzle clues.

But Teddy, when I ran through my theories, insisted that we present the evidence. Although he's pretty sceptical, I know he thinks doing something positive might help my recovery.

I use my finger to point at the clues. 'I won't tell you how to solve the clues, but I've listed relevant answers next to the puzzle grid, which is already filled in. It came out on the third of May.'

Dartington unlocks his hands, clicks his meaty fingers, and scans the words.

'*Strangler. Slaughterhouse. Death duties. Throttle.* Certainly, there's a theme here.' As he puffs out an elongated stream of air his lips quiver.

'Carry on. Look, it's the ones near the end.' My voice speeds up as I lean forward. Teddy's hand on my thigh helps ground me, slow me down.

'*Silver birch. Third May. Noon. Assassination. Amanda.* Are these the answers you mean? What does Silver Birch refer to?' Dartington looks at me and back to the words. He turns to his deputy who nods. 'Are you sure these are the correct answers to the clues?' he asks.

'Certain. And Silver Birch is the name of the property where I live. Where the murder took place.'

'And you're sure that your husband, Nathan, was the setter?'

'Yes.'

'Very interesting. This certainly provides a new angle for our investigation.' After a short pause, he carries on. 'Certainly, it's an angle with a difference. That's for sure,' he says with a wry smile.

'But don't you see? It was planned all along. He's been winding me up for months with loaded clues and answers. I thought it was him toying with me, payback with a difference.' It sounds ridiculous in the telling, but also very real.

'Can I take a copy of the filled-out puzzle and keep your list of answers? I'm not much good at puzzles. My wife dabbles though.' Dartington's eyes lock on to mine with a steely scrutiny before he stands up, scrapes back his chair, and extends a large hand. 'Thank you both for coming in and rest assured we'll be in touch.'

As we wander back out to the car, Teddy confirms that I definitely managed to catch the detective's attention.

But I'm not so sure.

101

AMANDA

Nathan always thought he was cleverer than everyone else. This has been his downfall. He knew his prints would be all over the murder scene. After all, he'd lived in the flat.

Even since Nathan was arrested and charged with Joseph's murder, I lie awake, rigid in the crook of Teddy's arm while he snores contentedly in the belief that it is all over. For me it'll never be over.

Text messages Nathan sent to Joseph showed that he had asked his best friend, my sponsor, to pop by at noon on May third. He asked Joseph to let him know how I was coping and if he'd hit a flimsy target with his sinister wordplay. Nathan shared the crossword puzzle joke with Joseph and when questioned by the police, Nathan never denied being the setter of the clues. I know he'll enjoy the notoriety when people read about the clues and acknowledge his undisputed genius.

The only thing that the police don't know for sure, was whether Nathan gave Joseph the date-rape drugs or if Joseph drugged me of his own free will. Nathan has denied all knowledge. He's never admitted to leaving wine on my doorstep and the police haven't been able to pin this crime on him. After all that happened, I realise it was most likely Joseph, but the police are treating this as history. Somehow, I'll have to as well.

The important thing is that Nathan has been charged with cold-blooded murder, aggravated by the fact his friend was trying to rape me. Driven to slaughter by jealousy and rage.

The puzzle grid helped convince the jury that the day's events might have been premeditated. But in itself, the crossword puzzle and the loaded answers weren't enough to convict Nathan of murder. Although it appears that Nathan had planned to turn up at our flat after he knew Joseph had arrived, this alone wasn't enough to send him down for murder.

Nathan claimed he had started to question both Joseph's loyalty and character. He knew his friend was a sex addict and soon guessed he had his sights fixated on me. Nathan followed Joseph to Silver Birch on May third, hung around outside before he went inside. He denied murder, saying that after witnessing Joseph's attempt at rape, he stormed out, claiming at this point Joseph was still alive.

The thing that became clear during the trial is that Nathan had it in for addicts. All addicts. Not just me. He blamed my addiction for the failure of our marriage. My addiction for goading Martin Hunter into rape. Then he blamed Joseph for his addiction to sex. Nathan felt a need to punish, give vent to his wrath and impotence and punish the sinners. A vigilante against all addicts.

Teddy wonders why Nathan didn't target Martin Hunter, although Teddy hates to speak my rapist's name. I tell him that Nathan has a lopsided logic. He probably felt Hunter had already paid, with the death of his son. Fate had meted punishment enough.

Framing me for manslaughter was clever, but also stupid. The blows, cracks to Joseph's skull needed much more force than my slight arms could have managed. Especially in a drug-infused and weakened state.

Hallucinations, faces, violence, screaming noises, cavort around my brain. I still can't remember anything from the day of the murder. It's as if my brain has shut down. I wrack my thoughts for flashbacks, and try to conjure up Nathan's face, his features as I lie frozen, comatose on bed. Teddy tells me it'll take time. He's confident that one day I might remember more. I may one day remember seeing Nathan pummel Joseph to death.

Perhaps I will. But then perhaps I don't want to.

Although the crossword clues provided indication of Nathan's warped mind, they didn't prove beyond reasonable doubt that he committed cold-blooded murder on May third. He was certain no one had seen him enter or leave the building. When the police finally contacted him later in the day, Nathan was in Clapham in a pub with his dog. He insisted he hadn't been near Highgate or Brewer's Hill all day.

But someone had seen him. Someone was able to identify the hooded stranger leaving the flat shortly after 1.30. The witness had no doubt. Nathan hadn't spotted them as they peered through the hedge that formed the boundary between Silver Birch and the property next door. Nathan had concentrated on making sure the street was clear when he entered and left the building, not giving enough attention to the houses either side, in his hurry to get away. But someone watched him scuttle off towards the Tube station.

Good old Mr Beckles. It was the first time in months that he'd managed to climb the steps and get back into the real world.

102

MERLONG

My new setter's name is Merlong. It tickles me that it's an anagram of Mongrel. No one at the paper needs to know who I am and where I'm living. I'll still be able to work from home, make a living and who knows? Perhaps one day I'll pop into the offices and show my face and let my colleagues know who the mysteriously named setter is. Then again, I might not.

It was with reluctance that I ditched Bagheera as my moniker. Bagheera had been Oliver's favourite cartoon character. A black panther who was minder, and protector of the man-cub Mowgli. But my new name, Merlong, heralds a new beginning.

Outside the window, an estate agent is using a mallet to bang in a *For Sale* board for Flat B, Teddy's flat. It is bright orange, like the sun, which today is golden and edged by a sizzling shimmering halo of heat. *Claxton Estates* is printed in thick unattractive black lettering across the swinging metal sign. Flat C, Amanda and Nathan's flat, is already on the market, but I doubt buyers will flock when they learn about the murder. It's priced well below the market value.

Merlong is barking, yelping at the man, jumping up and down

on his bony hind legs to get a better view through the window. He bares his teeth and when I rub my hand down his back, his angst increases. He's my new protector, and I'm his. He's my prize. He's such a sweet dog, thin and wiry haired. He needs protecting, the way he tries to protect me. I think of Oliver every time I feed and tuck my new pet in. Nathan says he'll have his dog back when he gets out. But that'll never happen. Nathan won't get Merlong back, and he'll never get out.

Merlong follows me round the flat. Up and down stairs, and below to the cellar which is sunk into the basement of Silver Birch where my recently redecorated office is kitted out with shelves, book collections, and wine. I've started my own wine collection, an immersive new hobby, and am planning vineyard trips around the globe. Marlborough County, New Zealand. Chianti region of Italy. Bordeaux in France. Even California. I've put up a world chart on the wall and marked the destinations. When I move, I'll take it all with me and keep the hobby going, but until then, it'll keep me busy while Nathan launches an appeal. He's unlikely to succeed, but I owe him support. Like the steadfastness he offered me when Oliver died.

Nathan is still in shock at having been charged with Joseph's murder. His innocent plea was based on the fact that all he was guilty of was sharing his wind-up ruse with Joseph, to whom he showed the crossword puzzle, the one that appeared on 3 May.

Today, it's on my calendar to visit Nathan in prison.

103

MERLONG

I arrive at the prison early, and sit in the car with Merlong whose tail is slumped between his hind legs. His watery eyes won't leave my face, and he emits a steady whimper. It's hard not to be moved by his abject misery whenever I leave him, even for a second.

When he finally accepts I'm getting out, he struggles to get into the back seat where he can watch for my return.

'Don't be silly, Merlong. I'll not be long.' I lock up, and try to soothe him through the window, where his tortured face is pressed against the glass and his anxious breath clouds his vision.

At the prison entrance, I sign in, and linger until I'm ushered to the visitors' room. I scan the space looking for Nathan. A few seconds pass, before my eyes settle on a small shrunken figure in the corner. Nathan gets up when he sees me, and his hands grip the edge of the table. With his shorn hair, and skeletal cadaver, I hardly recognise him.

'Tory. You came. I knew you would,' he says. His smile reveals small teeth which remind me Merlong's.

'I promised. You were there for me, I'll not forget. How are you coping?' I sit down on the hard orange chair, across from him.

He's keen to talk. Desperate to tell me his side of the story. His eyes light up as he gets started, and I sit quietly and listen. I owe him friendship, company after how he helped me. Kindness and evil can be unlikely bedfellows.

He runs through his version of the events of 3 May, and as he talks, his shoulders and demeanour start to relax. He speaks with confidence.

'I guessed Joseph would go round and visit Amanda,' he says.

'Why did he go round?' I ask.

'Joseph? I suggested he visit, see if the wind-up in the puzzle had worked on Amanda. It was just a bit of fun. Pretty clever if I say so myself.' He laughs. 'Don't you agree? You saw the clues, no doubt.'

Nathan still maintains his innocence, where murder is concerned, despite the evidence and the guilty verdict. He even lies to me. He's trapped by his own secretiveness, and duplicity. I've known Nathan a long time. We've worked on the London Echo crossword puzzles for as long as I can remember. He's clever, but deluded. He believes what he says, in his own voice, his own claims. He's confident when his appeal comes through that he'll show the world. Prove his innocence. We share compilers' traits, getting lost in private worlds of words and manipulation.

'Do you think Amanda was the one who really killed him?' he asks, pulling his hands together in tightly balled fists, and hunching towards me. Wiling me to buy into his story. He thinks he plays me like a card sharp, but it's hard to concentrate when Amanda's name is mentioned. My forgiveness will never go that deep.

It feels disloyal to tell him I know he killed Joseph, so instead I ask a question that's been festering. The question to which only Nathan will know the answer.

'Did you give Joseph the idea to use Rohypnol?' I ask.

'Perhaps I laid the seed,' he chuckles, before banging his palms hard down on the table. 'I told him how your loyal husband, Martin, used the drug to rape Amanda, and how it wiped her memory of events.' He hisses in the sarcastic telling. 'I told Joseph it was an easy way to get a girl into bed.'

'What made you think Joseph would use it on Amanda?'

'He was a sex addict. Don't forget I'd known him a long time. I wanted to test him. See how far he'd go with Amanda if he got the chance.'

'I'm confused. What made you think he intended to rape Amanda?'

Nathan tells me how Joseph, following on from their conversation, drugged wine and left it for Amanda.

'He didn't rape her that time, but I needed to know how far he'd go, if he got another chance. I'd entrusted him with Amanda's care, but soon became suspicious.'

'Hence, May the third plan.'

He talks with conviction. I promise him I won't tell the police, there's no need for them to know the date rape drug was his idea. But for me, it's the last bit of the puzzle. There's no doubt that Nathan is the killer.

He grabs my hands when I get up to leave, and begs me to come again.

'Maybe bring me some puzzles? Keep me busy till I get out of here.'

'Sure. Will do.'

I wander back to the car, and see Merlong bobbing up and down. His bark greets me when I unlock the car, as he scrambles through the gap in the seats to get back into the front.

I start the engine, stroke Merlong's head as he tries to find purchase on my lap, and I sit quietly for a moment. I wonder all along if Nathan meant to murder Joseph. Or if there was a time he meant to target Amanda, murder her instead. But with clever calculation, and not a small amount of arrogance, he found another way to punish his wife. To frame her for manslaughter.

As I drive away, I think life for me might be easier, my tortured thoughts less gripping, if Nathan had murdered Amanda.

Outside Silver Birch I park up, and although Merlong is panting to get out, I don't open the door. A sudden sight of Teddy with Amanda strolling up the path doesn't help my mood. They pause and smile up at the newly erected *For Sale* sign which swings in the breeze, alongside its sister board.

I'll be sad to see Teddy go, but not Amanda. I've got the grid ready for next Saturday's puzzle. New clues. New themes. New methods. She'll not get away that lightly.

My targeted clues will need some honing, but it's time to ratchet up the pressure.

ONE YEAR LATER

104

AMANDA

Teddy and I are both working remotely. The tumbledown chateau in the Dordogne has become our project. Our future. The first paying guests will be arriving next month.

Our flats sold quickly, considering. Teddy's, unsurprisingly, sold for way more than mine, but I didn't care. There is no price to put on escape.

Here in France, Teddy is in his element, so at home. He's replaced twenty windows, painted the same number of rooms, installed baths, showers, kitchen units. The list is never-ending, but at night, under a starlit sky we sip our drinks and do the crossword. Teddy has a glass of wine, and occasionally he lets me have a sip. He thinks I might be able, one day soon, to become a social drinker. But he'll only allow me to drink with food, as is the French custom.

Tonight, we sit by the swimming pool. Our bodies are damp, our hair wet, as we lounge side by side. We now download two copies of the London Echo puzzle from the internet. One for Teddy. One for me. Even though we fill in our grids separately, we work together, and although we compete to solve, we giggle when we crib, and share when we reach a block. If we get stuck, or bored, or decide to give up and take a dip in the pool, we share the answers. We never leave it unfinished before we go to bed. With the nasty conundrums, we google reluctantly as a last resort.

We've even taken up the challenge of a quick local crossword puzzle in French.

'Pen ready?' Teddy asks, his eyes already on the clues.

'Yep. I'll set the stopwatch. See how long it takes us.'

'Can I start?'

'Five, four, three, two, one. Go.'

* * *

Teddy grows unusually quiet. His boisterous enthusiasm becomes lidded. I know he starts at the bottom right-hand corner, whereas I still skitter at random all over the grid.

'What's up?' I ask.

Teddy's face is puckered, his lips tight and he's biting the inside of his lower lip. It's what I call his 'worry face'.

'Nothing.'

'I know you. It's not nothing.' It's true. I know him better now than I know myself.

'Look at the last few clues.'

The hot sun has baked the landscape for miles around. My carefully green-planted area that camouflages the pool surrounds with sturdy succulent bushes has dried up. Fading green is interspersed with rotting beige. The sprinkler system needs mending, and Teddy says he's made a mental note. But he works at his own pace, unwilling to leave a job unfinished unless there's a dire emergency, and even then, he doesn't panic. He's a 'live for the moment' type of guy, one of the things I love most about him, and the new pace of life suits us both. We toil by day and make love by night.

I read the clues. Slowly, the answers unravel before my eyes. A couple of them are so familiar, that my heart starts a steady thump.

A male attorney for the girl (6)

He'd hated war breaking out in the Tory Party (6,5)

A bird begins to warble with a steady trill of conversation. It sings out from the forest area that stretches back from our property. Overhead, a sudden fan of movement flickers past as a flock of geese squawk across the sky. Teddy sits up, shields his eyes with an outstretched palm and looks up. The sky is cloudless, and a distant haze of shimmering gold creates a scene like a painted canvas.

The next clues make up my mind, what I must do. What Teddy and I need to do. After I read them several times, and scribble down the answers, I decide. I lift my half-filled grid, stretch across, and pick up Teddy's copied section and with one almighty sweep, I rip the sheets of paper in half. Then half again. And again. And again. And again. Until tiny shreds of paper, like wedding confetti, float through my fingers and scatter round the pool.

'It's time to find another hobby,' I say, sifting through my canvas bag and lifting out a book. *Living in France. The language and the People.*

'Okay. How do you say, "Please may I have a loaf of bread"?'

Teddy laughs, gets up and nudges up beside me.

'How do you say, "I love you"?' His voice kisses my cheek and melts my heart.

* * *

I lie and look up through the skylight at the stars. The same stars that twinkle all around the world. Today, Teddy and I did our last cryptic puzzle together. Tomorrow will be a new beginning.

But as I try to sleep, the silence engulfs me, and I see the clues

The last ones I'll ever see. The setter was someone called Merlong, their name showing up against the grid.

The teasers worm around my head, like rotting maggots.

In France, cat and water make a mansion (7)

Children may be found playing it (4,3,4)

Warning, a busy insect about confrontation (6)

Sack member for having a weapon (7)

Made a threat involving loss of living (5)

Perhaps it's paranoia. Not letting go. Teddy says it's PTSD, post-traumatic stress disorder, but he pointed out the clues to me. He feels the loaded phrases too. As I close my eyes, the answers whizz across my vision, until they get trapped beneath my lids.

Chateau. Hide and Seek. Beware. Firearm. Death.

ACKNOWLEDGMENTS

Thank you to readers everywhere, who pick up each new book in anticipation of getting lost inside the intrigue of someone else's story. Readers, you are an author's greatest prize.

For me, being signed by Boldwood Books was the highlight of 2022. It has been the start of a whole new journey in my writing career, and I'd like to thank each and every member of the Boldwood team for their tireless and professional efforts in getting authors' books out into the world.

But a special thanks must go to Emily Yau, my editor. She believed in *One Down* on first reading, and with her insight and unbelievable attention to detail, she has helped bring the novel to life. I am so looking forward to working with her on many future projects.

On a personal level, I must thank Margaret Fitzpatrick for being my first reader, and whose opinion and input I trust more than anyone else's. She tirelessly works through my manuscripts, always encouraging, and making sage suggestions, in a gentle and positive way, on how the book can be improved. Thanks, Margaret. I don't think you realise how much I rely on you.

A writer craves approval and encouragement, in what can be the most lonely profession in the world. An author needs a few select people to let into their world of creation. People they can trust. Top of this list is my sister, Linda. She never fails to tell me that she knows I can pull it off. Whenever I doubt, she builds me up, confident every time that I'll reach my goal. Thanks, big sis.

Lindsay Pigott, my gorgeous niece, encourages me from start to finish. We share the same love of dark and macabre psychological thrillers, and she feeds me what will work, and angles to avoid. Thank you.

Everyone has a BFF (best friend forever), and I'm no different. Susan McCarthy, whom I met when only eight years old, asks me every day how the writing is going. Her pride at my achievements is shared without restraint. Thank you, Susan.

Finally, the biggest thanks in the world must go to the men in my life. Neil, my hubby, who battles me every day for the first look at the daily cryptic puzzle. Together we've solved some of life's hardest clues.

And finally, thanks to our wonderful son, James. He still says that one day he might get around to reading one of my books. But he's not promising.

MORE FROM DIANA WILKINSON

We hope you enjoyed reading *One Down*. If you did, please leave a review.

If you'd like to gift a copy, this book is also available as an ebook, digital audio download and audiobook CD.

Sign up to Diana Wilkinson's mailing list for news, competitions and updates on future books.

https://bit.ly/DianaWilkinsonNews

ABOUT THE AUTHOR

Diana Wilkinson writes bestselling psychological thrillers, including her debut novel *4 Riverside Close* published by Bloodhound. Formerly an international professional tennis player, she hails from Belfast, but now lives in Hertfordshire.

Follow Diana on social media:

 twitter.com/DiWilkinson2020

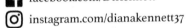 facebook.com/DiKennett

instagram.com/dianakennett37

Boldw⦿⦿d

Boldwood Books is an award-winning fiction publishing company seeking out the best stories from around the world.

Find out more at www.boldwoodbooks.com

Join our reader community for brilliant books, competitions and offers!

Follow us
@BoldwoodBooks
@BookandTonic

Sign up to our weekly deals newsletter

https://bit.ly/BoldwoodBNewsletter

THE

Murder

LIST

**THE MURDER LIST IS A NEWSLETTER
DEDICATED TO SPINE-CHILLING FICTION
AND GRIPPING PAGE-TURNERS!**

**SIGN UP TO MAKE SURE YOU'RE ON OUR
HIT LIST FOR EXCLUSIVE DEALS, AUTHOR
CONTENT, AND COMPETITIONS.**

SIGN UP TO OUR
NEWSLETTER

BIT.LY/THEMURDERLISTNEWS

Printed in Great Britain
by Amazon

41565970R00208